A MARIN
~Bed and Breakfast~

DOLORES
STREET

Black Rose Writing | Texas

©2025 by Dolores Street
All rights reserved. No part of this book may be reproduced, stored in a retrieval system or transmitted in any form or by any means without the prior written permission of the publishers, except by a reviewer who may quote brief passages in a review to be printed in a newspaper, magazine or journal.

The author grants the final approval for this literary material.

First printing

This is a work of fiction. Names, characters, businesses, places, events, and incidents are either the products of the author's imagination or used in a fictitious manner. Any resemblance to actual persons, living or dead, or actual events is purely coincidental.

ISBN: 978-1-68513-604-8
Library of Congress Control Number: 2025930454
PUBLISHED BY BLACK ROSE WRITING
www.blackrosewriting.com

Printed in the United States of America
Suggested Retail Price (SRP) $20.95

A Marin Bed and Breakfast is printed in Minion Pro

*As a planet-friendly publisher, Black Rose Writing does its best to eliminate unnecessary waste to reduce paper usage and energy costs, while never compromising the reading experience. As a result, the final word count vs. page count may not meet common expectations.

PRAISE FOR
A Marin Bed and Breakfast

"A clever, amusing, and satisfying read."
–**Carolyn Korsmeyer, author of *Little Follies***

"A tender and often sardonic exploration of love and loss, resilience and empowerment, and sexual awakening and enlightenment."
–**Steven Mayfield, award-winning author of *The Penny Mansions***

"Engaging and highly readable novel about modern love in its many forms."
–**Ruth F. Stevens, award-winning author of the *South Bay Series***

A MARIN
~Bed and Breakfast~

LILY
LOSSES AND OPTIONS

"New topic," said Lily Simone to the friends gathered at her kitchen's granite-top island for veggies and artichoke dip, "but what do you know about local realtors? Who's good?"

"Why?" asked Gail, laughing. "Is one of the kids ready to come back and buy?"

"Not exactly …" said Lily slowly.

"A high school friend?" said Margo.

Lily paused, broccoli in hand, eyes fixed on the bowl of dip. What an effing hard thing this was, even with two of her closest friends.

"What," said Gail, no longer laughing, "what's going on? You look like something's wrong."

The tears began to well up; Lily blinked carefully and none fell. "I need to sell," she said.

"No, what?" said Gail. "That can't be."

"Why on earth?" said Margo. "You don't have to downsize just because the kids are all on their own. I thought you and Don planned to stay forever."

"Is it that there're too many memories?" asked Gail. "Or too much space now that it's just you?"

More tears were ready to fall, and Lily's nose was activating as well. She gave another careful blink and a sniff. "No, no," she said, "it's not that. I love this house."

"Well, what then? Don left you a bundle, you should be set for trips to Tahiti."

There it was. In a rush, Lily said "Actually no. Actually no bundle, no trips, no nothing. He effing died next to broke." Finally delivered of this, she erupted into sobs as Gail and Margo stared at her in shock and then advanced to enfold her in competing and therefore not fully successful hugs.

"Omigod Lily, that's unbelievable!" exclaimed Gail.

"That can't be right," said Margo.

"When did you find out?" asked Gail.

"Do the kids know?" cried Margo.

"I haven't told them yet," snuffled Lily, frantically dabbing her eyes and nose with a napkin. It felt wrong to be wiping tears and snot with such a cheerful-looking paper napkin, all floral-printed in daisies and bluebells or something like that. The texture was all wrong—too crisp, too unabsorbent. Even a floral-printed hankie would have been more sympathetic, but Lily didn't normally keep a hankie in her pocket even now that she'd tried to wean herself from carrying packages of tissues in favor of the old-fashioned and more ecologically sound hankies. Her current hankie, a pale blue one with a crocheted edging, was tucked in her purse, next to the door.

"They don't know?" said Gail. "Oh, sweetie, are we the first ones you've told?"

"Well, the lawyer knows."

"But Don's been dead for months," said Margo. "I mean, passed away, sorry."

"You can say dead," sniffled Lily. "I mean, that's what he is, dead, after all. Anyway, yeah, I didn't see any reason to drag the kids along to meet with the lawyer, they were grieving their dad, and then I kept thinking I could find some way of handling this where I didn't need to involve them."

"Well, but why isn't there any money?" asked Gail. "You guys have always been very comfortable, almost from the very start. You have the lovely house, the Mercedes, Don's Corvette that you already sold, the nice vacations every year, the retirement accounts and investments and insurance and I don't know what-all else." Her eyes widened as she gazed at Lily. "Wait, is this why he …"

"Yes—maybe—I don't know," said Lily miserably.

And there wasn't really any way to know for sure about that. Don had been acting peculiar for quite a while before his diagnosis of an inoperable brain tumor, and he'd jumped off the Golden Gate Bridge the day after the news came that he didn't have long to live. His note had only said "I'm sorry," so Lily couldn't know whether that meant he was sorry to be making her a suicide's widow or sorry that he'd thrown away their life savings on crypto.

"What actually happened to the money?" said Gail. "There was always plenty while he was alive, or at least that was my impression."

Lily took another napkin. "I had no idea until the lawyer and I started dealing with the estate. You know how Don had all the financial know-how and I was never good at any of that. There was always money in the checking and savings, and I let Don handle all the rest. I mean after all, he was a goddamn stockbroker! He had an IRA and a 401K and we had insurance and we were going to get around to putting everything into a trust to avoid probate, so I thought we were doing just fine! But for some reason he emptied out just about everything and put it in crypto, and you know what's happened with most crypto, it's a disaster."

"I can't believe that someone as savvy as Don would've put all your money in crypto," said Gail. "Sure, try the waters, but all your savings? All your retirement money?"

"Exactly," said Lily. "It's crazy. I think it must've been his brain tumor talking. Because, to get at some of that retirement money, he wasn't even old enough to take it out, he wasn't fifty-nine and a half yet so apparently he had to pay a whopping penalty on it to the IRS. It was totally senseless. Even I would've known better than to do that."

"Well, of course you know better," said Margo staunchly. "You may not be a stockbroker or some kind of investment wizard like Don, but you're good at household finance. You don't go around wasting money."

Lily dissolved into another fit of weeping. "I know! I'm a native Marinite, so it's not like I grew up in wealth, we were a normal middle-class family back when you didn't have to be rich to live here. My parents taught me not to spend money I didn't have. But I thought I could rely on Don's income and financial expertise, and look how that's bit me in the butt."

"That's for sure," said Gail.

"But," said Margo, plunging a piece of purple cauliflower into the dip, "surely you don't actually have to sell the *house*."

"It's got a mortgage and there are property taxes and upkeep."

"Oh, come on, you bought this house over thirty years ago!" said Gail.

"Don refinanced a couple of times."

"So, then your payments are low and you've got a lot of equity."

"Think of the property taxes! I can't afford to stay without income," wailed Lily. "I'll have to move to Texas or something!"

Margo snorted. "Don't be silly. Only Republicans move to Texas. Democrats move to … oh, I don't know, Minnesota or someplace like that."

"Minnesota'd probably be too expensive. What about someplace like Arkansas or maybe Ohio?" said Gail.

"I'm a native Marinite—it seems sacrilegious even to think of leaving northern California!"

"Well," said Margo, "if you sold, you'd make a shit-ton given what housing prices have done since you and Don bought the place. Once you paid off your existing mortgage, you'd probably still have enough to buy a little condo and invest the rest. Maybe you could find an affordable condo in San Rafael or Novato."

"Novato! At that rate I might as well move to Arkansas."

"It's not *that* bad," said Margo. "One of my cousins lives in Novato and they have a perfectly respectable tract home."

"Well, my grandparents were Arkies," said Lily, "so I might even have relatives back there if they didn't all leave during the Dust Bowl."

"A minute ago you were threatening to move to Texas," said Gail.

"Oh, I know—I just don't want to have to go anywhere, but I don't see any way around it. I don't have many more months' worth in my savings and it turns out that I'm just about unemployable."

Gail and Margo again looked at her in astonishment.

"Why the heck are you unemployable?" demanded Gail. "You're a reliable mature person with a college degree."

"Have you tried to get a job lately?" retorted Lily, knowing that Gail lived on her investments. Gail's parents had bought oil-company stock long ago and over the decades this had grown to be a significant nest egg.

"No, but I've seen the 'Help Wanted' signs. People are hiring."

"Yes, but mostly at minimum wage, which isn't enough for me to live on if I keep the house. I haven't held a job since I married Don, which you know I did pretty much right after I got my AA at College of Marin."

"You did sort of do the old 'MRS degree,'" observed Margo.

"My degree was in French," said Lily immediately. "I could've transferred to State or probably even Berkeley if I hadn't fallen for Don." She was rather miffed that Margo could imply she hadn't been serious about her education. Margo was the one who had been more focused on boyfriends back then.

"Well, it all worked out fine," said Margo. "You had a happy marriage and got three lovely daughters too."

The marriage had been happy enough, Lily supposed, and she was certainly glad to have been able to focus on being a good mother to the girls, but … "Don't forget that that happy marriage is now in the past and my wonderful husband has left me practically penniless," she said sharply.

"Er … yes," admitted Margo, who cast her eyes down and busied herself with stabbing a new piece of broccoli into the dip.

"You know," broke in Gail, "I wonder if I have a possible solution for you. This is a gorgeous house with unused bedrooms, plus you're a whiz at whipping up the tasty hostess treats like this dip. And it's not as if there are a ton of places for tourists to stay when they come out to Stinson Beach, Bolinas, and Point Reyes. I mean, not a lot of places right along the coast—I'm sure there must be hotels in San Rafael and Corte Madera, but who wants to stay there if the plan is to relax on this side of the hills? What about turning the house into a bed-and-breakfast?"

"Omigod," said Margo, "she's right, you could *so* do that … if you feel like that'd be an acceptable solution."

Lily's mind was racing. After a moment of feeling just stunned at the notion of opening her home to strangers, she recognized that it certainly wasn't a stupid idea, it was purely a matter of whether she was willing. The house was a handsome old place with five bedrooms and three baths, and there might be some way of rearranging so that guests were all upstairs and she was downstairs.

"I'd have to think about it," she said slowly, "but you're right, that might possibly be a solution."

MEAGHAN
THE NEW TRUE BERNAL JOURNAL

Meaghan Simone looked up from her computer and gazed around the office with a feeling of great satisfaction. How lucky could she be! She'd somehow landed a position with this very cool local paper at a time when most newspapers were disappearing or going totally digital, and while the last of the earlier Bernal Heights community newspapers had folded back in 2012, she was confident that Carole Karpinski, the founder of *The New True Bernal Journal*, could totally pull off this slick, very hip, mixed print-and-digital neighborhood rag (but could you call it a rag if it was digital?). The office was small and funky in a good way (*not* funky as in stinky!), just one big room behind the garage in the downstairs of Carole's 1928 house, with a nice view into Carole's garden through a big sliding-glass door. Carole Karpinski was in her early sixties and had recently inherited the house from her parents, so now that she no longer had to pay a fortune in rent living over in the Marina District, she could use the rest of her inheritance for living expenses and to finance the paper. Or that was what she said, anyway.

"I was offered almost two million dollars for this house," Carole had confided to Meaghan, "but why would I sell my childhood home when keeping it means I no longer have to rent an apartment?"

Meaghan could certainly understand how Carole felt, because although her own parents had been perfectly willing for her to keep living in her old bedroom after college, she'd wanted to experience living and working in San Francisco, and the price to rent an apartment there was just horrifying, even for a girl from wealthy Marin County. And two million for Carole's house? It wasn't even a very special house, nothing like the big old coastal house Meaghan had grown up in. Carole's house was just another of those standard two- or three-story San Francisco houses with a garage on the lower floor next to the front door. Not that it wasn't a nice house, but there were hundreds like it all over San Francisco, with their bay-windowed stucco fronts and wooden rears. However, such houses were way out of Meaghan's own rental price range, so she'd moved in with her partner Shaun, who lived in a shabby studio that didn't look like it had been updated since about 1975. At least living with Shaun meant she didn't need to buy any furniture! The two of them shared a king-size mattress on the floor and had a big work table that served as a desk for both of them, and they ate their meals in the kitchen at a rickety table with just enough room for two place settings. Other than that, the décor consisted of a ficus tree in a large pot near the front window and some posters taped to the walls, all of which Shaun had provided. Meaghan had only had to bring her clothes, some toiletries, and her bike and laptop. She got her music via Spotify and her books electronically.

As she gazed around the newspaper office, Meaghan drank in its clean white walls, decorated with some big posters—framed, not taped up—that Carole had collected over the years. Carole had more than just one ficus tree in the office; she had one by each side of the sliding-glass door, like sentinels, and she'd also added smaller house plants like maranathas and spiderworts. The desks were all second-hand, but Carole had painted them in bright colors, so the office was a pretty cheerful-looking space, and in the bathroom there was a little electric table-top ceramic fountain that provided a soothing continual sound of flowing water. And Meaghan enjoyed the company of her fellow staffers, whose responsibilities involved art direction and advertising, while she and Britt Felker focused on reporting the news, learning about new businesses opening, old ones closing, and attending City

Council meetings to find out about anything that might affect the neighborhood.

While Meaghan missed walking on the beach every day and seeing the Pacific Ocean from her bedroom window, she was glad to have the chance to experience a very different lifestyle just an hour or so away from home. Well, it was more like three hours if you took the bus all the way. As she'd sold her car when she moved to the city, during her father's lifetime she'd met up with him in the Financial District for rides home. Now she generally took the bus as far as the Marin City hub and her mother drove over the hills to pick her up so that she didn't have to hang around forever in Marin City waiting for her transfer. Marin City might be in Marin, but while it was right there on the way from Sausalito to Mill Valley, it was still the poorest part of the county due to having been the only place where the black shipyard workers had been allowed to live following World War II. Meaghan and her family had some black friends, but people from significantly poorer social classes made them uneasy despite the fact that two of Meaghan's great-grandparents had come to California as dirt-poor Arkies and another of her great-grandparents had been an Okie. The fact that these great-grandparents had been born over a hundred years ago, had managed to prosper once the Depression was over, and (of course) were white, put them in a different category than people in Marin City who were still poor well into the twenty-first century. (Well, it was possible that the Okie wasn't entirely white, but he wasn't black; supposedly he'd had a Choctaw grandma. Meaghan had no idea whether this was true or not. She was just glad no one alive today in her family sounded like an Okie or an Arkie the way quite a few lower-income white Californians still did.)

Anyway, she thought, here I am and I'm a reporter in San Francisco!

The door opened and Britt Felker entered the office, saying "Something's up! Some dudes in suits showed up at Carole's front door while I was across the street interviewing a restaurant owner."

"Dudes in suits?" said Dontay, the layout guy.

"Yeah, suits," said Britt. "Not like Financial District suits, either."

"They were cheap suits?" said Meaghan, whose Financial District father had worn good quality haberdashery; Lily had made sure of that.

"Mormon missionary suits?" asked Lyric, the ad sales manager.

"Not Mormons, they were too old for that," said Britt. "I didn't see them very well, but Carole opened the door and let them in."

"Oh," said Meaghan. "Well, then they're probably insurance salesmen or something like that." Presumably Carole had an appointment with these people if she let them into her living area, after all. And since she wasn't bringing them into the office, evidently the meeting didn't relate to *The New True Bernal Journal.*

"Well, maybe ..." said Britt dubiously. "I just had kind of a funny feeling about them."

"That's probably because you want to be a crime reporter," said Meaghan. "Everything looks suspicious to you." Meaghan herself had no wish to be a crime reporter. She didn't even read mysteries, usually. For now, Meaghan was quite content covering her local news beat. Later, she thought, she might like to be a music journalist and write about her favorite bands, or even write novels, but for the present *The New True Bernal Journal* suited her very nicely.

AMBER
TIFFANY'S TROUBLES

Amber Simone was tidying up her studio at the end of a not-so-long day of putting together pieces of trash abstracted from recycling bins and forming them somehow into the shape of a seagull. She felt quite pleased with the result of her labors; this particular seagull was perched on the end of an old wooden piling and for the moment it was gazing saucily at yesterday's gull, which was in flight across the room. Several other gulls, along with cranes and even a few coots, also occupied the studio (though coots didn't sell as well). Amber's studio was not large, just an add-on sort of room in the one-bedroom mother-in-law unit or granny house she rented from one of her mother's neighbors, but it served her well for this kind of work. These seabirds were her bread and butter, selling pretty well to tourists and at the occasional craft fair, and they financed materials for other types of art project, such as those she constructed for the Burning Man festival each year.

Yes, everything was looking very good, other than her relationship with the enchanting but irritating Greg Stover, who had informed her earlier in the day that he really couldn't meet up for dinner after all because his son had some kind of ball game and he'd promised his wife (not yet ex-wife, but long-separated) that he'd go. Why this was, Amber could not imagine. Greg was no great fan of ball games and neither, as far as she knew, was his son Brayden; it was Greg's wife Tippy who was the sports enthusiast, so why didn't *she* take the unfortunate Brayden to this game, thereby leaving Greg free to dine and cavort with Amber? Before this ball game had arisen like the ghost of masculinity past, Greg had proposed that Amber join him to listen to his friend Joe's band, which had a gig at a bar over in Mill Valley. She'd planned to meet him at the downstairs flat he was renting in nearby Tam Valley—which was unfortunately just down the road from the big redwood house where Tippy and Brayden still lived—and from there the two would have headed for the comparative metropolis of Mill Valley (population 14,000 or thereabouts).

But no, that was not to be, and although she and the ridiculously handsome, sexy, Greg had been an item for several years now, she was getting more than a little tired of his failure to sever the knot with Tippy. Was Tippy really that clingy, that he couldn't drag himself away? Tippy was also, Amber thought, to blame for having named the poor kid something as stupidly trendy as Brayden; the miserable boy's classmates included Braedon, Jayden, Kaden, Aiden, and Grayden, not to mention Hayden and Peyton, while the rest of the class included the likes of Hunter, Cooper, Taylor, Madison, and Addison. Amber and her siblings had also been unlucky enough to bear ultra-popular names for their generation; she had suffered through being one of seven Ambers in her class, which had also been graced with a Megyn, a Mygghn, four Emilys, and an Emma, so she sympathized with Greg's kid on that front.

Amber was interrupted in her tidying by the phone, however; and she could tell by the ringtone that it was not Greg but her sister Tiffany. Tiffany had been one of only three Tiffanys in grade school, as most of the Tiffanys had been a few years older. Admittedly, once the Simone girls had reached high school, they'd experienced a wider mix of names—Tam High served Sausalito, Marin City, and Mill Valley as well as Tam Junction, Tam Valley, and the Pacific-facing hamlets of Stinson Beach and Bolinas—so there had been the likes of Demetrius, LaShonda, Jamal, Lupe, Micah, Lakshmi, and even a Susan.

"Hey, sis, what's up?" said Amber into the phone, her attention still largely on tucking things away and doing a little dusting.

"Wanna get together for supper?" said Tiffany, to Amber's surprise. Tiffany was married and not often available for impromptu dinners.

"Sure," said Amber. "That dork Greg has canceled our evening together in favor of watching Brayden play sports."

"Oh, that's too bad," said Tiffany glibly, "but he does have to be a dad. You wouldn't want him neglecting his kid."

"No, but it's not like Brayden is even into sports. This is Tippy's idea. Greg just bends to whatever family activity she suggests. He needs to make a cleaner break with Tippy, make it legal. Then do stuff with Brayden on a schedule and stick to things Brayden actually likes. Brayden isn't in the running to be the All-American Boy, he's a creative soul like Greg and me."

"Well, yeah," said Tiffany. "You're probably right. But since they're off being a nuclear family, how about Thai takeout for you and me? I could bring some over in half an hour or so. One veggie and one shrimp, maybe?"

"That sounds fabulous," returned Amber, who was now wondering what was up with Tiffany. While the sisters got along well enough, Tiffany was not exactly in the habit of inviting herself over with takeout; she was usually at home dreaming up something that she and her husband could eat whenever he got home from his job with one of San Francisco's countless tech startups.

Pondering this question, Amber closed up the studio and turned to putting her kitchenette in order. Not that the kitchenette was particularly messy—it rarely was—but Amber liked to greet guests, even her sisters, with a fresh centerpiece (whether floral or just some interesting branches), a choice of wines, and festive napkins. That was how Lily had brought them up, that within a few minutes they could make the kitchen or dining room look welcoming and attractive. So Amber cleared the tiny table of the few letters and miscellaneous items that sat on it, then brought forth a crisp tablecloth with an autumnal pattern of pumpkins and seasonal zodiac signs—her own design, printed by the online fabric design store Spoonflower—and set down plates, silverware, vintage salt and pepper shakers, wine glasses, and a bottle of Sriracha sauce. *Voilà,* very nice. That accomplished, she flung herself across the couch and began checking her phone for messages.

•   •   •

Tiffany was at Amber's door in surprisingly little time, given that she'd had to phone in the takeout order and pick it up on her way from her and Jason's apartment in the Strawberry area of Mill Valley prior to heading through Tam Valley and over the hills to Amber's place by the beach.

"Green curry shrimp and *pad see ew,*" she announced as Amber opened the door.

"Yum," said Amber. "Just set 'em on the tray there on the table." No point in spilling sauce on the tablecloth if they could avoid it; takeout boxes sometimes had drips of sauce on the bottoms. She examined Tiffany as she followed her sister into the kitchenette and concluded that yes, something was amiss. Tiffany usually looked so much the perfect young Marin County matron—the most conventional of the sisters, she always had her straight blonde hair perfectly combed, contained in a ponytail or pressed away from her face with a brightly colored sweatband, and she usually wore clothes that suggested she was just about to go for a run or play tennis or model for a fitness magazine. This evening her hair was a bit wispy and askew, and she was wearing baggy gray sweatpants that Amber was quite sure dated back to high school P.E. class; Amber was sure she had not seen Tiffany in sweatpants since Tam High days. "Chardonnay or Zin?" she asked. "Or I think I've got Pinot Grigio or Cabernet too." Amber believed in having a good stock of Napa and Sonoma County wines on hand.

"For right now I think I'll stick to water," said Tiffany. This was not her usual dinner drink, but more associated with the big bottles all of the sisters carried everywhere to ensure they were properly "hydrated."

"Tap or Calistoga?" said Amber, eyeing her sister.

"Oh, Calistoga, of course. Lime if you have any."

"How about lemon instead?" Amber didn't keep limes on hand, as her landlady had a lemon tree that she was allowed to harvest.

"Yeah, fine, it's all citrus."

Amber noted the obviousness of this fact as she rolled and sliced one of the lemons from her fruit basket. It wasn't as if she'd offered Tiffany a slice of grapefruit or kumquat or some other unlikely form of citrus for her water. She said nothing as she handed Tiffany the tumbler of sparkling mineral water, then said "Well, let's dish up and sit down. I'm looking forward to digging into that *pad see ew*."

"I keep thinking I should take a class in Asian cooking," said Tiffany.

"I'm sure College of Marin has Thai or Szechuan classes," said Amber. "Or even one of the Parks and Rec departments might, like San Rafael."

"You're probably right," said Tiffany, spooning up a helping of the *pad see ew*. She took only a tiny serving of the shrimp, which lay nestled in the white takeout box like pink corpses.

"Take some more," said Amber. "You aren't going full vegetarian, are you?"

"No, I'm still pescatarian," responded Tiffany. "I'm just not sure I can take a lot of the chilis tonight."

It wasn't, thought Amber, as if either of the dishes had to be spicy if Tiffany's digestion was feeling delicate. Just because they often ate scary-hot Thai and Indian food didn't mean they couldn't also enjoy a simple chow mein or pad Thai. "Well," she said, "it's a good thing you still eat seafood, because Mom would be very sad if we turned down her Christmas scallops."

They ate, and spoke of this and that, but the conversation lagged. At last, their plates emptied, Amber said "Let's move to the couch. So much comfier than these chairs, and we might see the last of the sunset."

"You do have a nice view," said Tiffany. "Jason and I love most things about our apartment, but it really has no view at all."

"How is Jason, anyway?" asked Amber, stretching out her legs in front of her as she settled into the couch and lifted her wine glass. "I haven't seen him in ages."

Tiffany's face crumpled. "Well, that's the thing, I feel like *I* haven't seen him in ages either!"

"What?" exclaimed Amber. "You haven't seen him?" Tiffany and Jason had been together since high school. The whole family liked Jason. "Is he *missing*?"

"No, of course he's not *missing*," said Tiffany. "Not physically missing. He comes home at night—eventually."

"Eventually? You mean like at three A.M.? Do you think he's having an affair?"

"No, I mean like by nine or so. He's such a fucking workaholic."

"Oh, well that's nothing new."

"Exactly, that's the problem!" exclaimed Tiffany. "I wouldn't mind if it was just now and then. I'm sure his boss appreciates it and there'll be a bonus at the end of the year. But it's nearly every night. I've talked to him about it and asked him to make more time for our marriage, and each time he agrees and then slides right back into being Mr. Type A corporate guy. We were starting to think about having a baby, but first of all he's always too tired to do more than eat and fall asleep, and secondly I'm getting fed up with being less important than his job, so I'm not too interested in bringing a kid into a situation like that."

"Maybe it'll just be temporary. These startups have periods of intense heavy lifting early on. Maybe things'll settle down in a month or two."

Tiffany heaved a sigh. "Startups don't settle down that fast unless they're about to self-destruct. We've been going through this for a long time now and I'm about ready to call it quits."

Amber's eyes widened. "You and Jason've been together forever! What about counseling?"

Tiffany fiddled with the ends of her ponytail, twisting them around her index finger. "Well, maybe to counseling, but I doubt it'd work.

Jason is just not a good candidate. He's like an addict—he tells me he'll change, and then after a week or so he's back to being Mr. Workaholic."

"I have to admit, I've been considering breaking things off with Greg, but that's different. You're married!"

Tiffany took a breath. "As for you and Greg, I'm surprised you didn't leave him ages ago. Married men who won't get divorced are just trouble."

"Well," said Amber, "married men who are separated are not exactly in the same category as married men who live with their wives."

"Yeah, but so many of them go back," said Tiffany.

Amber could hardly dispute that.

MEAGHAN
SURPRISES AT WORK AND AT HOME

Meaghan had awakened feeling absurdly content. Yes, here she was living in San Francisco, waking up beside her beloved Shaun, and soon she'd be off to work at *The New True Bernal Journal.* It was like a wonderful dream. She looked over at Shaun, who was still peacefully asleep, pink hair tousled, nose ring slightly askew. Soon she'd be introducing Shaun to her family. The idea was a little scary, because she hadn't yet told them that Shaun wasn't a guy, but her mother had always joked that it'd be perfectly okay if one of her children turned out to be gay, just so long as not all of them did. So that should be fine when the time came. Meanwhile, Shaun looked so sweet curled up there under the covers …

Meaghan quickly readied herself for work, then leaned down to kiss Shaun on the cheek. "I'm just about ready to leave for work, sweetie," she said, a little sad that Shaun's bartending job meant late nights and sleepy mornings.

"Ohhhh …" Shaun yawned. "Honey, I wish you didn't have to leave so early!"

"It's not *that* early," said Meaghan. "I don't have to be there till eight-thirty."

"That's so early," groaned Shaun.

"I'll be home in time for supper," said Meaghan. "We'll have some just-us time."

"I guess," said Shaun.

They exchanged a kiss, and then Meaghan was out the door.

Arriving at Carole Karpinski's and *The New True Bernal Journal* office, Meaghan set her backpack beside her desk and went to pour herself a coffee from the small coffee-maker near the sink, greeting her co-workers with a cheery "*¡Hola!*"

"Carole said to stick around this morning and not go out on any stories yet, she wants to meet with us," said Britt Felker.

"Did she say what it was about?" Meaghan added a squirt of honey to her coffee and took a cautious sip.

"No, but she seemed a little strange. Tense or something. She's been kind of jumpy lately, especially since those guys in the suits visited."

"Oh, those!" laughed Meaghan. "You really have an imagination. Guys in suits visit Carole and right away they're up to something sinister!"

"She hasn't been herself," persisted Britt.

"Yeah, she's been a little weird," said Dontay, "especially when she popped in this morning."

Meaghan smiled disbelievingly, and they all settled back down at their computers for a while. Meaghan could not imagine that anything could truly be amiss—maybe Carole was just feeling menopausal or something. Everything always hummed along pretty smoothly in the office, since after all it was a very small paper with only a few employees, so there was not really much to worry about. It wasn't like at larger papers where there was the danger of being taken over by some big corporation and then being downsized out of existence. So long as Carole could pay the paper's expenses, everything would be fine, and Carole had inherited quite a tidy amount, or so she'd indicated. Meaghan felt that this gig at *The New True Bernal Journal* was an absolutely ideal way to start her writing career.

Ten o'clock rolled around, and Meaghan was just getting herself another cup of coffee, when they heard Carole coming down the stairs from the private area of the house. Putting down the coffee carafe, she called out "Hi, Carole!" Meaghan always enjoyed their meetings with the publisher, who usually spoke enthusiastically about the need to bring back ultra-local journalism and help bring customers to the neighborhood's small businesses.

"Good morning, everyone," said Carole as she went over to the whiteboard where she typically wrote ideas and assignments. She looked weary, and her short gray hair was just a little untidy.

"Good morning Carole," said the newspaper staff, including Meaghan, as they pulled chairs nearer the whiteboard.

"Only, I'm afraid it's not really a very good morning at all," Carole went on. "I've got some very bad news to share."

The staffers looked startled, and one or two looked about to say something, when Carole continued.

"I'm afraid I can't continue to publish *The New True Bernal Journal*," she said. "The paper is defunct as of today."

"What?" demanded Britt. "What about the next issue? We're in the middle of putting it together."

"You'll have to stop work on it," said Carole. "I'm sorry, but this is due to circumstances beyond my control."

"Dang, lady," muttered Dontay. "Hey," he said more loudly, "we're getting paid, aren't we?"

Carole ignored this question. "Please clear out your desks of all personal belongings by noon. I'm very sorry, but we have to wrap this up pronto."

"That's crazy," said Britt.

"But Carole …" began Meaghan. "We all love the paper." She felt quite discombobulated at this news.

"I loved it too, but it's over. I don't have a choice about this," said Carole dismissively as she turned to go back up the stairs to her living room.

"Hey, you can't just leave like that!" exclaimed Dontay.

"What the hell happened?" yelled Britt.

"Carole …" cried Lyric.

Meaghan just stared dumbstruck at the entrance to the stairs, where Carole could no longer be seen. It was curtained off with strings of beads, which she'd always thought was very cute and retro-boho, but which now seemed a strange barrier to the private part of the house.

•   •   •

Returning to the studio apartment after packing up her personal items from the newspaper office, Meaghan expected she'd immediately be telling Shaun of the paper's demise and her sudden need to find a new job. While the studio was small and outdated in its features, it was still expensive; neither she nor Shaun were old enough to have benefitted from longtime rent control the way some of their older friends had. As recent renters, they paid market rate.

Since Shaun tended bar to support the beginnings of a career in documentary photography, Meaghan wondered whether she too might find work as a bartender. She knew the tips could be good, but did she know enough about mixing drinks? She wasn't sure that she did. She'd grown up reasonably familiar with the wines of Napa and Sonoma counties, as her parents had enjoyed going on winery tours and always brought home bottles of their favorite vintages, but she didn't think most people ordered wine when they went to bars. From going to parties with her classmates, she'd sampled various beers, as well as downing random concoctions made with vodka, tequila, rum, and gin, but she hadn't actually mixed many drinks on her own. Perhaps Shaun could teach her—or perhaps she could wait tables at one of the local restaurants. In either case, tip income would be vital to paying her bills, which included student loans that her father had pressed her to take out on the grounds that this would give her a credit history (it had worked for him, he'd said). He hadn't seemed to realize that student loans were a different animal for her generation than they'd been for his own.

These and other thoughts raced through her mind as she ascended the stairs to the shared studio—stairs carpeted in what must once have been a regal manner with a ruby red material, but which were now worn and stained. Recently, in fact, another tenant had flung the contents of a can of gray house paint all over the third-floor hallway, which even after two months looked like a fresh wet spill. At the time of the paint-flinging, Meaghan had found it kind of exciting, but she'd soon grown tired of seeing streaks and drips of paint all over a carpet that the landlord evidently felt could last another decade or two. She sighed and unlocked the studio door—hoping that Shaun would be home, but not quite ready to announce herself—and headed for the kitchen to make herself a sandwich.

"Meaghan?" came Shaun's voice, and then Shaun hesitantly entering the kitchen as Meaghan retrieved a package of cheese from the refrigerator to examine the label. *Havarti*, the label stated; well, that'd do.

"Hey," said Meaghan dispiritedly.

"Meaghan, I've been putting this off, but …"

There was something in Shaun's voice that might normally have alerted Meaghan to trouble, but between losing her job and picking out a sandwich-suitable hunk of cheese, her intuition was blunted. "What's up?" she said, expecting that perhaps Shaun hadn't paid the gas bill or something.

"Well, um, like I said, I've been putting off bringing this up, but I can't leave it unsaid any longer."

This caught Meaghan's attention somewhat more urgently. With the beginnings of fear, she said "Sweetie, I know I'm probably too picky about the laundry, but it's okay, I don't really care. I really didn't mean to nag you about it the other day—"

"It's not about the laundry," said Shaun. "Besides, you were probably right about the laundry. I never knew it was better to separate the whites from the colored, which by the way sounds racist when I say it, but it's laundry, not people."

"Well, you did turn all my whites gray," said Meaghan. "But I still love you."

"That's good," said Shaun; "that's good you still love me, because what I need to say isn't easy."

Meaghan was still having some trouble thinking very clearly about anything beyond her job situation, but she supposed that at least it didn't sound as if Shaun wanted to break up with her. That would've been terrible! "So … say it. It can't be that hard, can it?"

"Um, well actually it is. I've thought about this for a long time, long and hard. For a long time I kept thinking no, I shouldn't do it …"

"What, you decided to apply to grad school after all? You don't want to go someplace far away, do you? I could go with you …" said Meaghan in a hurry. Maybe if Shaun got accepted into an MFA program in someplace like Iowa, it'd be easy to get a job and a nicer apartment. Not that she wanted to leave the Bay Area! But still …

"No, it's not about grad school."

"Well?"

"Like I said, this is hard to say," said Shaun. "Okay, I've thought it through and I want to transition."

Still having trouble focusing on the situation to hand, Meaghan wrinkled her brow and said "Transition to what? Where? I thought you liked working at the bar."

Shaun's face took on a ghastly expression. "Meaghan! You aren't fucking listening! This is not about my fucking stupid job, I'm going to transition! I'm a man, goddamn it, and I'm done pretending to be a goddamn woman. Why do you think I go by 'Shaun' instead of 'Shauna,' anyway?"

The meaning of Shaun's words finally penetrated, and Meaghan shrieked "Shaun!" It was not a shriek of joy.

LILY
CONSIDERING THE HOUSE

Lily had taken a good hard look at her house since the conversation with Gail and Margo. She and Don had bought early in their marriage, and as it was one of the older houses in an area mainly built up after World War II—dating almost back to the days of refugees from the 1906 San Francisco earthquake and fire—it was a little unusual for that part of the coast. Its three storeys were built into the slope that led away from the beach, with the middle floor being the main and largest level and boasting a wraparound porch; the lower floor featuring a separate entrance and ocean-facing deck; and the upper floor hosting the three small and sloped-ceiling bedrooms formerly occupied by Tiffany, Amber, and Meaghan. With its cheerful sky-blue exterior and cream trim, set off by the small yard's plantings of ceanothus, agapanthus, rosemary, and cypress, it presented a charming face to the world. The main floor was likewise a welcoming space, with large windows and unusual unpainted board-and-batten walls that emphasized the beauty of the honey-toned wood. The house had been in some need of repair when Lily and Don bought it—this had made it possible for them to make a successful offer, with some help from their parents, when Don wasn't yet making a high salary. Then, over the years, they had gradually fixed and spruced up the property until Lily felt that it was really quite a dream house. She enjoyed decorating—perhaps she should have studied interior design rather than French—and had chosen a mix of folk art and prints, unusual but comfortable chairs, festive tiles and pottery, and had added mirrors here and there to make every room look just a little larger and brighter. Certainly, Lily thought, after more than thirty years spent perfecting her home, she did not want to give it up if she didn't have to!

Yet was it truly feasible to turn the house into a B&B? Lily wasn't sure. First of all, while Gail and Margo had seemed to think there was a shortage of rooms for travelers to rent along this stretch of the coast, a quick Google search had indicated that in fact there was no dearth of rentals. Hotels and motels and genuine B&Bs might be in short supply on this side of the hills, but it looked to her as if quite a few people in Stinson Beach (maybe fewer in reclusive Bolinas) had offered up rooms or even entire cabins and houses for rent. Prices ran the gamut, from under a hundred a night to well over a thousand. After looking through the listings, Lily began to feel as if she might be the only homeowner between Marin Headlands and Point Reyes who *wasn't* renting out rooms (well, neither were Gail or Margo, but they lived in cottages with no room to spare).

It did seem, however, that these rentals were focused on couples and families, and even on groups as large as ten or more, and that the guests were generally expected to bring their own groceries. A real B&B would offer a scrumptious breakfast, and wasn't seeking groups who wanted to rent an entire condo or cottage. Maybe there was still some degree of demand that wasn't being fully met—for example singles and couples who wanted to spend time on the beach or explore the coast while being able to come back to a comfy spot where someone else would make breakfast in the morning. Lily liked making breakfasts, and without Don or the girls in the house, she now had almost no reason to make waffles or bake coffee cake or prepare anything more elaborate than eggs or a crockpot of steel-cut oatmeal (the latter lasting her all week). It was true that she had sometimes resented having to make breakfast early enough to feed Don before he drove over the hills and across the Golden Gate Bridge to the Financial District, where he had had to be at work dreadfully early, especially during the period when he'd worked at the Pacific Stock Exchange, which pretty much operated on East Coast time. The girls, however, had usually been a pleasure to feed before school; even if they hadn't always been fully awake, they'd enjoyed their breakfasts.

That still, of course, left the question of whether she was willing to let strangers sleep in her home, even if she could attract any to come.

And so Lily wandered upstairs and down, deep in thought as she considered this problem. Upstairs, she could easily imagine converting the girls' rooms, provided that no daughter raised the roof at the idea of her childhood bedroom being rented to strangers. Tiffany was married and comfortably settled with Jason in that apartment in Strawberry, so she wasn't likely to object; similarly, Amber had been living in that neighbor's rental for several years. Lily was less sure about Meaghan, as she knew that the studio shared with Shaun was tiny—Meaghan's belongings were almost all still in her old bedroom—and who knew whether Meaghan and Shaun would last as a couple. Nobody in the family had even met Shaun yet, after all, whereas they all knew Jason well and even Amber's Greg wasn't exactly an unknown quantity. Whether Amber stayed with Greg or left him, she wasn't likely to want or need to move back home. So, apart from Meaghan's room, chances were good that the upstairs rooms were easily convertible, and there was a small bathroom in the fourth corner of the square upper floor, meaning that no one need come downstairs at night.

Well, at least not to use the bathroom. Lily was well aware that a guest might reasonably remember having left something important in the car, or alternatively a guest might stay out late and need to enter the main floor, which was where the master bedroom was located. Lily did not like the idea that guests—meaning strangers, not relatives or friends—might end up wandering about near her bedroom and bathroom during the night.

There were, she thought, two possible ways of dealing with this should she actually turn the house into a B&B. If she remained in the master bedroom, she could install a lock on the door. On the other hand, the lower floor did have its own separate entrance and was set up with a bedroom, bathroom, and kitchenette. The Simone family had mainly used the space as a rec room, storage area, and occasional guest suite. In theory, Lily could simply move down there and turn the master bedroom into an office. The question was, did she want to do that? It was, of course, part of her house, but it wasn't as nice as the main floor, apart from the fact that it opened onto the deck. The main floor was where she'd focused her decorating and where the majority of her married life had been spent. The master bedroom was redolent with memories … admittedly both good and bad ones, because although the marriage had been largely satisfactory, there'd been times when she'd wondered whether she ought to leave.

But, Lily thought firmly as she gazed about the lower floor and took stock of the furnishings, there was no point in thinking about *that*. It was quite enough that Don had developed a brain tumor, spent all their money, and jumped off the Golden Gate Bridge. There was no need to drag in any other less than desirable aspects of their marriage.

TIFFANY
MUSHROOM STROGANOFF

Tiffany glanced at the front door as she gave the mushroom stroganoff another stir. When on earth was Jason going to get home? He'd texted that he was on his way—he commuted on Golden Gate Transit since their apartment in Strawberry was convenient to the bus—so surely he ought to be showing up any minute. The stroganoff would be getting rather dry if it spent much longer on the stove.

She'd been feeling torn about their marriage for quite some time now. She still loved Jason and felt sure that he still loved her, but this was not how she felt marriage ought to be. This was not 1950 with the Man in the Gray Flannel Suit and the little wifey awaiting him in apron and high heels! It was not even 2000, when her mother had at least expected her father to do some minimal amount of housework (not that Tiffany was sure exactly what Don had done that was actually outside of a traditional dad's purview—he'd done some home repairs and gardening on the weekends). Tiffany felt that in her own generation, romance and hot sex should take a larger role, at least prior to the advent of children, and Jason was not around enough to carry through properly on that. She felt willing to do the majority of the housework since she worked only part time at a local boutique, but she'd married Jason for love, not because he was a meal ticket, after all.

Ah, at last there came the sound of the front door. What a relief! No dried-out stroganoff this time. Still, they had to talk.

"Jason?"

"Hey, Tiff," came Jason's voice. He didn't sound excited to be home. He rarely did. Sure, Tiffany knew he came home tired after these long days, but she felt he could muster at least a little joy.

"We're having mushroom stroganoff. I'm dishing it up now."

"Fine, give me a minute." He didn't even sound like he looked forward to eating. This had to stop. This was no way to live!

"Okay, but I don't want it to get cold."

"Yeah, I know. Leave it on the stove a minute more."

"It'll get dry on the stove. Do you want some wine?"

"Sure. Wine's good. I won't be so long that anything'll dry out. We don't always need to eat the minute I get home." His voice was faint; evidently he'd gone into the bedroom or the bathroom. Well, yes, he ought to use the bathroom and wash up first. Still …

"Okay, I'm pouring."

After a moment, Jason stepped into the kitchen. "Smells good," he said. He looked tired, but other than having taken off his shoes, he still looked work-appropriate in his chinos and polo shirt. Work appropriate for the tech industry, anyway. It was convenient that he didn't have to dress up particularly for work—certainly a more affordable wardrobe than her father's suits had been—but it meant that on work days he didn't look any different for home. He still looked like Mr. Tech Startup Guy, a look that had lost its luster for Tiffany. Not that she knew how else she wanted him to look—she wasn't a huge fan of his weekend T-shirts either.

"Let's hope it tastes as good as it smells," said Tiffany. "It's been on the stove quite a while."

"Oh, it's always good. You're a fantastic cook," said Jason, seating himself at their small table and raising his wineglass in a salute.

"Well," said Tiffany, serving the plates and sitting down herself, having poured Calistoga water into her own wineglass, "I'm glad you like my cooking, but you don't get it at its best when you're always coming home so late."

"It's still great food," said Jason. "I appreciate that you're such a good cook."

"I know, but I don't appreciate that you keep coming home late."

"We've already discussed this," said Jason. "This is just how it is right now."

"Well, the discussion isn't over," said Tiffany. "Marriage is a partnership, and in a partnership both parties have a voice."

"We do both have a voice," said Jason. "Neither of us can have what we want all the time, though. I'm the one who's supporting us financially and my job currently requires long hours." His tone was patient but there was an edge of the long-suffering to it.

"I'm tired of this. You could take some other job. I could work more hours if you weren't earning as much. I need you to be a real part of this marriage."

"I like my job," said Jason. "Sure, I don't always like the long hours, but it's a good job and I enjoy it most of the time. There's no way you could earn enough at the boutique to pay our rent, and we aren't even in a very big apartment."

"It's about our marriage, not about our money," said Tiffany.

"Yeah, but marriage is always about money. You can't have a successful marriage if the money isn't handled right."

Tiffany sighed. "I'm sure poor people have happy marriages too. I need you to be part of my *life*, not just be my financial partner." It seemed like she had explained this quite a few times. Why was he not getting her point? "Look, I love you, but if we aren't going to have quality time together, then maybe this isn't working." Her eyes flashed. "I think I'd better give single life a try."

Jason went pale. He stared at her for a moment, then said "Fine. I love you too, and I've been trying to make this work, but I guess it's time to tell you something. I love you tons, always have and always will, but I'm really more attracted to guys. I've never done anything about that, but I guess now I will."

MEAGHAN
AN UNEXPECTED INDICTMENT

Upon hearing Shaun's news, Meaghan had run out of the apartment and down the stairs and into the street. She knew, of course, that this wasn't any way to deal with the situation, but to first lose her job and then hear that Shaun was going to transition to identify as a man—well, this was just more than she could handle. She'd thought she was doing very well at "adulting," but this level of adulting felt way beyond her skill set.

As she stood on the sidewalk staring into the street, she realized, to her relief, that her small shoulder bag—where she carried her wallet and phone—was still hanging at her side even though she'd set her backpack on one of the kitchen chairs. Okay, this was good; she did not have to return immediately to the apartment and apologize to Shaun for her terrible reaction. Yes, she would certainly apologize, because she knew she'd been cruel to poor Shaun, but first she needed some space, some time to herself. She headed down the street to the nearest café and ordered a chai latte.

The hot and spicy sweetness of the chai latte was very comforting as Meaghan sat at the little table in the corner of the café (a table chosen for its relative obscurity in case she began crying too visibly), but of course it did not solve any of her problems. And what, exactly, *would* solve these problems? She needed a new job and she needed to apologize to Shaun, but merely apologizing to Shaun wasn't going to solve the sudden rift in their relationship. Shaun might be too hurt and offended to accept an apology, and even if Shaun accepted her apology, what was the future of their relationship? This was all just way too much uncertainty.

"Meaghan!" came the voice of Britt Felker, quite suddenly.

What the heck was Britt doing here? Meaghan didn't particularly want to talk to Britt right now, although she had enjoyed working with her former colleague. But this was just not when she wanted to chat with Britt.

"Meaghan!" said Britt again, now pulling up a chair at Meaghan's table and setting down her own drink, which looked like an espresso, for heaven's sake. Maybe she'd gulp it down and go away. But instead Britt said "You'll never believe what I've been finding out!"

"What?" said Meaghan dully.

"You know I was suspicious that something was going on when those dudes in suits showed up to talk to Carole."

"Yeah, yeah," said Meaghan. She didn't think she could produce a full sentence at the moment; when ordering her drink it had been all she could do to mutter "Chai latte, please."

"Well, I'd actually been doing a little investigation on the side into Carole and her finances, because I was a little surprised that somebody like her would suddenly start up a tiny local newspaper, especially at this moment in the history of journalism. It's not like she had prior experience in journalism, after all."

"So?" Meaghan thought it was kind of weird that Britt would investigate their employer, but she supposed that aspiring crime reporters probably stuck their noses into everything. In the short time she and Britt had worked together, Britt had taken the view that crime was probably rampant among the businesses that they reported on, whether it was graft or other white-collar crime, or getting merchandise that had "fallen off a truck" instead of buying it wholesale.

"Well, so after she suddenly closed down the paper—I mean, who on earth shuts down their newspaper or any other legitimate business *that* suddenly and with that little explanation—I got online and on the phone and did some digging, and it turns out that Carole's been indicted!"

"What?" said Meaghan incredulously. This could not possibly be true. People like former president Trump and people who embezzled huge sums of money got indicted. Publishers of tiny newspapers did not get indicted.

"Yes, she's been indicted! That means a grand jury has already met and thinks the prosecutor has a case!"

"But …" How could this be? Carole seemed like a perfectly normal person to Meaghan. Why would a prosecutor want to indict her?

"Carole's been nailed for laundering money for the Russians!" exclaimed Britt. "She did not inherit a fortune. That is, she inherited just enough that it didn't look strange to her friends that she began to have some money."

"But … the *Russians?*" uttered Meaghan. Like most people she knew, Meaghan had been shocked when Russia had invaded Ukraine, and so she'd become strongly pro-Ukraine. She had a Ukrainian flag pin and a sunflower pin on her denim jacket, and she and Shaun displayed a Ukrainian flag poster in their window.

"Probably not the Russian government, but Russian crooks, so basically the same thing," said Britt. "Her boyfriend's Russian, so that's probably how she got involved. She's just one of a whole crew of people who've been indicted."

"Carole has a Russian boyfriend?" Meaghan managed to say. Britt had finally sufficiently distracted her from her own woes that she could form and voice an entire sentence.

"Yeah, you probably never met him, his name's Yuri. San Francisco's full of Russians, after all. I don't know whether it goes back to the days of Russian fur trappers or just to the Russian Revolution, but where do you think Russian Hill got its name? The Richmond is full of Russians, likewise the Sunset, likewise wherever. Whenever things have been bad in Russia, people have headed for San Francisco."

"Things are always bad in Russia," asserted Meaghan.

"Well, sometimes it's worse than other times, but yeah, plenty of reason for Russians to come here over a long period of time. White Russians, Jewish Russians, dissident Russians, oligarch Russians, whoever."

"Wow," said Meaghan.

"So now Carole will either be arrested or allowed to surrender and be booked," explained Britt. "Then she'll be arraigned. I'm guessing she pleads not-guilty at that point; most defendants do. After that, it's usually pre-trial hearings. That's when she'd try to plea-bargain; that's actually how most criminal cases end, with plea bargains."

Meaghan was not that interested in the details of how the legal system worked; she wanted to know why Carole would get involved in money-laundering in the first place. Having a Russian boyfriend didn't seem like a good enough reason to get involved in organized crime, unless … "Is her boyfriend abusive or something? Was she forced into this?"

"Dunno," said Britt. "Probably not, but who knows? She might say he forced her when it comes to the plea-bargain stage. Depends on how loyal she is to him, I suppose."

"Isn't Carole kind of old to have a boyfriend?"

Britt laughed. "Don't be silly, Meaghan. Even people in nursing homes have lovers. Wait'll you're her age, I bet you won't feel ready to be done with love yet."

Meaghan burst into tears.

LILY
YES TO A B&B

"I'm doing it," Lily told Margo and Gail. "I'm going to give the B&B idea a try."

"Wow!" said Gail. "You've already decided? I didn't think you were that keen on the idea."

"Well, I can't go on much longer without income. Don really wiped out our finances."

Margo said, "I still can't believe that such a smart guy would be so dumb as to put all your money into crypto. That is, a guy who's smart about money like Don was. I'm sure plenty of people who are smart in other areas were dumb about crypto."

"I prefer to think it was his brain tumor talking," said Lily. "His doctor told me afterward that some brain tumors make people irrational or even violent. Don definitely went irrational."

"Yeah, it's just crazy—the stock market has mostly been good to us for years now, even if it did plunge during COVID, and Don was getting near retirement age," said Gail. "All the financial advice says to move your investments toward safer then, not to add new risk."

"He was *fifty-nine* when he died," said Lily. "So while he was getting near retirement age—he talked about maybe retiring at sixty-two or even sixty—he wasn't old enough to take money out of the retirement accounts without paying a huge penalty. Just a few more months and there'd have been no penalty—totally irrational!"

"I know," said Margo soothingly. "It's just terrible, such a shock to discover after he died, but you've been so strong."

Lily sniffed. She felt they didn't really need to have this conversation a second time. Time to pivot the topic. "It's not that I'm so strong, it's that I don't have a lot of options. Anyway, since I really don't want to sell the house and I'd only be likely to get hired at minimum wage being a Walmart greeter or something, your B&B suggestion seems like the best choice. Even though Google tells me that everyone under the sun on this side of the hills is renting out rooms, I can at least give it a shot and start testing the viability through Airbnb or Vrbo." She took a breath. "This house is pretty different than most of the other room-rentals around here, after all. Most of the existing rentals are Mid-Century or cute cottages, but this house is over a hundred years old, even if it's not quite Victorian. And I'll provide fabulous breakfasts, which means I can charge more than if it were just a bed for the night."

"How many rooms will you rent?" asked Margo. "Have you told the girls yet?"

"The girls don't know yet, so that might affect the number of rooms," said Lily, "but the only one who might suddenly want to move back would be Meaghan—she's in that pretty new relationship with some guy named Shaun that we haven't met yet, and she's working at that tiny-tiny ultra-local newspaper that frankly might fold at any time. All her stuff is still in her bedroom here, so for the time being I'm not going to rent her room; I just have a feeling it's safer to leave her an emergency landing pad. But Tiffany and Jason are solid, they've been together since high school, and Amber's got that place with her own art studio. Their two rooms should be fine to rent for starters."

"What about you? Are you staying in that lovely main floor master bedroom of yours?"

Lily sighed. "Well, I was torn about that. Staying in the master bedroom would mean I could rent out that whole lower floor with the deck, potentially even to long-term tenants. But I don't feel all that comfortable about sleeping so near strangers. I'm going to move downstairs and use the master bedroom as an office."

Gail clapped her hands. "That sounds smart. You're mostly separate from the guests except for check-in and breakfast, so if one of them is creepy, you're insulated."

"I'll have to have proper locks installed in any case," said Lily. This was one of the expenses she foresaw; there'd need to be locks with proper keys, some cost to redecorate the bedrooms, and maybe help from movers to get some things shifted to the lower floor. Later, if renting through Airbnb showed the venture was successful, she could switch to putting up a sign and advertising.

"It'll be an adventure, but I'm sure you can make a go of it," said Margo. "Who knows, you might even meet a new Mr. Right!"

Lily snorted. "I doubt it."

MEAGHAN
ALAS, SHAUN!

Meaghan had eventually staggered back up the stairs to the shared apartment, but Shaun was nowhere to be seen. And while Meaghan wanted to apologize for being thoughtless and unsupportive, she wasn't sure she was quite ready to put together a convincingly heartfelt speech. Her emotions were still so tangled and ambivalent—she wanted to support trans people in general and Shaun in particular, but that didn't mean she actually wanted Shaun to transition to male. Meaghan had had boyfriends in her teens, but their bodies hadn't interested her all that much, whereas Shaun's curves—her big round breasts and ample hips and even Shaun's rounded belly—aroused her almost every time she looked in Shaun's direction. Shaun's plump cheeks and little snub nose, too, enchanted her; well, just about everything about Shaun captivated her, whether physically or personality-wise. And while Shaun's personality might not change after transitioning (Meaghan hoped not), obviously Shaun wanted to make some serious physical changes. What if Shaun had those succulent breasts lopped off? It seemed highly likely. And while Meaghan supposed she might eventually learn to love a little beard or mustache on Shaun, she didn't want to even imagine Shaun with some sort of male genitalia taking the place of the lady-parts she'd been so enjoying exploring.

So, obviously, this was going to be a big problem. A big problem she had no idea how to resolve.

Meaghan sat for a while on the shared mattress, whose bedding Shaun had only barely pulled into anything resembling a properly made bed—the rainbow-striped comforter was rumpled and askew over crumpled sheets—and she stared hopelessly out the window. From where she was sitting, the overcast sky was the main thing visible beyond their Ukrainian flag poster; it was bleakly undifferentiated rather than offering a dramatic range of shades of gray (just one, not fifty!), and Meaghan felt this lack of variety in the clouds perfectly expressed the bleakness of her future. Here she'd thought she'd found both romantic love and sexual joy all beautifully encapsulated in a single, perfect, person, yet suddenly this perfection had been snatched away, replaced by a man-to-be who might destroy—would almost certainly destroy—Shaun's voluptuous bodily delights and turn her into someone Meaghan neither knew nor understood.

Oh, Meaghan thought, it might be tolerable if they were both fifty—Meaghan seriously doubted that there was much sex after fifty even though Britt and others had told her otherwise—but at twenty-two? *I'm too young for this,* she lamented repeatedly as she stared fixedly at the unsympathetic sky. *I'm too young, I haven't lived yet!* The notion that she might find a new, equally wonderful, securely lesbian partner seemed as improbable as the idea that she might find the male Shaun (Shaun 2.0?) as lovable as the female original. Surely her life—at least the romantic and sexual part of it—was more or less over!

In her distress, she reverted to a habit she thought she'd kicked; she began methodically pulling the hairs at her left temple, just above and in front of her ear. Next thing she knew, she'd created a messy little pile of them, like the beginnings of some dreadful kind of bird's nest, beside her on the comforter. (It suddenly crossed her mind to wonder why comforters were named as if they actually provided some form of comfort; the cheap but cheery rainbow comforter seemed to gaze mockingly up at her, taunting "LGBTQ" rather than giving her a loving Lesbian Solidarity hug.) She looked down at the hair pile, recoiling at the thought of lifting and disposing of it, then checked the skin on her temple with her forefinger. Smooth, nearly bald. Oops! She forced herself to scoop up the discarded hair and carried it to the bathroom, where she dropped it into the trash with a shudder. Maybe Shaun would think she'd just been brushing with unusual thoroughness.

Then again, would Shaun even care? Did Shaun want to continue a relationship with a person who wasn't enthused about the impending transition?

Heavens, Shaun might even be suicidal! What if her cruel failure to accept Shaun's pronouncement had been a crushing blow? No doubt Shaun had been struggling for months or years with her (his?) gender identity, and she, Meaghan, bad partner that she was, had been rejecting! Where was Shaun, anyway? What if Shaun was, at this very moment, flinging herself (himself?) off the Golden Gate Bridge just as Meaghan's father had done? Meaghan's eyes went wide with horror at the thought, and her stomach began to heave. Meaghan hadn't been living at home during the period when Don's brain tumor had been rendering him erratic and irresponsible—she'd merely (merely?) received her mother's sudden call announcing, in a choked-up voice, his death—and the idea that a loved one might suddenly, unexpectedly, jump off the bridge had lodged itself in a deep and hitherto mostly secret place in her psyche.

Meaghan lurched out of the bathroom and dug her phone out of her bag. But could she bear to talk to Shaun yet, even to do a wellness check? She didn't think so. Instead, she texted: Hugs! Love U! Without waiting for a reply, she called her mother.

AMBER
GREG AND HIS FAMILY

Amber scowled. That jerk Greg Stover had canceled on her yet again, and yet again it was because Tippy had signed Brayden up for some kind of sport that she could not imagine Brayden even wanted to do. Amber had not spent an enormous amount of time with Brayden, but as she and Greg had been together for nearly *four years*, she knew that Brayden, like Greg, was much more interested in music than in any sport she could think of. The kid played passable ukulele and was now learning oboe to play in the school orchestra.

"You know, Greg, I'm really sick of the way you keep canceling our plans every time Tippy crooks her finger and tells you Brayden has some kind of event to attend."

Greg's voice had been patient but verging on annoyed. "Well, he is my kid. Haven't you heard how it permanently scars a kid when their parents don't attend their games and concerts?"

"It does *not* permanently scar them if you occasionally miss something, Greg. It would only permanently scar Brayden if you never went at all and were a totally neglectful dad."

"Look, I don't live with Brayden anymore, so he needs to see me show up for all his stuff to make up for my not being there for meals and sleepovers and homework and whatever else he's doing day to day."

"You live down the street from him, Greg. He can walk over and see you whenever he wants. This is just one of Tippy's control strategies, to rope you back in."

"It is not, she's just making sure I don't drift away from my kid. I am not going to let him grow up to think I'm some kind of deadbeat who didn't care about him."

Amber had rolled her eyes at these repeated protestations of fatherly responsibility. Since the conversation was taking place via telephone, she stuck out her tongue as well, narrowly missing accidentally licking the device. However, as she'd swabbed the phone with a disinfectant wipe prior to picking it up, presumably she wouldn't have gotten any serious germs anyway. She said, "My father did not go to every school and after-school thing I did, and I am not scarred for life as a result. He was at work in San Francisco earning a living so that my mother could stay home and keep an eye on us. He was not there to watch me eat breakfast every morning, and that was just fine with me."

Greg said, "I don't know why you're defending your parents' outmoded traditional gender-role performance. It's not like you want to replicate it, and in any case it doesn't have anything to do with how Tippy and I are raising Brayden. It wouldn't have anything to do with how you and I would raise Brayden either. All three of us work, and what's more, all three of us work from home, so there's no reason Brayden can't have *all* of his parents come to his stuff."

Amber had stiffened. She had noted that Greg was speaking as if all three of them were Brayden's parents. And while she had nothing against Brayden as a person—he was a decent enough kid—she certainly did not consider herself to be a second mother to him. Brayden already had a mother who had borne him in the womb and in natural childbirth, who had suckled him until he was nearly three, and who was clearly busy mothering him all the livelong day. For an instant, Amber sniffed to herself that Tippy probably spent her working hours surreptitiously reading mommy blogs. But no, Amber knew better; she knew very well that in fact part of Tippy's income (besides the trust fund her grandfather had left her) came from writing her own mommy blog filled with affiliate links and discreet ads for parenting-related crap. As a part-time Influencer, that was probably why she was now dragging Brayden to all this sporting stuff, since he was too old to use in selling organic cotton diapers, gender-neutral cloth kiddie books, or plush dinosaurs. Now that he was in that nearly pubescent stage of life, evidently gender-neutral had to give way to showing he could be a Real Boy—given that as of yet he'd shown no sign of being either gay or trans, but merely a basic-issue male child.

"You aren't going to start being the gung-ho sports dad, are you?" she said. "Because it'd be pretty lame if after a lifetime of saying 'meh' to sports, you suddenly started rah-rah-ing Brayden to join Little League and play Pop Warner football."

"There is nothing wrong with letting the kid play baseball," said Greg. "For your information, I played baseball when I was his age and it did not turn me into a crazed macho man. I also swam, which is why I can dive just as well as you can. So long as Brayden doesn't mind, I'm not stopping him from playing any reasonable sport Tippy wants to sign him up for. It's fine with me if he plays whatever. So whether you like it or not, I'm going to go watch and cheer him on."

With that, the call had ended, leaving Amber in a state of aggravation.

LILY
FETCHING MEAGHAN

Lily looked around the upstairs with some satisfaction. Neither Amber nor Tiffany had left many belongings behind when they moved out on their own—or at any rate they had since retrieved most of whatever they'd initially left—and so it had not been very difficult to shlep most of what remained in their rooms down to the lower level. That is, shlep things that suggested teen girls, such as the bedding and some of the decorations. Lily had bought brand-new bedding for the guests (ouch, it was expensive—way more expensive than last time she'd had cause to buy sheets and blankets or duvets!), and now it was neatly installed on the beds. Tiffany's Barbies and My Little Pony figures, which had graced her dresser top since childhood, were now safely tucked away in a plastic bin, as were Amber's more goth-style posters, as Lily could not imagine that such items would appeal to most vacationers (and if any rabid Barbie or My Little Pony fans did arrive, she didn't want to have to explain to Tiffany that the beloved creatures had been stolen by collectors).

But—should she replace the curtains and rugs, or leave them for now? From the perspective of her wallet, Lily felt that these could probably stay, at least until there had been several nights' worth of paying guests and all her bills were paid.

Her thoughts were suddenly interrupted by the sound of the phone ringing downstairs. While she had had a cell phone for a very long time now, she and Don had never gotten rid of their landline, and it was that phone which was ringing so insistently. What with the loss of Don's income and their savings, Lily had indeed considered getting rid of the landline, but it was the phone she preferred to talk on, and what's more, she never had to worry that it would get lost or run down its battery. So … was this an important call or a robocall? She headed down the stairs to listen to whatever might be coming in on the answering machine.

"Mom, it's me!" came the voice of Meaghan, sounding unusually anxious. "Pick up the phone!" Lily's daughters knew that if she was home, they were much likelier to catch her with the landline than the cell phone, since the latter was usually buried in her purse or accidentally left outside on the deck.

Lily reached the phone with no difficulty and lifted the receiver. "Honey, what's up? You sound upset."

"I *am* upset!" exclaimed Meaghan. "Can I come home right now?"

"Darling, you can always come home," said Lily, "but don't you want to tell me what's going on?"

"Yes, but not right now. Right now I just want to come home. Can I sleep in my bed?"

"Of course, sweetie, you've always been able to sleep in your old bed"—Lily was mentally giving thanks that she had been so prescient as to leave Meaghan's bedroom alone—"but what's wrong? Did you and Shaun have a fight?"

"I don't want to talk about it on the phone, Mom, I'll tell you all about it when I get home!" exclaimed Meaghan. "Just tell me if you can meet me at Marin City or if I have to take the bus the whole way."

"Darling, of course I can meet you at Marin City," said Lily. "Just give me a call again when you're approaching the Bridge."

"Right, Mom. Thanks. I'm gonna head for the bus now." Meaghan hung up as Lily began to respond, which although a breach of normal phone etiquette was not too surprising to Lily.

And so, not knowing exactly how long it would take Meaghan to make her way to the fateful Golden Gate Bridge, as first Meaghan would need to get herself to one of San Francisco's Golden Gate Transit stops (was Meaghan calling from home? From work? From some other part of San Francisco?), Lily went back upstairs and made sure Meaghan's room looked particularly welcoming, and then headed for the kitchen to start some easy comfort food for their supper. A good hearty soup in the slow-cooker ought to fit the bill, she decided. Now, was there likely to be time to make cornbread to go with it? That was a little iffier, given that she didn't know which part of the city Meaghan was coming from. If it was from Bernal Heights, it wouldn't take Meaghan all that long to get to a Golden Gate Transit stop, but if she was farther from downtown, there was really no telling. Lily tried to turn her attention to the soup and away from the question of Meaghan's troubles and possible location, because really, what else could she do when Meaghan had provided so little information?

•   •   •

An hour or so later, Lily pulled up beside the Marin City Hub, which consisted of a rectangular green shelter surrounded by sidewalk and with a long semicircular concrete bench. Since the weather was neither rainy nor windy, Meaghan was seated at one end of the concrete bench, leaning forward with her elbows on her knees, her gaze apparently disconsolately fixed upon the backpack between her feet. She was wearing purple Converse Chuck Taylor high-top sneakers, a worn pair of black Levi's, and an old off-white hoodie with the hood up and mostly covering her hair. Lily had to honk to get her attention, whereupon Meaghan's head popped up, her arm followed in a tentative wave, and then she jerked to her feet, grabbed the backpack, and headed for the car. Lily leaned over to shove open the passenger-side door so that Meaghan could clamber in before an approaching bus could begin to assert its right to the space.

"Quick, honey, there's a bus behind me," she said, gazing at her offspring with concern as she held the wheel with her left hand and gave a quick hug with the right. "Mmm—tschk!" she smooched the half-covered cheek as Meaghan yanked the car door closed, and then she hastily pulled forward out of the bus's way.

"Hi Mom," muttered Meaghan plaintively as she sank down into the Mercedes's cream-colored perforated Nappa leather bucket seat.

"Sweetie, what's wrong?" said Lily as she maneuvered the car into a U-turn to get them out of Marin City. "It's Shaun, isn't it?" For reasons apparently but perhaps not solely geographic—Marin City backed up against the steep hills of the Golden Gate National Recreation Area— Donohue Street provided the only vehicular entrance and exit to the place, a fact that caused county planners some anxiety when they contemplated potential civic emergencies such as fire and tsunami.

"Um ..." uttered Meaghan desperately.

"Sweetie, I can't hear you," said Lily as she took Donohue across 101 over to the tail end of Bridgeway and turned left past the entrance to the Floating Homes Association, Kappa's, the Richardson's Bay Marina, and the Bayside Café (not to mention the approach to the Otis Redding Dock), onto the stretch of road parallel to the Mill Valley-Sausalito Path, which led to Northbound 101 itself and the brief bayside interlude prior to Seaplane Adventures, Terra Outdoor Living, and the Highway 1 turnoff.

"Mom, I just ..." faltered Meaghan as Lily followed Highway 1 once again across 101, this time westward rather than toward the yachts and houseboats of Richardson's Bay, quickly passing the Manzanita Park and Ride Lot to their left and the Transportation Department to their right, but slowing down somewhat as the road jogged on the approach to Coyote Creek and the several blocks of businesses that lined their way just before the sharp left that took 1, also designated in those parts as the Shoreline Highway, in a severely southwesterly direction into parts of Tam Valley.

"Sweetie, you can talk to me. Tell Mama all about it," prompted Lily, keeping her eyes to the road as they traversed the hilly, now redwood- and eucalyptus- and other vegetation-lined landscape with its short climbing residential streets rising from the highway, and veered due north for a few moments before the road squiggled northwest and southward and northwest again, then westward through the hills out of anything that could be considered Tam Valley (home of Greg Stover and also Tippy and Brayden) toward the mostly uninhabited forested hills with their turnoff options of the Panoramic Highway leading toward Muir Woods (to the northwest) and, many squiggles ahead to the southwest, the Green Gulch Farm Zen Center.

"I dunno where to start," moaned Meaghan, rubbing the area under her hoodie where she had so recently created that noticeable bald spot.

"What did Shaun do?" probed Lily. "Did he break up with you?" The turnoff to Green Gulch was, at this point, still well in the distance and the road was very wiggly, but of course Lily knew this road very well, and it was not all that heavily traveled once you got out of Tam Valley and away from anyone trying to get to Muir Woods. On weekends the road to Muir Woods could have bumper-to-bumper traffic.

"No!" burst from Meaghan. "Mom, it's not just Shaun, it's everything!"

"Everything, what do you mean, everything?" questioned Lily, trying to remain patient as this suffering child of hers continued to burp up useless fragments of non-information that provided almost no opportunities to offer either comfort or advice in the course of driving a mountain road.

"Everything!" repeated Meaghan, staring fixedly at the trees alongside the road.

"You need to be a little more specific," said Lily. "Tell Mama the whole story," she urged. Meaghan was usually willing to confide in her mother, but it was often hard labor extracting just what was bothering her on any given occasion.

"Oh, it's been just the worst day ever!" lamented Meaghan.

"I know, sweetie, but why?"

The entrance to Green Gulch passed on the left and they began to near the coast, approaching the Pelican Inn, the Redwood Creek Trailhead, and Muir Beach.

"Well ... first of all this morning I lost my job!"

"What?" said Lily, startled. "Why on earth did you lose your job?" Surely it couldn't be that hard to keep a job at the kind of tiny newspaper Meaghan had described to them. Granted that Meaghan didn't have a lot of prior work experience, but still …

"Carole closed down the paper, and Britt Felker says it's because Carole's been indicted!" Meaghan finally got out.

"What?" repeated Lily. She had temporarily forgotten her earlier suspicions that the newspaper might fold; or at any rate, it had never occurred to her that it would fold because the owner had been indicted. "What was she indicted for? Aren't people indicted for things like bribery and racketeering? Well, and for interfering with presidential elections, of course." Surely Carole wasn't involved in election fraud?

"Britt says she was laundering money for the Russians!"

Lily turned the car northward as they left Muir Beach; they were on the home stretch of the drive now, paralleling the coastline for the most part. "That's awful!" she put forward, after deciding against calling it wacko. "But honey, I know you really liked your job, but it's not your fault if Carole was indicted for money-laundering. I mean, you weren't involved in any way, were you?"

"No!" erupted Meaghan. "Of course not!"

"Well, then, honey-muffin, I know it hurts to lose your job, but when it's not your fault in any way, and you're just starting out after college, it's not as bad as it feels. Today's awful, but tomorrow or the next day you can sign up with Manpower or Kelly Girl and do some temp jobs until you find something else. You can type and you're good with computers; you're very hirable, at least in the City where there are jobs." *Yeah, unlike me living out here in my beautiful house and driving the expensive car Don gave me that isn't fully paid for!* "It'll be okay," she soothed, driving smoothly forward toward Stinson, carefully navigating all those too-familiar jogs in the glorious Shoreline Highway.

"But it's not okay!" wailed Meaghan. "Losing my job was just the beginning!"

TIFFANY
AN IMPORTANT TEST

Tiffany and Jason had been unsure what to do after Jason's unexpected revelation. Tiffany had burst into tears and run into the bedroom; Jason had remained seated for a moment and then run after her, attempting to soothe her, but his embarrassed ministrations were clumsy and ineffective as Tiffany wailed and pulled away from him. At last they had agreed that Jason would pack an overnight bag and go stay with his decidedly heterosexual friend Tyler, who was currently between girlfriends. This had at least given Tiffany some room to sob in peace, but it didn't exactly solve anything. Surely they couldn't continue to share the apartment if Jason was going to begin getting in touch with his gay identity! After several hours of tears, Tiffany began to wander the apartment, fretting over who would end up with what. Would she get the mid-century modern couch or would Jason? And what about the bed—should they just sell it and buy single beds to take its place? What about their photo albums, especially their wedding album? It was lucky, she thought, that they'd never gotten around to getting a dog or even a cat. She had kind of wanted a dog, especially since no sooner was Don's funeral over, than her parents' elderly toy poodle Gino had snuffled his last and left the family petless. But if she and Jason had gotten a dog, it would have to go with one or the other of them. Sharing custody of a newly acquired dog, especially if it were a puppy, would be very difficult. Maybe she could get her own dog, then, one who would make up for losing the love of her life. Not that a dog would take her out to candlelit dinners or bring her Valentine candy or father her children, but ...

And so things went for a short time. Tiffany called in sick to work although she knew she'd need the money, and Jason texted to warn her whenever he'd need to drop by their apartment. Tiffany knew that this could not go on for more than a few days, but she felt she needed to wallow a bit before going back to work, telling her family, and figuring out how to move on.

Then, in the midst of this gloom, it occurred to Tiffany that it had been strangely long since she'd had her period. She was using a contraceptive patch since that was considered a pretty effective and entirely reversible method of birth control, and it had always seemed pleasantly easy in comparison to some of the other options, but it was true that you had to be very careful to maintain your patch schedule and not to let a patch get loose or fall off. Her patch had actually fallen off not too long ago as a result of getting a little too energetic during a Pilates class, but she thought she'd taken care of that in a timely fashion, and besides, it wasn't as if she and Jason had been having all that much sex.

Still, what if ... Her stomach had been a little delicate lately too ...

Tiffany shuddered. She wanted to have children—ideally one girl and one boy—but the plan had always been to have them with Jason, sometime in the next few years, *not* right this minute. The question of her period couldn't be put off; she had to check! And so, into the apartment's small bathroom she went, to locate her small hoard of pregnancy tests. She looked in the mirror over the sink before opening the drawer with the tests, and although the room was dim—as was the entire apartment just now—she could see that her face had grown puffy looking, her hair tangled and askew. She barely recognized herself in this sad-looking reflection, given that she was accustomed to making sure she always looked sleek, fresh, and glossy-haired, the image of a prosperous, well-cared-for, regularly exercised young woman. Normally she looked as if she could step right into an influencer video and explain how skin cream or proper hydration or juice cleanses kept her in tip-top condition, but now she looked (she thought) like someone ready to beg for a bed at a homeless shelter. She opened the drawer and rapidly extracted a pregnancy test ...

•   •   •

"Amber, what'm I going to do?" lamented Tiffany, rocking back and forth in Amber's tiny living room.

"Well, Tiffany, you've got some obvious choices here," said Amber sternly. "You've got to pull yourself together and decide whether you want this baby." She wasn't sure why Tiffany seemed to think *she* was the one with all the answers; she wasn't the new Dear Abby or something, and in any case why wasn't Tiffany figuring this out with one of her various gal-pals instead? Amber felt that this was not the kind of problem you bothered your sister with until it was pretty much resolved.

"But I do want a baby, I just don't want one right now!" Tiffany gulped. "This is the absolute worst possible time for me to be pregnant."

"I don't know," said Amber, "I'd say seventh grade would have been a worse time than this."

"I was not having sex yet in seventh grade," retorted Tiffany.

"It still would've been a worse time," said Amber calmly. "Somebody would have molested you, or you would have had an inappropriate older boyfriend."

"I didn't even get my *period* until *eighth* grade," said Tiffany, "so even in those horrible circumstances I would not have gotten pregnant in seventh grade. Anyway, what about the fact that Jason says he's gay?"

"He wasn't saying that when he proposed to you," said Amber. "You've been together since you were, what, fifteen? He can't be all *that* gay. Maybe he just wanted to get back at you for nagging him about always being late for dinner."

"I do not *nag* him," said Tiffany. "Letting him know my needs and expecting him to be a true life partner is not *nagging* him. Besides, Jason would never pretend he was gay; he loves me, so if he says he's gay it must mean he really is." She paused. "Poor Jason. Poor me!"

"I didn't say he isn't attracted to guys," said Amber. "Apparently he is. But that doesn't mean he's not attracted to you too. Evidently he's bi. Lots of women stay married to men who are bi, especially now that there are drugs to control AIDS."

Tiffany did not feel that this conversation was going in a useful direction. Why was Amber being so difficult? She said, "It sounded like he's more attracted to guys than he is to me."

"Well, maybe he is. Maybe the whole thing is over and you need to get rid of this baby, find a new job, and start learning how to use dating apps."

Tiffany felt that they had reached an impasse. She still felt she had no idea what to do next.

"Tell you what," said Amber. "Let's walk over to Mom's and see what she has to say."

LILY
THREE-BEAN SOUP

Since Lily and Meaghan were so close to the house when Meaghan announced that losing her job was just the beginning to her terrible day, Lily suggested she save the rest of the story till they were home and comfy, perhaps even for after they'd eaten some of that good hot three-bean soup. And would Meaghan like her to whip up a batch of cornbread to go with the soup, since that was quick and yummy?

"I don't know," lamented Meaghan in tones of dramatic gloom.

"All right, then I'll start some cornbread after I dish up your soup; if you don't want any for supper it'll be there for later."

They drove the rest of the way in relative silence.

· · ·

"What kind of soup is it again?" inquired Meaghan as they settled in the kitchen and Lily took the ladle from its hook near the stove.

"It's that triple-bean and tomato soup I make, the one with cumin and fenugreek," said Lily. She had never known Meaghan to be deeply interested in cooking, but felt that it never hurt to feed her children a little knowledge of ingredients and techniques along with the food itself.

"Oh," said Meaghan.

"I think you've always liked that one."

"Yeah, I think so." Meaghan toyed with her spoon as she waited for her mother to fill her bowl. "It smells good, anyway."

"It's a good savory soup," agreed Lily. "And so easy to make. Do you cook much in San Francisco?" She began mixing the ingredients for the cornbread: yellow cornmeal and whole-wheat flour; sugar, salt, and baking soda; oil, milk, and egg.

"I dunno," said Meaghan. "Some, I guess. I mean, it's not like we eat takeout all the time." She busied herself eating the soup, so Lily let the topic of Meaghan's diet rest. After all, Meaghan looked healthy enough—neither fat nor thin, and her skin looked good. Lily wasn't as sure how to assess the health of Meaghan's hair, since it had been dyed and re-dyed in various colors ever since high school and Meaghan's quirky haircuts, sometimes chosen to disguise bald spots, never exactly provided the silky, glossy look that Lily associated with healthy hair.

Lily soon had the cornbread mixed and into the oven, so she set the timer, dished up some soup for herself, and joined Meaghan at the tiled breakfast bar. "All right, what else has happened?" she asked, once Meaghan had eaten a full bowl of the soup and turned down a second in favor of waiting for the cornbread. "You said that losing your job was just the beginning. What happened after that?"

Meaghan pushed her soup bowl out of the way and leaned on folded arms. "Well ..." she essayed. "Well ... um, we had to clear out our desks at work, and then I went home."

As Meaghan seemed to pause excessively at this point, Lily prompted "And?"

"Well, I was going to make myself some lunch, but Shaun was home."

"Okay, Shaun was home," said Lily patiently. "Is Shaun usually home for lunch?" She tried to remember what Meaghan might previously have revealed about Shaun's habits and schedule. Was there some problem with making lunch if Shaun was home? And if so, why would that be?

"Well," said Meaghan again (Lily refrained from repeating her own high school boyfriend's line of "That's a deep subject"). "Well, I don't know how often Shaun's home for lunch, 'cause I'm usually not, but I guess probably most of the time." (Why, Meaghan wondered, did her mother want to know about Shaun's lunchtime whereabouts?) "I mean, Shaun doesn't go to work until around suppertime."

"I see," said Lily, although she couldn't have said what she *did* see at this point. "So Shaun was home when you got there."

"Yeah," said Meaghan.

Lily was beginning to feel that she would never find out what was on Meaghan's mind. "And then?" she prompted.

"Well, Shaun wanted to tell me something and I wasn't paying very much attention because I was hungry and I'd just lost my job."

Indeed, Lily felt that at this rate, the cornbread would be done before Meaghan revealed anything. "What did Shaun say, honey? Just spit it out."

"Well," said Meaghan, yet again, then speeded up. "Shaun wants to transition, and I don't know if I can handle that!" She began to cry.

"Oh, honey—" Lily began to pat her daughter comfortingly, but mentally she was trying to figure out just what Meaghan had revealed. "Transition?" Then the meaning hit her. "Shaun is going to be trans?" she said incredulously.

"Yes!" sobbed Meaghan. "And I wasn't very supportive!"

Lily thought quickly. "Honey, I know you want to be supportive. *Naturally* you want to support your partner in difficult times. But it's not always easy to be supportive right away when a loved one surprises us with unexpected news. Sometimes it takes time to take in what they've said. Shaun can't expect you to jump for joy when he's just told you something like that. I don't suppose you had any warning, did you?"

"No!" said Meaghan.

Lily got up to reach for the kitchen Kleenex box. "Take some tissues, honey-pie."

Meaghan mopped at her face. "But what should I do? I don't want us to break up, and I want Shaun to be happy, but I don't want Shaun to be trans. I was happy with Shaun just the way things were!"

"Sweetie, that's only natural. You got together with Shaun being one thing and suddenly all your expectations are upside down." Lily paused. "You know, the two of you haven't even been together all that long. If Shaun's been pondering this for a long time, and was getting ready to decide, then maybe he shouldn't have let the relationship get going without first clueing you in to his situation. It'd be different to choose to get together with someone that you already knew was about to transition. It'd be a more informed decision on your part, I mean."

Meaghan exclaimed, in strangled tones, "People don't get together because they're making informed decisions, they get together because they're in love!"

Lily sighed. "Yes, of course love brings people together, but usually they like each other for a while before they fall in love. Even when people fall in love very quickly, there's usually some time before they're a couple. Time when one person can say 'I really like you a lot' and the other person can say 'I really like you too, but there's something you ought to know before we go any farther.' You know, like that they're about to move across country, or they've got herpes, or they want a sex change."

"People don't call it a sex change anymore, Mom."

"Well, you know what I mean. I can't always talk like I'm your age. We always used to call it a sex change. It's just a different name for the same thing. I'm not against it, if a person feels it's what they have to do. But it's hard on that person's loved ones if the person hasn't laid the groundwork, and it sounds like Shaun didn't prepare you to expect this."

"No, and I don't want Shaun to have a different body. Even though that's mean of me."

"Sweetie, it's not mean of you, it's just how you feel. I know it'd be simpler if you could be glad, but hey, it'd be simpler if Shaun wanted to stay the same sex. You just have to find ways to be kind. And maybe you and Shaun aren't meant to be a forever couple anyway. Not everyone marries their first love the way Tiffany and Jason did, after all."

Meaghan dissolved into further weeping at this.

Lily had been secretly relieved, back when Meaghan was in high school, that Meaghan had shown no sign of wanting to marry any of the boys she spent time with; Meaghan's apparent favorite, with whom she'd attended prom, was an overweight computer gamer named Andy Damien. While nice enough, Andy hadn't struck her as prime husband material the way Jason had. But perhaps Andy had merely been a late-bloomer and would be worth looking up now. Or maybe there was some nice boy that Meaghan knew from college?

"Why don't you go on up to your bedroom and have a little nap?" Lily suggested as the tears continued. "When the cornbread is done, I can bring you up a piece, but right now you look like you could use a little rest. Then maybe we can talk a little about Thanksgiving and what we want on the menu. After all, it's coming up next week and if you're still staying with me then, I could use your help planning it. The holiday's going to feel pretty different without Dad, after all."

Meaghan's weeping intensified at this reminder of the change in all their lives, and Lily moved close to hold her tight again.

•   •   •

"Hey, Mom!" came Amber's voice suddenly. "Tiff and I are here!"

Lily sprang up to greet her elder daughters. "Darlings! So sweet of you to drop by!" It was a little unusual for them to do that, or at least unusual for them to drop by together, she thought, but perhaps their arrival could provide a little break from Meaghan's troubles. "There's cornbread in the oven, so come on into the kitchen."

While Lily was in the other room greeting Tiffany and Amber, Meaghan took the opportunity to bolt upstairs to her bedroom. Flying straight to her old bed, she took no notice of the fact that Lily had removed all of their school pictures from the stairwell wall and painted the wall above the wainscoting a calming sage green.

"I've got Thanksgiving questions for you," Lily went on as Amber and Tiffany followed her into the kitchen. Picking up her own and

Meaghan's soup bowls to put in the sink, she added, "and there's soup in the crockpot if you haven't had supper."

Since it was barely five-thirty, Amber and Tiffany had definitely not yet eaten, so they accepted bowls of the bean-and-tomato soup. Then the timer went off for the cornbread, so Lily busied herself with checking it for doneness—yes, the knife came out clean—and popping the baking dish atop the stove for division into neatly cut cubes. One piece each for Tiffany and Amber, served on small plates with knives for butter—"There's honey if you'd like some—" and a piece for Meaghan, which she buttered herself. "I'm taking this piece up to Meaghan, she's in her bedroom not feeling too well."

"Meaghan's here too?" asked Amber, looking up from her soup. Crikey, that was unexpected on a weekday, but whatever.

"Yes, I picked her up at Marin City an hour or so ago," replied Lily. "She's already had her soup." She hustled out with the plate of cornbread before anyone could inquire further about Meaghan, feeling that Meaghan's situation could perhaps be left to Meaghan to explain, although preferably in a more coherent fashion than Meaghan had relayed it to Lily.

Meaghan proved to be lying face-down on her bed, the duvet crushed beneath her.

"I brought up some cornbread for you, honey," said Lily matter-of-factly. "I'm setting it on your bedside table."

Meaghan lifted her face from the covers and muttered "Okay."

•   •   •

"So," said Lily to Amber and Tiffany, "I've been thinking about Thanksgiving. It's our first one without Dad."

"It'll be kind of different without Dad to carve the Tofurky," commented Amber, who had always found Don's ritual carving of a hunk of Tofurky seriously humorous. The smoothly ovoid hunk of tofu and wheat, filled with its wild-rice and bread-crumb stuffing, bore no visual resemblance to a turkey, nor did it offer the same challenges to the carver, as all it actually required was to be sliced.

Tiffany wiped her eyes with her napkin.

"It's not going to be the same," agreed Lily, "but it can still be a lovely holiday. So the first question is, will everybody be there, or do either of you have other plans?" Tiffany and Jason had sometimes joined one set of parents, sometimes the other, for Thanksgiving. Lily hoped that this year she would host them, but she didn't want them to feel obliged to keep her company during her first Thanksgiving as a widow. She knew it might not occur to them to think of it that way.

Before Tiffany could respond—her face took on a stricken expression—Amber said "I'll be here, but we can't count on Greg. Tippy is really on his case to be around Brayden a lot lately, so she'll probably lean hard on him to do Thanksgiving with them."

Lily said, "Yes, she does do that, doesn't she? Are you sure he's really done with her? He doesn't really seem to be."

"No, and it's very annoying," said Amber. "I'm about ready to give him the heave. He's always whining that he has to go to Brayden's sports events, when I don't think Brayden even likes sports."

"Well, Brayden *is* his child," said Lily. "You wouldn't want him to ignore his son."

Amber raised her eyes to the ceiling and pouted for a moment, then said "Just don't expect him. He might be history by then."

"Don't sound like you're going to kill him," muttered Tiffany. "You know we'd have to testify in court if someone did kill him." While most of her thoughts at present were on her own situation, Tiffany had recently become a devotee of true-crime shows and podcasts.

"I am not going to kill him IRL," said Amber, "but I might put him to death in some other way."

"What do you mean, kill him IRL?" asked Lily hastily. "Please don't talk about killing people."

"I said I'm not going to kill him In Real Life," said Amber, "so it's not important whether I kill him in some other way. Not important to you, that is."

Lily supposed this meant Amber might be planning to kill Greg in some sort of online role-playing game, or to hold a mock funeral for him at the next Burning Man, or something like that. She decided not to ask for further details about Greg's possible fictional death.

"Anyway," said Amber, "Tiff ..."

"Yes, what're you and Jason planning?" inquired Lily. She liked Greg well enough, but she'd always had doubts about his marital status and it seemed that she'd been right about that.

Tiffany now, much like Meaghan, dissolved into tears. "We're not planning anything!" she wailed.

TIFFANY
NO PLAN

"What?" came Lily's horrified voice.

"We don't have a plan!" cried Tiffany. She felt almost as if she couldn't breathe, but somehow she got the words out. "We don't know what we're doing!"

"But Sweetie, it's not the end of the world if you have other plans for Thanksgiving."

"We don't! We don't have *any* plans!"

"Well, then why not just plan to come here? Or is there some problem with Jason's family? I'd be happy for them to join us, except that there are too many of them to seat at the table." Jason's blended family included four brothers and three sisters, several of whom already had children.

"We can't 'just plan' that," said Tiffany.

Amber took charge. "Tiffany and Jason's situation is in flux right now."

Lily looked shocked. "What're you saying? Is Jason's job transferring him? What do you mean?"

Tiffany moaned. Why did it have to be so hard to tell people what was happening? Why did Amber have to be so calm about other people's problems? Couldn't Amber just cry with her a little first and *then* be calm and supportive? Didn't Amber care that her life was falling apart? And what was their mother going to say?

"I couldn't hear you," said Lily, leaning toward her daughter. "Were you saying something, honey? I didn't quite catch it."

"Jason … Jason's moved out and … and I'm pregnant!" lamented Tiffany.

Lily gasped.

"Jason's decided he's bi or something," said Amber.

"Jason?" murmured Lily in disbelief. "*Jason* is bisexual?"

"I told Tiff that maybe he was just getting back at her for nagging him about always coming home late …"

Tiffany broke in. "I was *not* nagging him! I told him that maybe our marriage wasn't working out because he's never around enough to have a real partnership, so then he said he was attracted to men." She grabbed some handfuls of tissue from the Kleenex box.

Lily gazed at her middle daughter in alarm. "Jason's attracted to men—and you're pregnant too?"

"Yeah, but I didn't know that yet when Jason and I were … splitting up."

There was a slight pause. Then Lily said, "How did Jason react when you told him about the baby?"

"I haven't told him."

Lily said, "I thought he wanted kids."

"He does," said Tiffany. "He's always wanted to be a dad. But if he's not going to be a husband …" She grabbed more tissues. She wanted to ask for a glass of wine, but given her newly discovered pregnancy, that seemed like a bad idea even though it was possible she might not keep the baby.

"Maybe he'll be someone else's husband," said Amber. "Someone who's *his* husband."

"I don't know what to say," said Lily, and sat down heavily. "Well, except for 'have some more cornbread.'"

LILY

THANKSGIVING

Lily had intended to reveal her bed-and-breakfast plan to the girls whenever she saw them next, but their own revelations had taken precedence over any mere business decision, even one so intimately connected with the family home and how she was to support herself. For that matter, none of the girls had yet heard how Don's death had laid bare his mad despoiling of the family assets; they knew he had committed suicide after his brain tumor was diagnosed, but the full details of his erratic behavior and apparently compulsive purchasing of crypto remained to be told.

Perhaps, Lily thought, it had been a mistake not to tell the girls more right after Don's death, when they were all gathered for the funeral, but at that point she hadn't felt like burdening them with too many details of Don's illness, and she hadn't yet known that he had squandered their savings. Amber and Tiffany, living closer to home, had been somewhat aware that Don was going off the rails mentally, but they hadn't been seeing all that much of their parents at the time; Amber had been preoccupied with preparations for attending the annual Burning Man festival—making huge papier-mâché figures to take along—and Tiffany, while dropping in fairly often, wasn't always there when Don was home. Meaghan, as the youngest and also farthest away, had been home the least of the three since she'd been eagerly sampling the delights of post-collegiate life in the big city—although it was true that given the complications of public transit, she'd tended to catch rides home with Don when she did visit. When asked, a little guardedly, if she had noticed anything odd about Don during those drives home, Meaghan had professed to having noticed nothing in particular. To Meaghan, in other words, Don had seemed about the same as usual, inquiring about her finances, the cost of the shared apartment, and recommending that Meaghan think about buying Bitcoin once she had some extra cash. Bitcoin was, naturally, part of the crypto frenzy that Don had lost the family savings on, but to Meaghan it had just been one of a thousand vaguely familiar financial words and phrases, as she normally tuned out most of what Don had to say about money and investments.

Filled with such gloomy thoughts and regrets, Lily surveyed the house and her plans. It still wasn't quite clear whether either Greg or Jason might join the four women for Thanksgiving, although she supposed they would probably not. Her pals Gail and Margo sometimes came for Thanksgiving, as did other friends or relatives, but that was never a given, and this year Lily hadn't extended invitations to anyone beyond the immediate family. Yes, at Thanksgiving, she would definitely have to tell the girls all about Don and all about her plans; she could not reasonably put it off any longer than that.

Meaghan had stayed on into Thanksgiving week, and might perhaps have seen some of the changes in the house that Lily had gradually been making, but if she had noticed them, she hadn't said a word. Mostly, she seemed to be moping in her bedroom. Whether she was in touch with Shaun, Lily did not know; if she was, it must be via text. But then, Meaghan's generation rarely *spoke* on their phones anyway. They would use their phones to speak to their antiquated Gen-X parents like Lily and their even more ancient Boomer grandparents (basically anyone over forty-five, Lily supposed), but otherwise they were texting or using whatever the latest social media trend was. Lily had taught her own children that speaking on the telephone and not merely texting was still an important and polite means of communication, so perhaps they did make more actual *calls* than was usual for their peers, but at the same time, she figured that so long as her children communicated somehow, there was no need for her to keep track of whether they favored Facebook, Instagram, WhatsApp, SnapChat, Discord, or some medium she'd never heard of; they were adults now. After all, none of her kids had apparently been involved in sexting or online bullying or any of the other alarming things that seemed to be afflicting the current high school generation.

But ... poor Meaghan, so cut up about Shaun's decision to transition! Lily supposed that if a sex-change was in the cards, better that it occur when the relationship was young rather than after thirty years of marriage, so that Meaghan could get out (if that was her choice, of course) before getting too attached to this Shaun. Lily told herself that whatever Meaghan decided, it would not be a terrible thing; if Meaghan left Shaun, a new boyfriend would soon come along, while if Meaghan stuck with Shaun, well, it wouldn't be dreadful to have one lesbian daughter (if that would in fact technically mean that Meaghan had become a lesbian). Lily's thoughts on this subject were not particularly clear in their gender politics; so long as Meaghan was reasonably happy, that was what counted. After all, Tiffany and Jason had the traditional heteronormative thing down—

But no, they didn't after all, because now Jason was gay or bi and sleeping on Tyler's couch unless he was persuading Tyler to be gay or bi too—Lily didn't think Jason could possibly be truly innately gay after all these years with Tiffany, so he must simply be bi-curious and therefore for all she knew maybe his friend Tyler was also bi-curious.

Lily sighed and gazed up the stairs to the realm of Meaghan's bedroom and those two other bedrooms that she was now putting off further converting into rentable space. What on earth was Tiffany going to do? Especially now that she was pregnant! Lily considered herself to be pro-choice, and she was sure her daughters felt the same, but she nonetheless felt strongly that being pro-choice didn't mean being eager to abort potential grandchildren. Tiffany was going to have to make a decision about this very soon, and Jason would need to be involved even if he wasn't going to stay married to her.

Meanwhile, the remainder of the Thanksgiving menu had to be worked out and the last of the foodstuffs purchased. The groceries had better go on the credit card …

•   •   •

Thanksgiving Day arrived, bringing with it an increased chill in the air, a morning nippiness that Lily associated with Northern California winters—a harsher, wetter nip than the nip of their coastal summers. The Simones typically ate their feast in mid-afternoon, which allowed for potentially attending other people's feasts in the evening—not that any of them usually did that—so the cooking began in the morning hours, apart from anything that had been prepared the night before. In recent years, the family had moved toward pescatarian menus after first abandoning red meat and then mostly leaving behind fowl, so they had been experimenting with Tofurky. However, Lily was not that impressed with the venerable turkey substitute, so this year she had bought a sizable hunk of salmon instead. This, she felt, would go well with a rice pilaf, roasted root vegetables, mashed and sweet potatoes, sauteed spinach with raisins and pine nuts, a cranberry-based chutney, and whatever Amber and Tiffany brought in the way of bread or desserts. Meaghan had made a basic pumpkin pie the night before, and both Amber and Tiffany were quite competent in the kitchen, if not to the extent that they could be termed chefs or foodies.

And so Lily began her labors in the potato realm, boiling her russet and sweet potatoes in separate pots preparatory to mashing the russets and layering the sweet potatoes with butter, brown sugar, pecans, and spices. She'd made the chutney the day before and with Meaghan's help would make the pilaf, roasted vegetables, and spinach closer to dinnertime. Right now, though, she was willing enough to let Meaghan sleep in while she herself drank coffee and prepped whatever could be prepped this early in the day. They'd use her lovely French jacquard tablecloth, all autumnal oranges and purples, with a wreath of eucalyptus, wheat ears, and mini pumpkins as a centerpiece that embraced a majestic three-wicked beeswax candle on a stout stand of myrtlewood. Napkins in similar colors but a different jacquard pattern to the tablecloth came out of the table-linen drawer, and a set of classic dark-brown stoneware "Ruska" dishes from Arabia of Finland, which had been a wedding present, were moved to the table.

The dining area, graced by large windows on two sides—some divided by muntins, others not—carried out the main floor's theme of unpainted wood, with the interior walls done in batten-and-board like the living room, mostly stained a tobacco hue. Though small as dining rooms went, its view onto the luxuriant plantings out back gave a sense of spaciousness at the same time as the hundred-year-old wood and a stained-glass pendant lamp offered coziness. With the seasonal cloths and wreath accenting the rich tones of the wood and the deep umbrous shade of the stoneware, Lily felt that whatever each member of the family's current problems, she was at least providing a restful setting for their holiday meal.

•   •   •

A few hours later, Amber and Tiffany had arrived—each *sans* partner and each carrying sumptuous desserts. Lily had directed them to put these desserts on the living-room coffee table for now, and after a short interval of snacking on olives, pistachios, and brie, all three daughters joined her in carrying food from the kitchen to the dining area.

Lily and Don had always dressed up a bit for the holiday—nothing elaborate, but fancier than their usual around-the-house wear—so Lily continued this tradition with a russet silk blouse under a long columnar jumper of navy-and-black wool, accented by a chunky necklace of big ivory-colored beads in diverse shapes that had been carved from some sort of exotic nut (she no longer recalled exactly what, beyond that the necklace had been described as "fair trade" by the shop). Amber and Tiffany had made some effort to follow her example as well in their own quite different styles; Amber was sleekly got up in black top and leggings under a dress sculpted from numerous random-sized pieces of recycled purplish fabric, while Tiffany wore beige leggings under a tunic-length gray angora sweater that had the merit of ensuring she did not look half-nude (Amber had once pointed out to her that beige leggings on white women could easily give this unfortunate impression). Meaghan, on the other hand, had not brought a wardrobe of outfits with her when fleeing San Francisco, and there were not all that many clothes in her old closet, so she was wearing her black Levi's with a long-sleeved black T-shirt.

•   •   •

Lily leaned over to light the candle—although it was mid-afternoon, only a rather subdued light entered from the windows—and the four women seated themselves.

"Amber, will you start the salmon?" Lily asked. "And Tiffany, the mashed potatoes, Meaghan, the chutney." She herself started the spinach and then the pilaf on their rounds.

"We forgot to make biscuits!" exclaimed Meaghan suddenly. Baking-powder biscuits were often on the family's holiday table, and were eagerly devoured with plenty of melting butter.

"We can't make everything every year," said Lily, adding quietly, "Remember, this year there are only four of us."

"It's so weird with no men!" exclaimed Tiffany. "It's all wrong having Thanksgiving without either Daddy or Jason!"

Lily sighed. "I thought we might spend some time thinking about Dad today, but maybe we could take at least a few bites first." She really did not want to start the meal by recounting his worst actions.

"Dad used to make a real show out of carving that stupid Tofurky," observed Amber.

"Well, he did have a sense of humor about it," said Lily. "I might have given up on the fake meat earlier if he hadn't enjoyed acting the Lord and Master of All Tofurky."

"He was really silly about it," said Meaghan wistfully. "Waving the knife and fork in the air before he started."

"Remember how one year Jason tried to fight him for the honor of being Master Tofurky-Carver?" said Tiffany.

"Dad wasn't going to let some upstart son-in-law take on that job," said Amber.

"They were funny together," said Lily, remembering the two men pretending to duel at the end of the table. Don's sense of humor hadn't exactly been his most notable characteristic, but on the occasions when it did emerge, she had usually enjoyed watching him loosen up and caper about.

They were quiet for a moment and then Tiffany said "I miss Jason! I wish he'd go back to being my real husband."

"Have you decided about the baby yet?" asked Amber.

"I have only known about the baby for a week!"

"Well, you do have to decide pretty soon ..." said Amber.

"It's not a *baby* yet, it's an *embryo*," Meaghan said.

"Whether it's a baby or an embryo, Jason ought to be part of the decision," said Lily. "Have you told him yet?"

"No," said Tiffany, looking on the verge of weepy. "If it's a girl, I want to name it Taylor Swift."

"That sounds like you're keeping it," said Amber. "Taylor Swift Johnson?" she said with a note of disbelief. "Hey, if you took back your maiden name, you could call it Nina Taylor Swift Simone!" This was the kind of joke that Amber would have shot down immediately had it come from Don, but which she occasionally brought forth on her own with complete confidence in its brilliance.

"That's ridiculous," asserted Tiffany.

"I miss Gino," said Meaghan.

"Poor Gino!" echoed Tiffany, clearly glad for a change of mammal to lament.

"He was such a good dog," Lily offered.

"Always underfoot at the table looking for scraps," said Amber.

"Yeah," said Meaghan fondly, "always right there. I miss him so much!"

"He was a good dog," said Lily again, "a little naughty sometimes, but a good dog."

"I miss him sleeping on my bed with me," said Meaghan.

"He slept on *my* bed more when we first got him," claimed Tiffany. "He used to snuggle up with me."

"He wasn't supposed to sleep on *anybody*'s bed," said Lily, "but he was hard to say no to."

"He was a perfect dog," declared Meaghan.

They pondered the defunct Gino's perfection for several moments. Then Tiffany said, "Tomorrow's Black Friday! Who's up for some retail therapy? And what does everybody want for Christmas? Where should we go, Corte Madera or San Francisco?"

Lily stopped chewing and sat bolt upright, her eyes wide. Could she get this mouthful of spinach—so savory with the addition of raisins, pine nuts, and butter—swallowed quickly enough?

"You look like you're about to choke, Mom," observed Amber.

Lily bolted the spinach; luckily she'd already chomped the pine nuts and none went down the wrong way. "No, no," she responded, "but I'm not going to be going out shopping tomorrow."

Tiffany looked at her as if she'd gone mad; the two had always enjoyed shopping together, whereas Amber and Meaghan had usually been somewhat less likely to join them. "Mom!" she wailed. "It's Black Friday! There'll be Christmas music! We could go to Union Square and see the Macy's Christmas tree! We could go to Gump's! We could go have drinks at the St. Francis—well, nonalcoholic for me, but the St. Francis!"

Amber and Meaghan exchanged glances; Black Friday was not quite their preferred day for visiting Union Square, as crowds sometimes made them uneasy, especially after they'd seen news reports of over a hundred people being trampled to death during Halloween festivities in Korea.

"Honey," began Lily; "honey, not this year."

Before she could go on, Tiffany cried "But it's *retail therapy!* We *need* it! This is the year we really need it! We're bereaved!"

Amber gazed at the ceiling and Meaghan fidgeted.

"Honey," said Lily, "'retail therapy' isn't for bereavement. Retail therapy's for when you had a bad day or something."

"But we need to buy Christmas presents even when we're bereaved," said Tiffany. "And listening to Christmas music and seeing the big tree and watching the ice skaters will make us feel better."

"Well, maybe," conceded Lily. "It also might make us feel lonely and sad that Dad and Jason and Gino and whoever else aren't with us."

"Shaun!" put in Meaghan.

"Yes, and Shaun, and maybe even Greg," said Lily.

"I'm ready to cut Greg off for good," said Amber. "I'm about ready to cut off his dick."

"Well, maybe," said Lily, who had heard this periodically from Amber before. "Anyway, there's another reason I'm not going Christmas shopping tomorrow. There are some things I need to tell you. Maybe I should have told you earlier, but ..."

All three daughters looked at her in surprise. The air became charged with a new tension, one surpassing earlier moments of nerves and angst.

"What is it?" they wanted to know.

"Well, girls," said Lily, "I'm just about broke. Dad was going kind of crazy before he died. I guess it was the brain tumor, but he was *not* acting rationally all the time. He did some strange things." She wasn't going to go into detail to her daughters about some of his strangeness, but the malfeasance had to be revealed. "Basically, Dad spent all our money before he died."

All three daughters stared at her, dumbfounded. Then they began to bring forth disjointed questions and exclamations.

"But ..."

"But Dad ..."

"But he can't've ..."

Lily broke into their stumbling objections, noting simultaneously that half the salmon remained uneaten on the serving plate, no doubt long cold at this point. "I'm afraid he put everything we had—

retirement savings, insurance, the laddered CDs we used to have, you name it—into various kinds of crypto, and especially into forms of crypto that have tanked or been subject to scams. If there's any good crypto out there, he doesn't seem to have invested in it, just whatever is train-wrecked." She took a breath. "There was still some money in the checking account when he died, but that's gone to pay bills. You know I sold his car—well, that money won't last much longer. I'm putting things like groceries on my credit card so that I can pay things like the utilities from checking. So, obviously I can't go putting almost any money into Christmas shopping."

They continued to stare at her in shock. Then Amber said, "What're you going to do? How do you get out of this? It's not like any of us are making much money yet to bail you out!"

Lily attempted a smile. "I've tried looking for work, but I guess I shouldn't have spent so many years as a housewife. I don't have a lot of employment options, especially around here. And so I've come up with an idea that might just possibly work to bring in some cash."

"What on earth would that be?" asked Amber, who knew how few jobs there were along this stretch of the coast and how lucky she herself was to pay far below market rate on her rent. "You're going to do phone sex or something?" she said brusquely, aware of her mother's surprisingly limited computer skills.

"Oh Amber," said Tiffany, "don't be mean. Mom can't do phone sex!"

Lily giggled just a little, and Amber said "How do you know she can't do phone sex?"

"Well," said Lily, "I am not planning on doing phone sex, I'm going to try turning the house into a bed-and-breakfast instead."

MEAGHAN
THANKSGIVING SURPRISES

Meaghan could hardly believe what she was hearing. A bed-and-breakfast?

"Mom," she said, "what about me?"

Her mother turned, frowning slightly. "Sweetie, I began planning this before you came to stay. I would've told you about it earlier, but you've been so upset about Shaun. Have you noticed that I've been doing a little fixing-up on Amber and Tiffany's old bedrooms?"

Tiffany leapt in. "What've you done to our bedrooms, Mom? I have my Barbies and my My Little Ponies in there!"

Their mother was prepared for this. "I haven't done anything terrible to your old bedrooms, and your Barbies and My Little Pony figures are perfectly safe downstairs. After we're done eating, you can go up and look, but the main thing I've done is box up your things and put new linens on the beds. I thought the two of you could help me figure out how we should redecorate."

"Mom!" yelped Tiffany, but without rancor.

"I didn't do anything to Meaghan's room because I figured I didn't know whether she was going to be in San Francisco long term or not—don't look at me that way, Meaghan, I was right about that, wasn't I? Besides, you usually stayed overnight when you visited."

Meaghan said, "I might be moving back in with Shaun." She was terribly afraid that it might not happen, but for now she had to hang onto the hope that Shaun would rescind the decision to transition, forgive her, and take her back.

"Well, of course," said her mother, "but for now your room is all yours. Tiffany, you aren't planning on moving back home, are you? That is, you can if you need to, but I'll want to know."

"I've got the apartment in Strawberry," said Tiffany, although they all knew there was no way she could afford to keep it on just her wages from the boutique. Still, Jason hadn't said he would stop paying the rent ...

"All right," said their mother. "For right now, at least, Meaghan has her bedroom here. Meaghan, honey, I know it has to be hard deciding whether to stay with Shaun. I know I've said this before, but he really should have told you he wanted to transition before you got together. He must have had some idea that that was what he wanted well before that—you've only been together, what, about six months?"

Meaghan was beginning to feel that surely her head would explode if her mother continued in this vein. "Mom! Stop being so PC about calling Shaun 'he'!" She had temporarily blocked out the fact that she'd never gotten around to coming out to her family or mentioning that Shaun was female. "Shaun's still a girl, she hasn't transitioned yet!"

Everyone gazed at Meaghan in astonishment at this outburst.

"Dang, little sister, way to come out of the closet!" said Amber.

"Meaghan!" said their mother, rather faintly.

"I was not in the closet!" protested Meaghan. Surely it wasn't really a surprise to them that she was gay, even if she hadn't happened to make a big announcement about it. She hadn't been *hiding* her identity; she'd just been moving gradually along to becoming certain of it. Her college friends all knew, and so did some of her high school friends. It was not a secret, it just wasn't what she felt like talking about at home.

"Coulda fooled me," said Tiffany.

"Oh, I don't know," said Amber, "it makes sense to me apart from that Meaghan never *told* us. Andy Damien as prom date?"

"Andy was a nice boy," asserted their mother, never mind that she hadn't envisioned Andy Damien as a suitable spouse for Meaghan. "Do you ever see Andy anymore?"

"Mom, Andy went to San Jose State, not SF State," said Meaghan.

"What an odd choice," commented Lily. "San Jose!"

"It's not odd," Meaghan returned, a little huffily. "He's down there doing game design or something. He's doing what he wants."

"I just meant that it's not very close to Marin," said Lily. "San Francisco or Berkeley or even Sonoma would be closer."

"Mom, San Jose isn't all that far either. Marin County isn't the center of the world."

"Why are we talking about Andy Damien?" interjected Tiffany.

"Has he become an incel?" inquired Amber.

"Amber!" said Lily.

"He seemed like he might," said Amber. "Especially if he and Meaghan weren't really a couple."

Again, Meaghan felt as if her head might explode. "He is not an incel!" she shouted, although in truth she really had no idea whether Andy Damien might technically be involuntarily celibate. She was sure, however, that Andy was not one of those incels who resented the sexually active to the extent that they bought guns and committed mass murder—or even who "merely" harassed women online. She wouldn't have gone to the stupid prom with him if he'd been that kind of guy. They'd hung out together in the high school library!

"All right, I think that's probably quite enough about that poor Andy Damien," said her mother. "I'm sure he's having a very nice life down in San Jose or wherever. Why don't you show us some pictures of Shaun instead? It'd be nice to know what he—I mean she—looks like."

Amber said, "If Shaun is transitioning to male, then we should say 'he' since that's how he identifies. No matter what Meaghan wants."

Meaghan looked up from her phone, which had been conveniently reposing in her pocket until Lily's request, and glared at Amber. Then she passed the phone to her mother. "That's Shaun." She had chosen one of her favorite pictures of her partner, in which Shaun was making a mildly goofy face but looked, in her opinion, incredibly cute.

Lily examined the photo, her features forming a slight frown. "Thank you," she said as she passed the phone back to Meaghan.

"Let me see," said Tiffany, leaning over.

Amber reached for the phone too. "Huh, kind of like Andy Damien's sister," she observed.

"Andy doesn't have a sister," said Meaghan sharply, retrieving the phone and stowing it rapidly in her pocket.

"Brothers from another mother," said Amber.

"How are we going to afford Christmas?" broke in Tiffany before any more comments on Shaun or Andy could arise. "I was really hoping we could go to Tahoe again."

Their mother sighed. "We're not going to Tahoe this year and you'll just have to be satisfied with whatever I can come up with in the way of gifts, since the B&B won't be underway until January." She sighed again. "Is everybody done with what's on the table? Do we want dessert now or later?"

Amber said, "We need to have my poached pears now, and we can have the rest later. I made 'em with cinnamon and no wine, and a chocolate sauce."

Everyone agreed that this sounded like a good immediate topper to the meal and that Meaghan's pie and Tiffany's cookies would be splendid later in the day.

"After we've had the pears, maybe we can go for a little walk on the beach and then watch a movie," suggested Lily.

"We could watch one of those movies that Dad couldn't stand," said Amber.

"Or one of his favorites," said Tiffany.

Amber went to the living room to fetch the pears, and the rest of them bussed their dishes to the kitchen.

Meaghan felt some unruly tears slide down her cheeks. She didn't know whether she'd rather watch one of Don's favorites or something that only the women in the family liked. She wished that he had never died and that Shaun had never decided to transition. And that Gino was at her feet right now pleading for treats.

"While we're eating our poached pears," said her mother gently, looking in her direction, "let's make a list of things we're thankful for."

LILY
PREPPING THE HOUSE

After Thanksgiving, things seemed to settle down a bit, Lily thought. Not that anything had really gone back to normal, but at least now they all seemed to know what each member of the family was dealing with. Meaghan had arranged to go back to San Francisco with Amber to pick up some more of her things, with the understanding that she and Shaun would meet up at a later date to talk. Amber was still talking about wanting to break things off with Greg, but didn't exactly seem to have done it yet. Tiffany had taken on extra hours at the boutique in preparation for Christmas, and continued to turn down alcohol just in case she ended up keeping the baby.

Lily herself had plunged deeper into preparing the house for its new career as a B&B. She had conferred with Amber and Tiffany about options for redecorating their bedrooms, and although rejecting Amber's suggestion that she do one of the bedrooms as a dungeon to attract the BDSM crowd, she was at least willing to consider the idea that one bedroom could be done in a "cottage-core" theme and the other in a "dark academia" theme with candles, skulls, and leather-bound books. Tiffany wavered between liking the "cottage-core" idea and asserting that most people these days wanted a minimalist style of décor with everything in gray and white.

Lily's own impulse for redecorating the bedrooms involved using seashells and other beach-themed items; after all, anyone coming to stay would be wanting to spend time walking on the beach and enjoying the coastline. "People who like minimalist or 'dark academia' décor probably have that at home," she had said, "so they probably want something a little different when they stay at a B&B."

Amber had opined that beach-themed décor was standard everywhere that beaches could be found, and was therefore trite, but she'd admitted that tourists kept loving it decade after decade. After all, she herself made most of her income selling sculptures of seabirds to those same tourists. Very few of the tourists wanted to buy anything more unusual that she produced, even the pieces that managed to find a place in the Sausalito gallery that sold many of her seagull figures.

Lily had pointed out that the new sheets she'd bought were all a radiant high-thread-count white, and that since the house as a whole included some maritime elements without being either trite or suggesting Florida or Hawaii, the bedrooms could suggest beach or coast in a subtle, cozy manner. Mainly, she had to do this without spending a lot of money.

And so she got out some of the decorative items that hadn't been on display for a while, and found some fun things at flea markets. She added white lace curtains to the windows, swapped out the old rugs for new, and put a painted scene of tropical fish in the upstairs bathroom. (Sure, they were tropical rather than local fish, but cold-water fish were just not as charming! People did not decorate with pictures of salmon— at least not in the greater Bay Area—or rockfish, herring, or bat rays.) Maybe she would get Amber to stencil some California poppies on the walls, or something like that. Perhaps some whale-themed or sea otter- themed items would be nice.

Lily arranged with Airbnb to begin listing the two rooms for January, and began, with Meaghan's help, relocating many of her own belongings to the lower level, a space that hadn't been as much used once the girls had moved out and were no longer using its main room as a play area and for ping-pong. She was rather enjoying seeing how to reimagine the former guest bedroom down there into a new bedroom for herself, one with little reference to Don and their years together.

After all, while in ways she missed him, felt the sweet pain of recalling their best times, in other ways she was ready to leave the past behind, especially those months of erratic behavior and strange comments. Mourning, she reflected, happened differently for different people. Although she wasn't yet sixty and hadn't lost all that many friends, enough friends and family members had died that she had already experienced a range of griefs. A few were searing; others calmer. Some tormented her for a long time, like that of a high school friend who had committed suicide, while others soon subsided. Grief for Don was proving to be an odd mix of emotions, but most of the time she found she could function quite normally. She didn't feel a need to display his picture all over the house, and in fact put away the wedding portrait that had adorned their dresser for so many years. For now, she didn't need to look at him; later, at some unknown future date, she might want to again.

MEAGHAN
LAKEISHA BOUDREAUX

Without a job to go to each day, and with her relationship with Shaun uncertain and perhaps permanently destroyed, Meaghan was not entirely sure what to do with her time. Yes, she did enjoy having free time, time to read and think over her life and future, but she was also a person who liked having things to do. She was not by nature lazy, but preferred to have projects, concerts to attend, friends to meet up with, and places to explore. She was fond of her parents' home and had always enjoyed roaming the shore and hiking the western end of the Dipsea Trail, but she'd been thoroughly enjoying life in the City, where she could bike, skate, go to movies and clubs, and get around pretty well with public transit so long as she planned out the timing. This return to her childhood home felt both comforting and limiting.

And what was she going to do once her mother started taking paying guests? For now, she had her bedroom, but did she really want to stay in a bedroom on a floor occupied by total strangers? Sure, her mother had had a locksmith come out to add real locks to all of the upstairs rooms, including the bathroom, but wouldn't it feel like being in a hotel? A hotel room without its own bathroom, too! Meaghan hadn't stayed in many hotel rooms that lacked their own bathrooms. If her mother was going to rent out part of the house, she couldn't see why it had to be the upstairs. Why not rent out the bottom floor instead, which was really perfectly usable as a separate apartment? That way nobody's bedroom would have to be redecorated, she wouldn't have to share a bathroom with strangers, and there could be a long-term tenant who would mind their own business and not have to be fed breakfast. However, her mother seemed to have considered that option and decided against it for some unknown reason, so Meaghan was not about to bug her to change her mind. Apparently her mother thought it could be fun to be an innkeeper, and if her mother thought something might be fun, it wasn't always easy to persuade her that it was a bad or stupid idea. Besides, if her mother was as broke as it sounded, there was no question that something had to be done right away.

And so Meaghan spent her days partly up in her room reading, and partly outdoors reacquainting herself with the beach and the various paths along the shore and up into the hills. Since she too was broke now that she was unemployed, she had no idea what she could give her family for Christmas, unless she distributed some of her old paperbacks, collected sea-glass and driftwood for them, or dug up her childhood square loom and made everyone some potholders. (But did she still have any of the colored loops? If not, where did one buy them and how much did they cost?)

One day in mid-December as she meandered along the coast, the sound of the lapping waves keeping her company, she noticed a figure walking toward her. This was a little unexpected; while in warmer weather a person could expect to see quite a few other walkers between Muir Beach and Point Reyes, especially near the towns of Stinson Beach and Bolinas, in December there were naturally far fewer people out, especially during the week.

As the distance shortened between herself and the figure, Meaghan realized that this person looked somewhat familiar, although when people were bundled up for winter in jackets or coats or whatnot, it could certainly be harder to tell at a distance, especially if the person was someone you hadn't seen in several years. Could that really be Lakeisha Boudreaux? She and Lakeisha had gone to Tam High together, where they'd been friendly without being especially close, but Lakeisha was from Mill Valley, not the coastal settlements, as her father, a successful musician, had figured that if Mill Valley was good enough for the likes of Jerry Garcia, Janis Joplin, Bonnie Raitt, Huey Lewis, and various other famous performers, it was good enough for him. Not that Mill Valley residents never made it to the other side of the coastal hills, of course … it was just that they were more likely to come in warmer weather.

"Lakeisha?" queried Meaghan once they were within easy hailing distance.

"Meaghan Simone?"

Well! Evidently it really was Lakeisha Boudreaux. Meaghan was intrigued. She had always admired her classmate, who had had a knack for drawing manga-style comics, and she would have liked to have known her better. "I never expected to see you over here," she remarked.

"What, you don't think I might like to walk on the beach?"

"It's December!"

"So? I see you walking here too, Girlfriend."

Meaghan was surprised to feel a jolt of libido at hearing herself called "girlfriend." It wasn't like anyone meant much when they used the word in this casual way, after all. But Lakeisha *was* very attractive, and in a very different way than Shaun. At the moment, most of her was covered up in warm clothes, but she looked as if she was still just as pretty as she'd been in high school. Elfin, in Meaghan's view. "This is where I grew up," she said. "I'm visiting my mom. Is your family still in Mill Valley?"

"Yeah," said Lakeisha, "but I don't live with them. I went to Cal Arts and now I'm thinking about moving back up here, just not with my family."

"Cal Arts!" Meaghan was impressed.

"Yeah, down south. Just north of L.A. It's hot there."

"Are you walking anywhere special right now, or just walking?"

"Mostly just walking, I guess," said Lakeisha. "Why, you wanna walk together for a while?"

"Sure," said Meaghan. "I haven't seen practically anybody except family since Thanksgiving. Things are kind of weird right now, 'cause the newspaper I was working for in San Francisco went out of business."

"Newspapers aren't doing too well these days, I hear," said Lakeisha. "Not enough ad revenue and people want to read free online."

"Yeah, but this was a small neighborhood paper. The owner was indicted so she had to give it up!"

"Indicted, that's crazy," said Lakeisha. "What the heck for?"

"Money-laundering for the Russians," said Meaghan. "I would never have guessed."

"No, I guess not," said Lakeisha. "That's truly cray-cray."

In conversation like this, the two high school friends walked for the remainder of the afternoon, until at last they stopped for coffee, and after that said their goodbyes, having first exchanged phone numbers. Apparently Lakeisha was still drawing manga, and had begun to make a surprisingly good income from selling manga books online. When she heard that Meaghan occasionally tried her hand at fiction, Lakeisha had suggested that Meaghan look into self-publishing.

"There's a bunch of ladies out there making a bundle writing all kinds of niche stuff," she reported. "If they can do it, and if I can make what I'm making publishing manga books, then maybe you could turn your stories into money too."

"That'd be super cool," said Meaghan. She wasn't sure she was ready to make a living selling stories online, but then again, maybe it was possible. She definitely wanted to know more.

TIFFANY
A READER OF ROMANCE

Prior to Thanksgiving, Tiffany had experienced some mild hints of morning sickness, but as Christmas approached, the nausea really began to hit hard. Fortunately she hadn't had to spoil Thanksgiving with bouts of barfing—Thanksgiving had been difficult enough without that—but now it was really getting hard to keep much down. Was this just what it was like being pregnant, or was her emotional state adding to the churn in her stomach? She knew that not absolutely everyone had morning sickness when pregnant, but certainly it was common; her mother had told her that all three of *her* pregnancies had involved morning sickness. Therefore, she must have inherited this tendency to it, but still, had her mother really been this sick? Eating crackers and drinking ginger ale was not exactly doing much to settle her stomach.

All the nausea was not helping her to work more hours at the boutique, either. While it was not a store that typically experienced a heavy Christmas rush, it always did see increased traffic after Thanksgiving, as shoppers often wandered in seeking stocking-stuffer gifts like scarves and jewelry. Tiffany had not told the owner of her pregnancy, given that she hadn't made up her mind about keeping Taylor Swift Johnson (or Taylor Swift Simone, should she end up taking back her maiden name); she felt that although Maeve Ritchie was a fairly sympathetic boss, there was no reason to involve Maeve in her personal problems unless it turned out to be absolutely necessary.

Nor had Tiffany yet told Jason of the pregnancy. Jason was still bunking over at Tyler's, and they communicated mainly by text of late, mostly regarding when Jason could stop at the apartment without seeing Tiffany. Jason always ended his texts with multiple heart emojis and protestations of his undying love for her, but Tiffany did not see the use of that if he was actually more attracted to men. She had told Amber that she was not interested in being the baby-mama for a pair of gay men, thank you very much! If Jason wanted to be her husband and have babies together, he could just give up working late and give up dreaming about other men. Anyway, lots of pregnancies ended in miscarriages, so even if she were to decide to keep this baby, there wasn't a lot of point in telling any other people about it until she was at least three months along. People seemed to figure that the greatest number of miscarriages occurred before then.

All the same, she and Jason had agreed to exchange Christmas presents. They'd been together since they were fifteen, so even if they did divorce, it didn't seem right to stop giving gifts yet. They would just limit the gifts to one each this year, which was also what her family had decided to do given their collective lack of funds. (How she wished she could have persuaded her mother to go down to Union Square with her, if not on Black Friday, then on some other day! But Lily had been firm about avoiding the temptation to shop.)

And so, avoiding the apartment in Strawberry as much as possible, Tiffany was now spending a good many of her hours seated at the nearby Starbucks and other cafes distracting herself by devouring romance after romance on her e-reader. For her, the key to these romances was that by definition they all ended happily—no Romeo and Juliet tragic endings here—and the variations were proving to be endless.

Growing up, Tiffany had naturally read a certain number of romances—those by Janet Dailey and Nora Roberts, for instance—but she had not delved deeply into the genre, preferring books that were being marketed as chick-lit, especially Sophie Kinsella's lighthearted *Shopaholic* series. Romantic comedies, anything advertised as a "beach read," and the occasional thriller rounded out her typical reading, although she was not averse to random examples of Young Adult fiction, some Agatha Christie, or a sprinkling of self-help and New Age nonfiction. And, of course, there had been her recent appetite for true crime.

Now, however, most of these interests fell precipitously by the way; even rom-coms were left behind. Instead, Tiffany had discovered a vast world of romance subgenres, many of which were only available as e-books. She discovered "clean and wholesome" romances featuring cowboys, small-town men, and the Amish (although for the most part she avoided Christian romance, the Amish were intriguingly exotic). She discovered romances in which firemen, Navy SEALs, Marines, and forest rangers took charge (these were typically sexier). Billionaires too proved to constitute a surprisingly large population in the world of romance, sweeping their secretaries, nannies, and other low-income women utterly off their feet. (Were there so many billionaires in the real world? Tiffany doubted that even über-wealthy Marin County boasted a large supply of them; perhaps Atherton or Saudi Arabia were the real stomping grounds for live billionaires.) Multi-cultural romance too had a certain appeal; while Jason was a tall blond of Swedish and Dutch descent, Tiffany found she enjoyed rooting for interracial couples, interfaith couples, and international couples. Historical romance, if it included pirates, Highlanders, or cavaliers (but not plantations, Puritans, or references to Henry VIII) could draw her attention; gently paranormal romance might also, as did (occasionally) romances involving sexy vampires.

She could not, however, bring herself to sample even a single LGBTQ+ romance. While she had no doubt that it was a fine thing for LGBTQ+ people that romances were written catering to their preferences, the notion of subjecting her wounded heart to anything in this realm pained her. She supposed that Meaghan, for instance, probably delighted in lesbian romance but avoided anything involving trans people; just so would she herself stay clear of the entire LGBTQ+ arena. Nope, she was going to start in on a whole new subgenre she had just run across: secret-baby romance. She could hardly wait to start reading the first one—maybe this would quell that terrible nausea!

LILY
CHRISTMASTIME

As Christmas approached, Lily thought hard about how she could make this holiday nice despite her lack of funds, and perhaps a little calmer than Thanksgiving had been.

Not that Thanksgiving had been awful—while a little tense at times, it certainly hadn't been anything like those awful Thanksgivings that people joked about, where there was always a drunk uncle behaving inappropriately and people arguing over politics. Lily was grateful that these things were not problems in her family, and she had listed this as one of the things she was thankful for, along with being thankful for having three wonderful daughters, still having a roof over her head and food to eat, and not living in Ukraine or some other war-ravaged place. The girls too had managed to come up with some things they were thankful for. Amber had said she was thankful not to live anywhere with unexploded landmines, and that she was thankful for the efforts of all the giant African rats trained to find the landmines (Tiffany had stared at Amber in disbelief during this recital, and Amber had had to explain all about how these rats had a remarkably keen sense of smell and were too light to detonate the landmines when standing on them sniffing for TNT). After some moments, Tiffany and Meaghan had begun saying they were thankful for whales and sea otters and kelp forests and redwoods. Tiffany had then said that she was thankful Jason was letting her stay in the apartment for now, and that California had not made abortions hard to get the way some states were doing. Meaghan had said she was thankful that her bedroom was still available to her and that she had had the chance to live in San Francisco and work at a newspaper for at least a little while. Lily had then added that they could all be thankful for being in good health and sound mind, although in her own mind she questioned whether being thankful about TNT-sniffing rats was entirely sane if, like Amber, you didn't live anywhere that needed their services.

Lily was not too worried about coming up with festive meals for Christmas; she still had plenty of staples on hand—no shortage of flour, sugar, rice, or potatoes, for instance, so she felt she could afford to make her usual scallops for Christmas Eve. Mulled cider wasn't expensive to make, nor were cranberries exorbitantly priced. She and Meaghan set to baking dozens and dozens of Christmas cookies, which they placed in Tupperware and mostly stowed in the chest freezer for the time being; you could never have too many home-made Christmas cookies on hand.

On the other hand, they were accustomed to having a nice tall Christmas tree and had many ornaments for decorating their trees, but the price of fresh Christmas trees had gone up drastically over the years, and even quite a small one could cost a surprising sum. After fretting about this for several days, she and Meaghan had gone to a nursery and picked out a living conifer that had not reached more than three feet in height (a baby tree, they termed it). After loading it with some of their favorite ornaments, they hung some of the rest from door handles, cupboard knobs, and from lengths of swagged tinsel garland.

"It's quirky, but it'll do," Lily had said to Meaghan, who had shrugged and nodded. After all, while the majority of their Christmas ornaments were designed to be hung from a tree, they did have others that could sit on shelves and table-tops, plus wreaths that could go on doors and windows, stockings to hang for each member of the family, and plenty of pine cones, table runners, and holiday wall hangings.

"What're you going to do once you start having customers?" Meaghan asked as they worked on arranging the decorations.

"What do you mean, when I start having customers?" asked Lily. "Be a little more specific. What do you want to know?"

"Well, about decorating for Christmas. It's not their house, I mean."

"No, but people always enjoy seeing decorations in stores and restaurants, and at other people's homes," said Lily. "I think we'd probably decorate just about as usual, don't you think? Besides, I don't think I would probably have any guests right at Christmas. I could close for a week or two, I suppose." It wasn't something Lily had really thought about before, but she supposed that it would probably make sense to block off certain periods of the year when she simply wasn't open for business.

"I wish we still had grandparents," said Meaghan. "Then we could just go have Christmas with them."

"Do you miss them a lot?" Lily's parents had died relatively recently, whereas Don's had been gone much longer.

"Kind of," said Meaghan. "Not a *lot*-lot, I guess, but I wish they were still alive."

Lily had turned and folded her youngest into her arms. "So do I, sweetie, so do I."

•   •   •

Since the family had decided on a one-present-per-person rule, Lily's list in that arena was mercifully short, and she had fulfilled it by shopping in her cupboards. Before Don's death had caused her to have to worry about her spending, she had often bought decorative candles in various sizes, shapes, colors, and scents, so she had a good collection of these tucked away awaiting use. She knew that all of her daughters also liked candles, so this was an easy set of presents to provide. Even Margo and Gail and other people to whom she normally gave Christmas gifts could definitely be given candles; the only potential downside was that it might look odd if anyone happened to give *her* candles this year. Well, she didn't think she was giving anyone a candle that they had previously given to her; that would be much more of a faux pas than if she and someone else simply both happened to give each other candles on the same occasion. She was just not going to worry about it. Anyone who couldn't handle potential regifting or mutual-gifting of good candles clearly did not have enough else to worry about.

•   •   •

When Christmas Eve finally arrived, Lily felt that, with Meaghan's help, she had managed a setting almost as festive as in years past, even if it was a lower-budget one. Many of the candles that she had not tucked into cute holiday gift bags (or that were not reposing in handsomely wrapped boxes) were arrayed and lit on tables and shelves throughout the living and dining rooms; there were also battery-operated candles glowing safely on the windowsills to greet neighbors and travelers until the wee hours. Rather than Thanksgiving's autumnal jacquard linens, now a rich ruby-red tablecloth was decked with crisp placemats, red-and-green napkins, and a set of classic Spode Christmas-tree patterned dinnerware. This time a wreath of bent twigs laced with real-looking artificial berries sat at the center of the table, circling a majestic candle whose hue matched the tablecloth. Beside the wreath, Lily had placed wax figures of elves (presumably Santa's rather than Tolkien's, and certainly not the Elf on a Shelf or the dreadful Erlkönig), along with a few reindeer. CDs of holiday music played in the living room.

Once again, Amber and Tiffany arrived bearing desserts and without male companions; the weather was now cold enough that they wore heavy coats and woolen scarves, although neither had bothered with hats or gloves. Lily greeted them wearing a cream-colored cashmere cowlneck and long plaid wool skirt, plus a necklace of sparkling garnets and peridot; Meaghan wore a plain white cotton turtleneck with her black Levi's.

"Jason's at his parents'," said Tiffany; in the past, the couple had gone to one set of parents for Christmas Eve and the other set for Christmas Day.

"I'm sorry we won't be seeing him," replied Lily, wondering when, if ever, she would see her son-in-law again. Even if he was truly attracted to men, she couldn't help feeling that he was Tiffany's soulmate. But perhaps that was just wishful thinking. Could he be Tiffany's soulmate if he was more attracted to men?

"Greg has let me down *again*," proclaimed Amber. "He's spending Christmas with Tippy and Brayden."

Lily sighed. "Greg does not seem to be on the verge of ending that marriage, dear."

"He's such an idiot," said Amber.

Since no one else was very eager to discuss Greg's failings or his ongoing lack of divorce papers, the subject was dropped and Amber and Tiffany set down their desserts and bags of gifts, peeled off their coats and scarves, and set to arranging the gifts under the tree.

"This is cool," said Amber, "a living tree! It's been a long time since we had one of those."

"It is, isn't it?" said Lily. "I don't know why we stopped doing that— oh, but I do know! We ran out of space to plant them."

"I miss the big trees," said Tiffany. "I mean, I know the living trees are nice and probably more ecological, but it's not like you can get a seven-foot tree in a pot."

"We picked out the best living tree at the nursery," said Meaghan.

"And I think it's simply lovely," said Lily hastily. "Who knows, maybe next year we can have a big tree again, but this one is very pretty. Meaghan and I tried to use all our favorite ornaments and not bother with the plain ones. I hope you both approve!"

Amber and Tiffany indicated their acceptance of the small tree, and of the decorating in general.

"If you'll all help me bring in the serving dishes from the kitchen, we'll have the scallops ready to go in hardly any time," Lily went on. She had made a family tradition of featuring scallops as the Christmas Eve main dish; while at Thanksgiving the meal was always a hearty one, for Christmas Eve her menu focused more on elegance than on heavily laden plates. This time the scallops were paired with a lemony rice pilaf with sliced almonds and bright green young peas, plus a colorful side dish of julienned red cabbage and carrots with lots of fresh ginger. Cranberries made a return appearance, this time as a sauce with slices of apple and tangerine, and while golden unfiltered apple cider was mulling on the stove with cinnamon sticks for after the meal, Lily had opted for a choice of Chardonnay or Martinelli's pale sparkling nonalcoholic cider to enjoy with the scallops.

After a dessert course of small squares of Amber's gingerbread with whipped cream, slivers of Tiffany's cherry cheesecake, and a sugar cookie or two each, all of which were eagerly consumed, Lily and the girls loaded the dishwasher, refrigerated a minimum of leftovers, and reloaded the CD player with a different selection of holiday music. The light and dark honeyed wood of the living room's board-and-batten walls glowed in the soft light of the many candles, the Christmas tree lights, the wood-stove's warming fire, and two old-fashioned oil lamps. Everyone settled on the couch or adjacent with their mugs of mulled cider.

Lily looked around at her daughters, all curled up looking cozy in their winter dress-up togs—Amber in purple crushed velvet over her standard black turtleneck and leggings, Tiffany in cream with a red ribbon tied in a bow just below her breasts, and Meaghan who had now strung a length of gold tinsel garland around her neck. It was true that Lily would have liked to have been able to afford one of those new e-bikes for herself, and she knew that Tiffany wasn't the only one (even if the only one to have said it) who lamented that they wouldn't be spending the next week up in Tahoe skiing, but they had all been very good about not whining this evening and not fixating on their woes. Maybe everything would be all right soon. Bravely, she began to say "We are blessed, aren't we?"

At the same time, Meaghan said "Gino would be in my lap!" and Tiffany said "Christmas isn't the same without Dad!" and Amber said "Greg totally missed out on the scallops."

"Okay, I guess we'd better open the presents," said Lily, casting her eyes to the ceiling and rummaging in her pocket for the hanky she would probably be needing.

MEAGHAN
SHAUN'S GOODBYE

Once Christmas was over and that quiet interim period leading up to New Year's had begun, Meaghan took stock of her situation. Staying with her mother was all very well in the short term, and nobody in the family had been too freaked to learn that she was gay, but she desperately needed to figure out what was happening with Shaun. Hiding out in one of the remotest parts of Marin County would neither repair her relationship nor, probably, get her a new job. Meaghan knew that she'd better see Shaun very soon, because as it was, Shaun was mostly ignoring her texts and definitely did not answer the phone when she tried to call.

That being the case, Meaghan caught the so-called West Marin Stagecoach to get herself back over the hills to her transfer point in Marin City and thence to a Golden Gate Transit bus and finally to San Francisco's Muni. She could have asked her mother to drive her to Marin City, of course, but that wouldn't really have shortened the trip in quite the same way as being picked up at Marin City sometimes did; the West Marin Stagecoach ran the least frequently of the three transit systems, so from her mother's house the easiest thing was simply to verify the Stagecoach schedule and not leave the house a moment earlier than necessary. Still, it wouldn't be a quick trip at the speeds typical of the various buses—and that was fine with Meaghan. Missing

Shaun didn't allay her deep sense of dread regarding their upcoming conversation.

And so, as the Stagecoach lumbered along on its route east through the hills and woods—on the same route that Meaghan and her mother had driven somewhat faster in the other direction in the Mercedes the week before Thanksgiving, and the same route that Meaghan and Amber had driven shortly after Thanksgiving on their trip to fetch some of Meaghan's belongings—Meaghan gazed out the window, fixing her attention on the trees, and then at the signs of habitation as they approached Marin City. Then, once aboard Golden Gate Transit, she was surrounded by late commuters—not a very full complement of them since after all it was mid-morning between Christmas and New Year's, but still a set of men and women largely wearing suits under their raincoats or their down-filled puffer coats, since the bus was headed for San Francisco's Financial District.

The reminder that her father had taken these buses to work, on days when he didn't drive the whole way and pay a fortune in bridge tolls and parking, made Meaghan even more melancholy than she already was in her dread of what might come of her meeting with Shaun. Why had her father ended up with a brain tumor, and why had that apparently prompted him to lose all of her parents' money? Meaghan had always found Don's love of finance and money vaguely boring. Not that she had ever objected to the comforts his work provided for the family, but she had always thought of his work as just another of those dull but well-paid occupations typical of so many Marin County breadwinners—it had mattered little to her whether he supported the family by working in the financial world or by being an executive with a large company or by being in charge of some company's personnel. She would have much preferred for him to make his money like some of the other Marin County dads—like Lakeisha's father, for instance— being a rock star or jazz legend or movie producer or even a sculptor. But there it was, her dad had been one of those financial guys in an expensive suit, who might even have known some of the people who were seated near her on Golden Gate Transit bumping along the slow rise out of Sausalito toward the Golden Gate Bridge …

And oh god, was she ever going to get used to crossing the bridge again now that her father—her very own sort of boring but endearing dad—had jumped or fallen from it?

Meaghan shuddered. She had no idea just where along the expanse of the structure he had climbed up and gone over. No one had told her the specifics, and maybe even her mother didn't know exactly where it had happened. People walked across the bridge every day, and the relatively low railings had made it easy for people in despair to go over before the bridge patrol or pedestrians could stop them.

In fact, decades of suicides had finally led to a decision to build a metal net twenty feet below the railing in order to catch people and give them a chance to reconsider. This net had actually been under construction when Don went down, but evidently he'd made a point of avoiding the completed areas and the construction workers, even though construction was nearing completion. He'd walked along that long, long walkway, a small figure on the vast and iconic structure with its eternally renewed International Orange paint, and had found a spot where the net wasn't yet in place to catch him and break his fall (as well as probably breaking quite a few bones on its unyielding metal).

Meaghan hadn't paid a great deal of attention to suicide prevention efforts before her father's death, as the few people of her acquaintance who had killed themselves were simply faces recognized from school, not friends, but after his death she'd noticed more news stories about the progress of the net's construction, and learned that studies had shown that most people who had been deterred from suicide never made a later successful attempt. Relatively few people were so determined to die that deterrence was a mere delay …

Meaghan closed her eyes for the entire length of the bridge, and then, once she could hear and feel that the bus had left the tollbooth well behind and was securely traversing the streets of San Francisco, took a look again at her surroundings. The street was lined with rows of two-storey stucco-front houses that looked almost exactly like Carole

Karpinski's house in Bernal Heights. She turned her thoughts to wondering what was happening in Carole Karpinski's life and whether Carole was now in jail or what.

· · · ·

"Well, look what the cat dragged in!" Shaun said as Meaghan entered their apartment.

It had begun to rain, and so Meaghan was not looking her best, but she knew Shaun's comment was not about her dripping hair. "Shaun!" she exclaimed plaintively.

"I don't know why you're here," her beloved retorted. "You've been gone over a month, you came and took some of your stuff when I wasn't home, and you haven't paid any of our bills since the middle of November. We were supposed to be splitting the bills fifty-fifty, right? The landlord wants the January rent, and are you even going to cough up what you owed for December? I had to borrow to cover the December rent."

Meaghan was horrified. She hadn't been thinking about their rent or utilities, but on the other hand she *had* tried to stay in touch with Shaun via text, and Shaun had not reminded her of these responsibilities. Was it really her fault that she hadn't sent money to cover any of this? Well—maybe it was, but after all, she'd just lost her job! She'd lost her job, then Shaun had announced she was a trans man (and therefore not "she"), and then once she'd gone home it had turned out that her *mother* was practically broke. Where was she supposed to come up with this money from? Amber didn't earn much, Tiffany had apparently split with Jason and therefore lost most of her income too, and their grandparents were now all dead.

"I don't—um—have any money!" she coughed up. This was not what she'd come back to San Francisco to discuss! And couldn't they move out of the apartment's claustrophobic little hallway, in which the front door faced the door to the ancient bathroom (probably little renovated since the 1950s, and old-fashioned looking even for that decade), and the presence of their bikes beside the bathroom door made reaching the kitchen (to the right) or main room (to the left) something of an obstacle course. "Can we—can we, like, sit down or something?"

Shaun tossed her—his—their? head and said "Oh, well, I suppose we *could* sit *down*. If you really want to. If you think that'll help."

"Um, yeah," said Meaghan, "it would. I mean, it might. It probably would."

"Well, then let's sit out *there*," said Shaun, gesturing to the main room, "'cause I've got stuff all over the kitchen chairs and I don't want you moving it or sitting on it."

They made their way out to that larger room with the king-sized mattress and the table that had served as their shared desk; Shaun took a seat at the table, which left Meaghan with only the mattress to sit on, unless she wanted to sit directly on the floor. She felt odd sitting on their mattress again (where she noticed that Shaun had not been very recent in laundering the sheets or very careful about placing them on the mattress), but there wasn't much of anywhere to sit on the floor since the king-sized mattress took up so much of the space.

"I'm sorry I was so insensitive," said Meaghan in a rush. "I didn't mean to hurt your feelings!"

Shaun stared incredulously at her. "You stiff me a ton of money on rent and utilities and now you're whining that you didn't mean to hurt my feelings?"

"Well—I mean—I'm sorry about the money too!" said Meaghan.

"You go and turn into the worst deadbeat roommate ever—"

"No, Shaun, I promise I'm not a deadbeat roommate, you're wrong—"

"I am not wrong, bitch," snarled Shaun.

"But Shaun—" how could Shaun be saying this—"I love you! And you love me! We love each other!"

Shaun continued to fix her with a steely gaze. "You are so full of shit, Meaghan Simone. You are so infantile. If you really loved me, you wouldn't go running off to Mommy when I tell you who I really am, and you wouldn't leave me in the lurch owing a ton of money to the goddamn landlord. You are the most piss-poor excuse for a girlfriend in the *universe!*"

"But Shaun!" breathed Meaghan. "No, I really do love you!"

"No you don't," said Shaun, "and I don't love you. We are through. Once you've paid me what you owe, I never want to see you again, Ms. Little Rich Bitch from Marin County. My friends don't want to see you again either. Don't come to the bar, 'cause the people I work with don't want to see you again. Nobody I know wants to see you ever again."

Meaghan gasped. This was getting crazy-bad. She'd thought Shaun's friends liked her. She knew she'd made mistakes, but she was sorry! She'd said so! Why would Shaun turn their friends against her before they'd even talked things over?

"You are the absolute worst," continued Shaun. "You have absolutely no grasp of how to be a human being. You're a lightweight pseudo-liberal fake-lesbian trans-hating piece of pond scum. So listen up, baby, I want you to get your bike out of here and anything else you own out of here in the next like twenty minutes. I found somebody else to share the rent with starting January first and I want your stuff gone *now*. If you or your mommy haven't paid up on your share by January seventh, I'm taking your ass to Small Claims Court. Understand?"

Meaghan felt faint. Lightheaded. This couldn't be. Surely it must be a dream! A nightmare! Shaun couldn't possibly be saying such things to her—Shaun was a kind, loving, funny person.

"Get your butt off my bed, Meaghan Simone," said Shaun. "Get up and get packing. There can't be all that much left, 'cause you never brought in that much to begin with and you already snuck out with most of what you did bring."

Meaghan stumbled to her feet and then dug in her backpack. "But I brought you something! I brought you a present." She pulled out a box covered in shiny wrapping paper printed with a repeating pattern of Santa's laughing, white-bearded head. It held a large vetiver-scented candle, the very candle that her mother had given to her on Christmas Eve, which her mother had received from Gail the year before. "Here," she said. "Keep it."

AMBER
MEAGHAN AND THE BIKE

Amber looked skeptically at Greg. They were seated in Greg's downstairs Tam Valley flat, a surprisingly dark habitation even at the best of times due to the house having been built into a hill and Greg's only windows facing southeast toward the driveway and a wooded incline. On this rainy winter afternoon, it was even darker than usual, and Greg's lamps weren't providing much illumination; Amber felt as if they were trapped in a cave watching it rain. There had been times when the flat had seemed romantic and cozy to her, but it had been a while since she'd thought that. The décor tended toward dark wood paneling on the hillside wall, with a few lengths of fabric hung here and there near the bed, plus Greg's guitars and electric piano arrayed like idols around the main living area.

"You've got a gig on New Year's Eve," she drawled, with no enthusiasm whatsoever.

"Yeah, you should come," said Greg. "Why're you looking at me like it's a bad thing?" Greg didn't have gigs regularly; while he and friends played at local bars and restaurants now and then, he—like his wife Tippy—was a trust-fund baby and supplemented his income from the trust primarily by running a small record store. The store earned modestly, and the same could be said of his gigs.

"Look, you're fabulous, but not on New Year's Eve," said Amber. "New Year's Eve sucks for musicians' partners. We just sit there like idiots and can't hear the music because the rest of the room's whooping it up."

"Yeah, I get that," said Greg, "but it's not like I always have a gig on New Year's Eve. It's not my favorite time to play either, but it's always good when we get a booking. Plus, the money's better on New Year's Eve."

"Well, I'm just saying it's not how I was hoping to spend New Year's Eve."

They were silent for a moment, and then Greg said "You've been pretty sour lately. What's going on?"

Amber sighed noisily. "You're still married to Tippy, for one thing. I'm really tired of that. But also, it seems like my whole goddamn family is falling apart. First my dad gets brain cancer and offs himself. You know *that* was just great. Then Tiffany tells me she and Jason are splitting up because Jason's gay and oh-by-the-way she's pregnant. Then Meaghan loses her job and freaks out because her partner, who to our surprise turns out to be a lesbian, is actually a trans man and therefore not really a lesbian, just hasn't left his sex-at-birth behind yet. Finally, Mom says Dad spent all their money on crypto before he died, so she's broke. So yeah, maybe I'm in a sour mood lately."

Greg's expression during this recital underwent a series of rapid changes, and at the end he muttered "Whoa!" Looking at Amber in some puzzlement, he said "When the hell did all this happen? How can I not know most of this? When did your family turn into a daytime soap opera?"

Amber closed her eyes for a moment. Surely she must have told Greg at least *some* of this before? Then again, they hadn't seen much of each other lately. "I don't know when all of it happened, other than Dad jumping off the bridge, but it's all been coming out just in the last month or so. It's crazy, so don't add to my stress."

"That's wild," said Greg. "That's so unexpected, babe." He appeared somewhat at a loss for words.

"Well, so don't go pushing my buttons," said Amber, "because it won't end well."

"Babe, sometimes you push your own buttons," said Greg unwisely.

"I'm telling you …" Amber began, when suddenly her phone began to ring. "What the hell?" she muttered as she dug in her bag for it, then looked at the screen. "What's up?" she said hurriedly once the phone was to her ear.

"Amber, you have to come get me!" came Meaghan's plaintive voice.

"What?" demanded Amber, making gestures of mystification to Greg. "Where are you and why do I have to go get you?"

Meaghan sounded tearful. "I'm in San Francisco! I'm in the lobby of my building with my bike because Shaun threw me out and it's pouring rain and Mom's car doesn't have a bike rack and Tiffany's at work!"

"Oh fer god's sake …" Amber knew that she would have to deal with this. Irritating though Meaghan could be at times, when she needed help Amber was the sister she normally turned to, and for the most part Amber accepted this. "Okay, I'll head down. I'm at Greg's right now so maybe it won't take quite so long, but in the rain, who knows."

Meaghan breathed a word of thanks, and the call was over.

"What was that about?" inquired Greg.

"More craziness. Evidently Meaghan went down to talk to her trans lover and he kicked her out of their apartment. She says she's in the lobby of their building with her bike, and I guess I can't blame her for not wanting to deal with getting the bike on and off at least three different buses in the rain."

"I'm having trouble imagining Meaghan with a trans lover," commented Greg.

"Well, evidently Meaghan had trouble imagining it too," said Amber tartly. "She thought she'd found some kind of lesbian heaven, only it wasn't."

Greg shook his head. "Poor kid. Poor both of them, I guess. Do you want me to come along? I mean, you might want some help loading the bike in this rain."

Amber considered this. She hadn't planned on dragging Greg along on this venture, but if he was willing to make himself useful … "Okay, I guess it couldn't hurt. I don't know how busy her street will be, and we might have to double-park in front of her door or something."

"Okay, then," said Greg. They got up and Amber threw on her raincoat. Greg took a good look out the window and pulled a pair of red foul-weather bib trousers out of the closet. "It's gonna be nasty out there loading the bike," he observed as he pulled on his gear. "You'll probably need to stay in the driver's seat while I help Meaghan with the bike."

Amber did not object.

•   •   •

The rain was heavy after years of drought, and Amber had to drive relatively slowly on their way to the southbound freeway. Once Highway 1 joined the 101, they were soon rising from the low-lying stretch beside Richardson Bay to the exposed hilltop ridge above Sausalito, where rain lashed the windshield. Soon there came the bridge—Amber refused to let herself wonder which section her father had plunged from—and slowly they made their way across to San Francisco, above Fort Point and through the Presidio area and on to Cow Hollow and down Van Ness past Market on into the Mission and further south toward Bernal Heights.

"Damn, this is a long drive," said Amber at one point, since she didn't often drive into San Francisco to begin with and certainly didn't normally do so in heavy rain.

"There's a reason we don't go into the City much," observed Greg.

But eventually they were in front of Meaghan's building, and indeed they had to double-park while Amber called Meaghan and then Greg got out of the car to hold the door while Meaghan wheeled her bike out onto the sidewalk and over to the car, where she and Greg lifted and secured the bike to the rack. Then they both hustled into the car, splattering rainwater on the seats and on Amber.

"You guys are wetter than a pair of otters," she said.

"I'm drenched, and I was only even out there a few minutes!" proclaimed Meaghan from the back seat.

"Otters like being wet," said Greg. "They've got those thick pelts. I'll bet they never get wet to the skin."

"I'm definitely not an otter, then," said Meaghan.

"No, you certainly aren't," said Amber, getting the car underway again and flicking off her hazard blinkers.

•   •   •

Once back in Marin, Amber dropped off Greg at his place in Tam Valley, and the sisters continued on through the trees toward the coast.

"So Shaun threw you out," Amber commented after a while.

"It was horrible," said Meaghan. "I think Shaun hates me now. And I owe a bunch of money because I forgot that I needed to send money for utilities and December rent! Shaun says she's—he's—going to sue me in small claims court if I don't pay up in a week or so. Amber, where'm I going to get the money?"

Amber attempted to keep her eyes to the road in the dimming light of late afternoon, but said "Shaun is a friggin' jerk. You really know how to pick 'em, don't you."

"It's not Shaun's fault that she's—he's—trans!" said Meaghan. "Or that I forgot about the bills."

"I didn't say any of that was Shaun's fault, I just said Shaun's a jerk."

"Shaun's not *usually* a jerk ..."

"Shaun's a jerk right now, so get used to the idea."

"I don't suppose Shaun's any more of a jerk than Greg sometimes is," essayed Meaghan.

"Greg is a jerk who also just volunteered to come out in the rain and help you load your bike onto my bike rack," said Amber. "Humans are often jerks. Some of them are also not-jerks."

"Do you think Shaun might take me back someday?"

"Forget Shaun. It's abusive to throw you out in the rain like that. Let Shaun learn how to be male on his own time. He couldn't expect you to know how to be supportive out of nowhere."

"But where'm I gonna get the money?" Meaghan persisted.

"We'll find it somewhere. Come on, we may be broke but we're not in poverty. Mom's still got her credit cards, and so do we. Or she could get a loan. We know people who have money. It's not that dire. We can figure it out."

With this, Amber pulled up at their mother's house and they hurried in, leaving the bike on the bike rack.

"Mom!" shouted Meaghan as they burst in. "I'm back!"

Lily appeared from the kitchen, spatula in hand. "Sweetie! You're drenched! Well, you're both wet, but Meaghan, you need to change into dry clothes pronto. But first, guess what? I have a renter coming!"

LILY
AN IMPENDING GUEST

Lily didn't mean to cut off anything her daughters were about to say, but the news of her upcoming guest filled her with excitement, if also a touch of trepidation.

"It's one person," she said eagerly, "a woman named Blossom Hinckley. She's booked a three-week stay starting right after New Year's! Can you believe it?"

"Wow!" said Amber dutifully.

"Meaghan, you run upstairs right now and change," Lily went on. "I'm not having you catch pneumonia after being out in the rain like that. How did you get *that* wet?"

"Go change," said Amber, "I'll explain."

Meaghan, who had been yanking off her wet Chuck Taylors, hurried away; her wet jacket was already on a peg near the door.

"I'm so excited about this booking," said Lily, "because heaven knows I need the money, but I'll need some help from you and Meaghan to finish pulling together that bedroom. I'm thinking this Blossom Hinckley can have your old room since that's got a good view of the water. I wonder what she has in mind that she's booked for so many days? Anyway, what's Meaghan been doing out in the rain? I thought she was going to be in San Francisco all day talking things over with Shaun."

"Well ..." said Amber slowly, "Meaghan did go to San Francisco, but the meetup with Shaun didn't exactly go according to plan."

"No?" said Lily, unsure in any case just what Meaghan's plan had been beyond talking with Shaun and perhaps beginning to sort things out. "What happened?"

Amber updated her on Shaun's reaction to Meaghan's return, concluding with "And so Shaun threw Meaghan out and is threatening to sue her for the unpaid rent and utilities, with the result that Meaghan lugged her bike downstairs and called me because I've got a bike rack on my car. Then Greg and I spent our afternoon driving down to pick her up, and the two of them loaded up the bike in the pouring rain while I got to sit there warm and dry like the driver of a getaway car."

Lily said, "Well, Greg's of some use, at least!"

"Yeah, he volunteered himself like a good knight in shining armor. I can't complain about that."

"But this mess with Shaun!" Lily had expected that Shaun would feel hurt at Meaghan's reaction to the news of the impending transition, but all the same she had supposed that, given time to think things over, Shaun would realize that Meaghan's shock was not about being anti-trans, but was simply the shock anyone might feel at hearing totally unexpected important news. Especially news that revealed how different someone was than you had always thought! Lily hadn't taken the news about Don's crypto extravaganza with loud shrieks, but she might have, had she been Meaghan's age.

"I told her Shaun's a jerk," said Amber, and then, "Is there something you need to take care of in the kitchen?"

Recalling why she held a spatula, Lily rushed back into the kitchen, followed by Amber, and immediately turned off the stove. "I'm making a frittata," she said sheepishly, sliding the spatula under the egg mixture and expertly flipping it. "Doesn't look burned, anyway," she added with a critical look at the crispy brown surface, and popped it into the oven. "Want to stay for supper? With a salad, there'll be plenty for three."

"Yeah, I could stay," said Amber. "What's in the frittata this time?"

"Oh, the usual suspects—onions, garlic, peppers, cherry tomatoes, cheese. I may have put in some other things that I've forgotten. Will you throw together a salad from the refrigerator while I finish all this up?"

Amber assented, and in a few minutes supper was ready and they had called Meaghan to come downstairs. She arrived in the same old off-white hoodie sweatshirt that she had worn the day Lily had picked her up at Marin City before Thanksgiving, but instead of the high-tops that were drying near the door, her feet were encased in a pair of ridiculously large pink-and-white bunny slippers.

"I'm going to need some help putting the final touches on things before this Blossom Hinckley arrives," said Lily as they ate. "The house is mostly ready, but we'll need to do a deep-clean of the top two floors and make sure that the bedroom and bathroom are in tip-top shape. Meaghan, I'll want you to keep all of your bathroom items in your bedroom, so that our guest doesn't feel that she's intruding."

"What do we know about this guest?" inquired Amber. "Besides her name, that is."

"Not much," said Lily. "I'm glad we're starting off with a woman, though, and with a stay longer than just a couple of nights. I'm hoping that Airbnb has verified everything necessary—that's part of what they're for, after all."

"I wonder why she wants to spend January here," said Amber. "It's not exactly the best time of year to go to the beach."

"Maybe she's a marine biologist," offered Meaghan.

"Here?" scoffed Amber. "A marine biologist would probably want to stay closer to Point Reyes. Or just be at some other part of the coast."

"Well, then maybe she's a painter," said Meaghan. "Or somebody who just got divorced and wants to stay in a remote coastal village for a while."

"We're not all *that* remote," said Lily.

"If I'd just gotten divorced and wanted to stay someplace remote, I'd probably rent an abandoned lighthouse," said Amber.

They continued to come up with possible reasons why Blossom Hinckley might have chosen to spend January on the damp, chilly coast of Northern California, until, supper over, Amber said her goodbyes and headed for the door. "We can unload the bike when it quits raining, or at least when it's light out and only drizzling," she said.

MEAGHAN
LAKEISHA RETURNS

On New Year's Day, Meaghan felt she really had to get out of the house for a while. Not because there was anything wrong with being there, but simply because she'd been indoors quite a bit lately and after helping her mother seemingly perfect every surface, every nook and cranny, every pillowcase and towel both upstairs and on the main floor where guests would check in and have the opportunity to lounge in the living room if they didn't care to do so in their bedrooms ... well, Meaghan felt she needed and deserved a break. Especially after she and Amber had caught sight of the brand-new Keurig upstairs and had told their mother that it was all wrong to have bought a coffeemaker that used single-cup non-compostable packaging. If this was going to be a bed-and-breakfast, then guests ought to come downstairs for their fancy breakfasts and not make their own separate wasteful and non-ecological coffee upstairs! (Their mother hadn't taken this criticism very well.)

Therefore, Meaghan had bundled up in warm clothes, even wearing cap and gloves, and headed for the shore. The morning fog was clearing, but she knew the air would remain cold. There probably wouldn't be many people out, and that suited her just fine.

She'd been trying to avoid thinking about Shaun these past few days, and to some extent that was working. After all, she'd had Shaun on her mind almost continually from the time she'd learned of the impending transition till the day Shaun had so vehemently rejected her; she couldn't go on like that week after week. Perhaps, with the new year, she could find a new job or at least some new way of earning a living, and she couldn't do that if her mind was constantly on Shaun.

Instead, with her feet crunching the wet sand a little as she walked close to the water, she put her mind to the idea that Lakeisha had planted in her mind before Christmas. Could she actually turn the stories she occasionally wrote into an earning proposition? Would people really pay to read stuff that was published online? Lakeisha had seemed to think so, and Lakeisha was making money selling her manga-style books. As Meaghan understood it, Lakeisha made the books available for sale online but the physical printed books arrived in customers' mailboxes. Which made sense, because manga was all about pictorial storytelling, and Meaghan didn't think most people wanted to read graphic novels—manga-style or otherwise—on e-readers. Just because it was *possible* to read some of them on e-readers didn't make that the ideal way to enjoy the story. But it had sounded like, for stories that were just text, there might not be any need to sell printed books in order to make money.

Meaghan was vaguely familiar with some of the platforms where this could be done, of course—she'd read e-books from the library, and she was aware of at least a few of the popular options for subscription-based reading. But she hadn't really taken the trouble to learn much about any of this yet despite her interest in journalism and creative writing. She'd mostly taken the view that all of these platforms changed pretty frequently and some of them went out of style or stopped existing at all (as a kid she'd had several blogs, some of which were even written for school, but then blogging had gone out of fashion despite some people still diligently writing their blog posts). Basically, she had always figured that she could learn more about current online platforms when the time came to use them. Was that time now?

In musing about this question—and about whether the stories she'd already written were good enough to attract readers—she almost didn't notice a familiar voice calling out "Girlfriend! Meaghan Simone! You out here again braving the cold? And it is dang cold out here today!"

"Lakeisha!" she exclaimed, turning toward the sound. "I was just thinking about you!"

"You were just thinking about me?" demanded Lakeisha, jogging down toward the water's edge where Meaghan had been walking. "Girlfriend, what makes you think of me in particular on this chilly morning?"

"Well—" began Meaghan, beginning to blush a little (why was it so exciting to hear Lakeisha call her Girlfriend?)—"I was thinking about our conversation last time we saw each other."

"Oh yeah?" said Lakeisha merrily. "And why is that? Are you so lonely out here staying with your ma that you've got to cast about in your mind for conversations you had weeks ago just to feel like you have a social life? Or am I just so dang exciting?"

Meaghan giggled—but just for a second. "Well—um—it *is* a little lonely compared to when I was living in the City, but after all I *did* live here all my life till I went to college. So it's not like I'm not used to it. I was thinking about what you were saying about publishing. You know, about selling your books, but also what you were saying about how maybe I could sell some of my stories online too."

"Oh, you think you might have the bug? You're thinking you could learn to do this too?"

"Um, maybe! You did say a lot of people these days are making a living selling e-books or something like that."

Lakeisha gave a bit of a shimmy, and Meaghan thought she looked very cute in her red parka. "Yeah, I did say that, didn't I? Well, Girlfriend, you were saying you wrote stories, and I remember you wrote some back when we were in high school too. You were definitely into it back then. So why the heck not give it a try? I think I was talking about publishing whole books, but even if you have just short stuff, well these days there are ways of monetizing that too."

Meaghan giggled again. "Monetizing! You sound like you took a finance class or something."

"Well heck yeah! No, I did not take a finance class, but I know about monetizing my creative labor."

"I need to earn some money, so I guess maybe I need to learn how to monetize my writing. It's either that or, like, get a job in a café or something. Or work for my mom now that she's going to run a B&B. Only then I wouldn't earn any money, I'd just be helping around the house."

Lakeisha looked at her. "If your ma's gonna run a B&B, yeah, she's prob'ly gonna expect you to help out if you're living there. That stands to reason. She's gonna want you to help dust, or make beds, or do grocery runs, or whatever. So then you're really gonna need some income from some other source, or else twenty years from now you're gonna be the two ladies who run a B&B together. So yeah, selling stories online on oh, I dunno, like Substack or Patreon or Wattpad or whatever might be a very good plan."

Meaghan shuddered. "There's no way I'm gonna be running a B&B with my mom twenty years from now! Yikes! I mean, she's into the idea 'cause she needs money too, but no way am I going to … well, devote my life to helping run a B&B." There were so many reasons Meaghan did not want to run a B&B long term that she could hardly begin to enumerate them, they were so pressing in her mind. All that laundry! All that shopping! Never having time to go hiking or biking or skiing! Never going to bars and clubs and spending half the night dancing! Becoming a female incel! The idea was just suffocating.

"Well then, Girlfriend, I say you oughta give this a try, because hey, you write anyway, and you can write while you're staying with your ma. Now depending on which platform you choose, you might have to start out letting people read your stuff for free, because you have to develop your fan base so that people want to start paying, but if you write stuff that people want to read, well, then before long you can probably start monetizing."

Every time Lakeisha said "monetizing," Meaghan wanted to start laughing—it was such a funny-sounding word—just like every time Lakeisha called her "Girlfriend" she felt a weird little spark of sex, as if her Lady Parts (as she and friends often called them) were starting to quiver with excitement. She hadn't felt much like laughing in weeks, and she certainly hadn't been feeling any delightful quiverings of the Lady Parts since Shaun had announced wanting to transition to male. Just for the thrill of it, she let the muscles of the said Parts flex a few times—there was no way Lakeisha would know, so it was perfectly safe.

"I want to learn how to do this," said Meaghan eagerly. "Anything you can tell me about how to monetize stories online would be just so great!"

"Well," said Lakeisha, "first of all, what've you got and what genre is it? I mean like how long are your stories and what're they about?"

This was something Meaghan hadn't had much of a chance to discuss in quite some time. Or at least she hadn't felt like discussing it with her family. She and Shaun had sometimes talked about their ambitions, but Shaun had been the one with more to say. "Most of what I write is short," she said, "although I have some ideas for whole novels. And mostly I write fantasy, 'cause that's pretty much my favorite kind of fiction." Not that she didn't read other genres, but there was just so much amazing fantasy being written that she wasn't finding a lot of time for things like contemporary fiction about real life. Especially now that her own real life was taking such a rocky path.

"Fantasy, that's good," said Lakeisha, "fantasy definitely sells. Especially longer fantasy, but people also read a bit of short fantasy. What kind of fantasy? I mean, there are a ton of subgenres out there, so you need to think about your niche."

Meaghan thought. Did she have a favorite kind of fantasy? Had she mainly written one kind or was she all over the map? "Well, I love elves and dragons, but I also like urban fantasy."

"Are we talking epic fantasy for the elves and dragons, you know, like sword-and-sorcery? Or something else? Dark urban fantasy or not-so-dark? Shape-shifters?"

"Oh, I like all of that," said Meaghan, excited to learn that Lakeisha was so familiar with some of the subgenres she enjoyed reading. "I've written some stories with baby dragons, and some about human girls falling in love with gorgeous elf princesses."

"Ooh, you have sapphic interspecies romantasy?" exclaimed Lakeisha. "I would so definitely read that! There is just not enough of that out there."

Meaghan found herself grinning delightedly. "I could write more! Do lots of people read that?"

"Enough that people are selling it, but I think this is a market with room for more content. That is, romance in general is a huge market with a lot of competition for all those readers, but if you niche down enough you can do pretty well. I mean, come on, there are actually people selling books about women who go for orcs."

"Eww," said Meaghan, "I don't think I could write about anyone falling in love with an orc."

"That was just an example. I'm not into orcs either. But sapphic romantasy could definitely use more authors. My books sometimes have a sapphic romantasy subplot, but the main plot is more adventure-focused. You know, quests and stuff. Sometimes time-travel."

"This is so exciting!" said Meaghan, her eyes shining. "And I didn't know you were into sapphic romantasy. That is so cool!"

"Oh, Girlfriend, am I ever into the sapphic romantasy!" said Lakeisha. "I am all over that stuff!"

Meaghan could hardly breathe—Lakeisha was calling her Girlfriend again and announcing she was a total fangirl of sapphic romantic fantasy. This was a sapphic erotic fantasy coming to life—was she dreaming? She was starting to tingle all over at the thought of Lakeisha reading one of her stories. Maybe she would write a story just for Lakeisha! And while the winter clothes meant she couldn't see very much of Lakeisha's figure, in high school Lakeisha had been quite the slender little brown elf, just adorable. Not at all like pale, chubby, curvy

Shaun, but just as cute. (Cuter? Nobody could be as cute as Shaun, could they? Or if anyone could be, maybe Lakeisha?) Meaghan said, again, "That is so cool! I never knew! Okay, I'm totally going to lean into writing more sapphic romantasy. I mean, I might still write a little about baby dragons, because they could just be so *adorbs*, but sexy elf-girls … so hot! And maybe sexy witches meeting sexy elf-girls. I can hardly wait!"

AMBER
NEW YEAR'S EVE

Amber was not happy about the prospect of spending New Year's Eve watching Greg and pals performing. As she'd pointed out to him, it was one thing to enjoy hearing him play at other times of the year—at Burning Man, for instance—but New Year's Eve was a crappy time to try to enjoy anybody's music, because any live venue would be filled with throngs of people focused on getting drunk with their friends. It'd be noisy, and not from loud music, but simply from people shouting at the people seated across the table from them. She'd wanted to have an evening more conducive to coupledom and regaining Greg's full attention. Because ... she was seriously tired of this vying for supremacy. There had been times in the past, pre-Greg, when she'd shared a partner with another person—once even with them all together in bed, which had been pleasantly kinky—but those had been brief affairs and the parameters had been clearly defined. This, however, just seemed to be getting more and more like yet another tired story of a man who couldn't quite leave his failed marriage, and for that she had only scorn.

When she arrived at the venue—not Mill Valley's renowned Sweetwater, but a fairly new place looking to build its audience— Amber discovered that the people she knew were all seated together. Not that this was entirely surprising, given that the only familiar faces she was seeing were the family and friends of the band members (evidently everyone else she knew in Marin County had gone elsewhere), but she saw, to her dismay, that Tippy was among them, decked out in a top covered with white sequins.

Greg had not said Tippy was going to be there.

Amber considered leaving, but friends were already calling out welcomes and gesturing for her to come their way. It would look bad if she left at this point; Tippy would appear to have won, and she, Amber, would look like a sore loser. Amber was not about to be pegged as a sore loser, or indeed as any kind of loser. She strode up, thumbs in the front pockets of her black leather pants, and took a seat next to Tippy.

"Hey, Tip," she said in offhand tones, "how's it shakin'?" It wasn't as if she and Tippy knew each other well, but they certainly knew each other by sight, and from time to time they encountered each other at the grocery store or in other spaces of neutral territory.

"Bitchin'," said Tippy.

"Cool beans," replied Amber dryly.

Conversation restarted among the group as a whole, and Amber ordered a Lagunitas.

"How's Brayden these days?" she inquired after a moment. "I hear you've got him in sports now."

"Yeah, it was kind of a surprise, but all of a sudden he took an interest, so we had to support that," said Tippy. "No football, we don't want him getting concussions, but other than that we're pretty okay with whatever. He's been playing tennis, but I think he's losing interest and pining for baseball season."

"Huh," said Amber. She didn't want to ask too many questions about Brayden in case that made it sound like Greg hadn't kept her up to date on things.

"We really want to work on his skiing while school's still out," said Tippy. "We've got Tahoe season passes like we always do, so he should be able to make good progress if there's decent snow this year."

Amber felt a pang of mixed anger and envy. In the past, she had had the chance to ski with her family after Christmas most years and often skied with Greg as well. Her parents had usually bought lift tickets, or even season passes, for everyone in the family, so her relatively low income had never been a deterrent to skiing since she already owned all her own gear. Was Greg going to spend all his ski time this year with Tippy and Brayden, or would she still have a chance to go with him? The thought of missing out on the winter's skiing was surprisingly painful. While not an expert skier, she'd skied since childhood and was pretty good, enjoying a mix of blue and black-diamond runs every year. Each of the Tahoe-area resorts had its own charms; did she prefer Heavenly, Northstar, Kirkwood, Squaw, Sugar Bowl, Mt. Rose, or one of the others? She probably didn't have a favorite, but she was already missing skiing—the crunch of snow under her boots, the long anticipatory (or relaxing) rides up the lift with their views of the trees and snow, the feel of her skis atop the powder, the pleasure of the turns on the way down whether gentle or around moguls ... the bracing air, usually not *too* cold and often even in the forties on sunny days ... Amber managed a generic response about how she couldn't wait to get back onto the slopes.

Conversation in the group eagerly took up the topic of skiing, as most of the group were avid or at least occasional skiers or snowboarders, and this went on for some time before giving way to talk of sailing, never mind that few had their own boats. Someone ordered shots for the entire group and although soon the band began to play, even the partners of the musicians were not strongly attentive to the music, because—as Amber had pointed out—who really listened closely to the music at a New Year's Eve party?

•   •   •

Later in the evening, after several more drinks and some visits to the restroom, including with Tippy, Amber was feeling much more in the swing of things. Who cared whether Greg did this or that? She and Tippy were starting to sing along with some of the musical numbers—not raucously, of course, but audibly enough, with their arms around each other's shoulders despite the fact that Tippy's white sequins were rather scratchy against Amber's bare forearm. People at some of the other tables were much noisier, occasionally hooting as if they were in a sports bar watching their favorite teams, so there was certainly not anyone in the crowd to care if Amber and Tippy sang along with the band, especially given that they both managed to sing in tune even after knocking back quite a few drinks.

"Amber!" said Tippy at one point, "We gotta do this more often!"

"Dang, girl, maybe you're right!" replied Amber.

"I need more Girls' Nights Out!" said Tippy. "I mean, Greg can come too, but no Brayden. Brayden's at his Grammaw's tonight. He should go there more often, I'm telling you. This Mommy Influencer shtick is starting to get to me."

"I can imagine," said Amber, who couldn't imagine ever wanting to be a Mommy Blogger or anything of the sort. How had Tippy tolerated posting endless mommy-related drivel all these years?

"You should come up to Tahoe with us," Tippy went on. "Brayden can have his own room and spend all his time at Ski School, and you and Greg and I can do our own adult things. I mean yeah, ski some, but we could hot tub and things."

"I'm into it," said Amber. "Love hot tubs and hot springs. Calistoga!"

"Omigod yes," breathed Tippy. "We have to do this. Hot tubbing in Tahoe for ski season, then Calistoga. Massages!"

"Love massages," said Amber. "Massage oil."

"Lots of massage oil," agreed Tippy. "With Vitamin E."

"Lots of Vitamin E."

"Flavored. Flavored massage oil."

"It's good stuff." (Depending, Amber thought but did not say, on the flavor.)

"I love to lick off a good flavored massage oil," said Tippy. "Maybe I should switch from Mommy Influencing to Sex Toy Influencing."

"You could," said Amber. "You totally could. The world needs more Sex Toy Influencers."

"I don't think I could do it on Instagram, though. Meta's so puritanical. Maybe TikTok."

"There are places," said Amber.

"Has Greg ever showed you our little sex den?"

Amber sighed. "No, you're always home. Or Brayden is."

Tippy gazed deep into Amber's eyes. "Well, then tonight's the night! Brayden's at his Grammaw's all night, it'll be just us grownups. We can run through the house naked if we want!"

Amber was somewhat surprised by this invitation after years of being kept mostly away from Tippy's orbit; it was true that she and Greg enjoyed a lively sex life, but this turn of events was unexpected. "What about Greg?" she asked. "Is he coming?" She was open to joining Tippy in the sex den, but did Greg know Tippy was inviting her?

Now Tippy looked surprised. "Well duh! He's the designated driver. It'll be a super after-party." She turned to the rest of their group and announced "After-party orgy at Tippy and Greg's, be there or be square!"

Okay, thought Amber, *this should be interesting!*

LILY
BLOSSOM'S ARRIVAL

Lily was making what seemed like it must be the fourth round of dusting the main floor of the house; her new guest Blossom Hinckley was scheduled to arrive soon and she wanted everything to be perfect, wonderfully inviting. Meaghan had been around during the morning and had helped with a few chores—watering the plants and such—but then took off to meet up with someone named Lakeisha whom Meaghan had described as a friend from high school. Lily didn't recall any friend named Lakeisha from Meaghan's high school years, but of course she hadn't known *everyone* her kids had hung out with in their teens; the family lived too far from Tam High, and the school's students fed in from too many towns, for her to have seen all of them, or even very many of them. It had been similar when she herself had attended Tam High. As her family had lived in Mill Valley, the kids who lived there and in Sausalito could relatively easily gather at one another's homes (easy bus connections for those without their own cars), but it had been harder to hang out with kids who lived farther afield. That wasn't something that had really occurred to her and Don when they'd bought the house on the coast, that their kids might have few playmates close to home and need cars once they got to high school in order to participate in all the after-school events.

Not that this had really been a problem. There had been at least *some* kids in their own community, and it hadn't exactly been a burden to take the girls to Tam Valley Junction or Mill Valley for dance or gymnastics class, or to Sausalito for sailing lessons. It was just that she hadn't gotten to know all that many of the girls' acquaintances. Perhaps this Lakeisha was from Marin City, since Lakeisha sounded like an African-American name and the rest of the county was so white.

Anyway, Lily didn't begrudge Meaghan leaving the house to hang out with a friend for the day. Meaghan's departure meant that Lily could put on her favorite music—listen to Eighties tunes from her own high school years—and take time making minor adjustments to vases and knickknacks, straightening the rugs, ensuring that none of the pictures on the walls had gone a hair askew. She'd already moved the more valuable knickknacks down to the lower level, since you couldn't be sure a guest wouldn't turn out to be a kleptomaniac (or just clumsy and break stuff), but that still left plenty of nice things to display to present a welcoming, homey, appearance. The colorful ceramic jars in the kitchen, for instance, in case guests happened to wander into that area. Or the decorative plate with a fern pattern that sat on a wooden plate-stand in the dining room. The stained-glass lamps. The decorative pillows on the built-in daybed that functioned as a living-room couch. She had turned the main floor's master bedroom, her old bedroom, into an office, and while the lace curtains on the windows there still seemed a little bedroom-like, they looked charming nonetheless. The master bathroom on that floor, admittedly, would never look like anything but a master bath—it was large and in fact consisted of two adjoining bathrooms, one with an old-fashioned clawfoot tub (the side painted with flowers) and one with a shower. But guests didn't need to know that there were actually two baths in one; the door to the second could be closed, so that guests wanting to use the downstairs toilet would only see the one just off the office, where she had placed a vase of dried flowers and a nice guest towel. Since people these days tended to prefer showering to tub baths, she didn't think there would be much demand from guests for that floral clawfoot; the upstairs shower should be quite sufficient, just as it had been (most of the time) for the three girls.

Lily smiled. Even though she was a little sad to have moved her personal things to the lower level, she was excited at the prospect of beginning a new adventure, maybe even a new chapter in her life. She hoped Blossom Hinckley would be a perfect first guest—respectful and courteous, but also friendly. It wouldn't be much fun to start off with a sourpuss, or someone who wanted to retreat into the bedroom as if it were a monk's cell! She wouldn't mind if there were occasional later guests like that, but please, not the first one.

And then the doorbell rang. She'd made sure to put a sign directing visitors to ring, because how else was she to check them in? She dropped off her dustcloth in the kitchen and hastened to the door.

•   •   •

"I'm Blossom Hinckley," said the tall woman at the door. "I've booked a room."

"Yes, of course, come in!" said Lily, smiling. "I'm Lily Simone and you'll be staying in the Dolphin Room." Rather than numbering the rooms, she and Meaghan had decided that it would be much nicer to name them, and so the Dolphin Room door was graced with a leaping dolphin that Amber had made.

The two women went into the new office, where Lily briefed her guest on the rules of the house, information about the area, and offered a plate of snickerdoodle cookies she had baked that morning. Blossom Hinckley was about Lily's own age, slim and perhaps even athletic of build, with short straight dark hair. Wearing a long camel-hair coat and cream beret when she entered the house, she now removed them to reveal a cream cable-knit turtleneck and gold corduroy trousers tucked into knee-high honey-toned boots. Lily noted with approval that this was a very concordant ensemble, although she wasn't sure that there would be much call to wear a camel-hair coat on this side of the hills unless to attend winter parties. It was more of a go-to-San-Francisco (perhaps to the opera!) kind of coat than a walk-on-the-beach coat, after all.

"You'll have the upstairs almost to yourself, at least for the time being," Lily said. "My daughter Meaghan is temporarily back in her old bedroom, but she's usually very quiet. She's my right-hand helper with the bed-and-breakfast." This last was a spur-of-the-moment invention, as while Meaghan did help, it was clear that she had no real desire to be involved, and assisted purely from a sense of obligation. However, Lily wanted guests to have the best possible initial impression of her daughter, since not all of them were likely to be enchanted with her sometimes ratty and disheveled appearance, or the fact that she would not be at their beck and call like a maid.

"That sounds lovely," said Blossom Hinckley. "Have the two of you been in business long?"

Lily had hoped this question would not arise, but there it was. "Actually, you're our first guest," she confessed. "We're very excited to have you and hope you'll let us know how we're doing." She paused an instant, then plunged forward. "What brings you to the area in January? Meaghan wondered whether maybe you were a marine biologist or something like that. Not that it's any of our business, but we did have fun speculating."

Blossom Hinckley laughed. "I'm afraid I'll have to disappoint her on the marine biology front."

Since Blossom Hinckley didn't immediately go on to explain her true reasons for arriving in January, Lily quickly said, "That's quite all right, and I shouldn't be asking you unnecessary questions when you haven't even had a chance to bring in your luggage yet! Did you have a long drive to get here, and would you like a hand?"

"Oh, this afternoon's drive wasn't all that long. Just up from San Francisco. And there's not really much for me to bring in for tonight. Tomorrow I might bring in a bit more stuff from the car. But am I parked legally, down on the street in front of the house?"

Lily explained that while it was okay to park briefly on the narrow street, it would normally be best to park behind the lot, on the next street up the hill. "That's a wider street, where there's some space by the garage. You can enter through the back gate and through the back yard to the porch. Here, I'll take you out to show you; it's a little complicated the first time you see it, but once you've walked it, you'll know exactly where you're going." And so she led Blossom Hinckley out onto the balcony and through an ornamental gateway to the back yard, from which the garage and gate to the upper street could be seen.

"This is quite the fabulous garden!" commented Blossom, gazing about in admiration. "I must admit that the photos of the garden were part of what drew me to choose this particular B&B."

"Thank you!" said Lily. "It's been a labor of love over the years." She wondered, looking out at it, how she'd manage to maintain it properly now that Don wasn't around to help. While she enjoyed gardening, it was a big job to keep the various plants looking their best. The young palm tree, for instance, had to be trimmed from time to time so that the dead fronds didn't look shaggy and dirty (and attract rats). Some of the shrubs needed regular shearing to maintain their shape. She couldn't expect Meaghan to be around to help with all this forever; would she need to hire help? Lily put the thought out of her mind and took Blossom Hinckley back into the house to show her the Dolphin Room.

TIFFANY
JASON AND JIMMY CARTER

"It feels funny to be back in the same room with you again, Jase," said Tiffany unsteadily. There they were in their living room in the apartment in Strawberry, sitting awkwardly, not close to each other, but across from each other with their Christmas presents sitting on the coffee table between them. The sun was filtering in the living room window in a cold, wintry sort of way, and their intentionally minimalist décor, all white and gray, looked stark rather than stylish now that it was missing some of Jason's personal items. Jason himself was looking larger than she remembered, a tall figure taking up his entire chair, wearing chinos and a rugby shirt with a heavy waterproof jacket.

"Way to go, Tiff, that's not a very encouraging start!" said Jason. "What about, like, Happy New Year or How was your Christmas?" He frowned unhappily, peering at her from under lowered eyebrows.

"Well, how *was* your Christmas?" She missed him, and there he was looking gorgeous as usual, but really, weren't things pretty much over between them?

"My Christmas kind of sucked, because you weren't there," said Jason. "My parents didn't exactly know how to talk to me without you along. They kept asking if you were all right and why we weren't having Christmas together this year."

"What'd you tell them?" Tiffany avoided saying that her Christmas hadn't been that great either.

"Same as at Thanksgiving, that we had some things to work out."

"That's not very informative."

"Tiffany, it's not like my family needs to know every detail about our marriage, especially right now. Why, did you tell *your* family everything?"

"Well, I told them more than you told yours!"

"Oh, great," sighed Jason. "I'm not sure I want to know exactly what you told them."

"Okay, then you don't need to know what I told them."

"Tiffany, I don't want to fight with you. You know I love you. I've always loved you."

"Yeah, that's what you say," said Tiffany. She was starting to feel the nausea again. When the heck would it subside? And should she get an abortion or not? She knew that if she was going to do it, the sooner the better, but she hadn't been able to bring herself to make a decision during the holiday season.

"That's what I say because that's the truth," persisted Jason.

"How can that be the truth if you're really more attracted to guys?"

Jason rubbed desperately at his hair, as if trying to give himself a receding hairline. "Love isn't the same as attractions," he said. "It's not like I'm not attracted to you. I've always loved you *and* been attracted to you."

"You said you were more attracted to guys," said Tiffany stubbornly. She felt that if she focused on this one problem, maybe her stomach would settle. Or was it making things worse? It was hard to concentrate when feeling so queasy.

"Yeah, I know I said that," said Jason. "I wasn't lying that I'm attracted to guys, but I said it because I was getting mad that you kept getting on my case about my work schedule. I mean, I'm attracted to lots of people, male and female. It doesn't mean I chase after them."

"That doesn't seem very likely," said Tiffany. She told herself he must be making this up.

"What, you've never heard of being attracted to people and not pursuing them? Ever heard of a guy named Jimmy Carter?"

"You're comparing yourself to President Carter now?" laughed Tiffany. "Give me a break! President Carter is a saintly man—I bet he'll be the first official saint who wasn't Catholic. Besides, he never said he was attracted to other guys."

Jason leaned forward, his eyes intense. "I can't believe you're being so prejudiced. It's not important whether Jimmy Carter was attracted to men or women, the important thing is that his marriage was more important to him than whether he was attracted to other people."

"Well, fine," said Tiffany, "but I still can't believe that you're comparing yourself to President Carter."

"Well why wouldn't I want to be like him? A guy who always valued his marriage and who built houses for poor people—not to mention that he was president of the United States."

Tiffany could not believe that they had gotten into such a bizarre argument. "He was president before we were even born!" she exclaimed, irrelevantly.

"Tiffany, honey, you have to stop worrying about President Carter—why did I even mention him?—and try to accept me the way I really am."

"I—" Tiffany's nausea finally won out and she bolted for the bathroom, but didn't quite make it there. Luckily, one of the appliances they had bought the year before was a rug shampoo machine.

LILY
NECTARINE JAM

"This spiced nectarine jam is really something!" commented Blossom Hinckley at the breakfast table on her first morning at the new B&B. "I never would have thought of pairing jam with pancakes and fruit, either."

Lily beamed. "It's a local jam," she said. "One of my friends makes it, and the jam and pancake combo recipe is one she got from her mother. I've been making the nectarines-and-pancakes for years—my family loves it—so in addition to keeping the jam on hand, I usually buy and freeze the fresh nectarines so that we can enjoy this even out of nectarine season. Since you're the first B&B guest, I couldn't resist starting you off with one of our favorite hearty breakfasts."

"This is hearty, all right, but I suppose it can't hurt to start off my stay with a real treat," said Blossom. "I'm looking forward to doing some hiking and exploration today."

"That's an excellent plan," agreed Lily. "It'll be chilly, but we're not expecting rain, so the hiking should be very good. I take it you've brought good sturdy boots and all?" The previous day's boots were definitely not hiking boots, and at the moment Blossom was wearing forest-green woolen Halflinger house shoes with cork soles, so those were obviously not for hiking either.

"Yes, they're still in the car along with some other things."

"The Dipsea is our most famous trail, but there are also others," Lily went on. "You'll have lots of options right around here, not to mention if you go up to Point Reyes. Have you spent much time along this part of the coast before?"

"It's not the first time I've been to this part of Marin, but I really don't know it well," said Blossom. "It's funny how a person can live in the Bay Area for decades and only get to know certain parts very well."

Lily smiled. "I suppose that's natural when the Bay Area encompasses—how many counties? I don't even know offhand. And I have to admit I seldom leave Marin unless I'm going to San Francisco or up to Napa and Sonoma. Well—or to Tahoe to ski, I suppose." She was enjoying having a chance to talk a little more conversationally with her guest rather than having to focus on being purely informative. She hoped she wasn't overdoing it.

"Oh, do you ski?" asked Blossom. "I love to ski."

"I enjoy it," said Lily, "but I wouldn't say I'm an avid skier. We used to go up to Tahoe every year after Christmas, but part of the fun for me was the chance to sit and drink hot chocolate while I watched my girls fly down the mountain."

Blossom laughed. "How many daughters do you have?"

"Three!" replied Lily. "Amber lives nearby, Tiffany's over in Strawberry, and Meaghan's just back home for a while after her situation in the City didn't work out as planned." She paused an instant, then said "Do you have kids too?"

"No," said Blossom Hinckley. "That wasn't really in the cards."

"Oh!" said Lily, blushing. "I'm sorry to hear that. I mean, if you wanted them."

"I'm happy enough not to have any at this point," said Blossom. "If I had any, I'd be terrified for their future. As it is, it's enough to worry about humankind more generally, and hope I'll be long dead before people render the planet completely uninhabitable."

Lily looked down at her hands, as if checking her freshly applied pale peach nail polish could avert global warming and climate catastrophe. "I try not to think about how it'll be for my kids after I'm gone," she said, although that wasn't really true, just not something she'd been thinking much about lately, what with more immediate personal crises to deal with. "I donate to charities that are working to fix things," she added, although that wasn't currently even slightly true. She'd had to suspend all her charitable contributions once she'd seen the true state of her finances, and it felt strange to realize that now she was no longer supporting the Sierra Club or Greenpeace or any of the rest.

Blossom Hinckley did not directly respond to these comments, but instead continued to eat her pancakes with the spiced jam, alternating the bites with sips of coffee.

It occurred to Lily that this situation of having a single guest at a bed-and-breakfast was probably somewhat uncommon; that while it might be ordinary at a typical Airbnb where the host only welcomed the guest upon arrival and then disappeared, at a bed-and-breakfast (even one run with the help of the Airbnb company), even single guests were likely to breakfast in the company of other guests, not eat under the eagle eye of the host. She was unsure of the etiquette in such a situation; obviously the host needed to ensure that the breakfast was satisfactory and not lacking in anything important, while on the other hand a solo guest might want to be left alone to eat in peace. She said, "If you'd rather not talk during breakfast, just say so and I'll go do something else. I know some people just hate to be disturbed at breakfast."

Blossom looked up and smiled. "I'm not one of those people who can't tolerate the slightest bit of breakfast conversation. I may not be the chattiest breakfast companion, but at least I don't snarl when spoken to."

Lily was quite relieved to hear this, as with only one guest it really seemed more natural to be able to speak with her. "That's good, I wouldn't want to impose. Your comfort is paramount!" She tried to think of further suitably innkeeperly phrases, but apart from the old Motel 6 "We'll leave the light on for you" slogan, nothing came to mind, and the last thing she wanted to do was recite a budget motel catchphrase to her guests. Plus, she couldn't recall whether Blossom's booking data had indicated that the stay was for business or pleasure.

"My wife was the one who sometimes needed to be left to herself at breakfast," Blossom continued. "Not every day, just some days. I needed to be able to tell if it was one of those days."

"Oh!" said Lily, slightly surprised to be learning at least three significant pieces of information in one fell swoop. "You're not married anymore?" she asked cautiously.

"Julie died last year," said Blossom.

"Oh my goodness!" exclaimed Lily. "I am so sorry! That's ... well, I know that every grief is different, they're not all the same, but it's strange—my husband died last year too."

"Unexpectedly or did you know it was coming?"

"Very unexpectedly. That's what led to my opening the house for guests."

"I'm very sorry," said Blossom. "Loss isn't easy, is it."

"No, and sometimes I get really tired of my friends telling me how well I'm coping. They mean well, they want to be supportive, but ..."

"They can't truly know."

"Exactly. Especially since I can't tell them absolutely everything that's on my mind, because not everything is mine to tell. Family stuff, I mean."

"Yes," said Blossom gravely, "there's always stuff that can't be told, or can't be told to certain people, or under certain circumstances. Some things are just confidential for one reason or another."

•   •   •

Lily had been a little surprised to hear Blossom Hinckley call family troubles "confidential"—while she didn't think she ought to recount her daughters' recent woes to Gail and Margo yet, she assumed that eventually these matters would seem tellable, at least to close friends who had known the girls since infancy. However, when Blossom revealed later on that she was a lawyer, it was obvious why Blossom would use terms like "confidential" for the kind of family secrets that were no longer ultra-secret in most families.

After that first breakfast, Blossom had gone off exploring and not returned until evening, but as Meaghan preferred to breakfast in the kitchen on her own unpredictable schedule rather than joining the scheduled breakfast in the dining room (organized according to Blossom's preference since no other guests had yet arrived), breakfast soon became a time for Lily and Blossom to chat. Lily learned that Blossom had lived in San Francisco for the majority of her life and was half Chinese, her mother having come from Taiwan in the early Sixties, and that Blossom and Julie had met while attending UC Berkeley. Following Julie's death early the previous year, Blossom had taken a leave from her law firm and was now contemplating whether she should retire and leave San Francisco in favor of some other area—for instance, the Marin coast or perhaps somewhere further north like Sonoma County or even Mendocino.

"Wouldn't you get lonesome moving far away from all your friends and colleagues?" asked Lily.

"Possibly," admitted Blossom, "but I could visit them if I wanted. Besides, that's part of what I want to figure out—would I regret leaving or would it be refreshing to make a new start?"

Lily felt that she herself remained a loyal native Marinite who wouldn't at all like to move to some other county or state. Although there was a lot of talk lately about coastal erosion and the potential rise of the sea level as more and more polar ice melted, she didn't think this was likely to threaten the house during her own lifetime, or at least not before she was in the market for some sort of assisted living community. Her house was surely at least twenty feet above sea level and possibly even higher, unlike some of those newer houses that were right on the beach and endangered by the slightest wave from a far-off tsunami. But these were not matters that she saw any reason to mention to Blossom, or at least not unless Blossom began to show a desire to buy a property too close to the water. In that case she would probably warn Blossom to reconsider. Instead, she said "What sort of things do you think you might do if you retire and leave San Francisco? That is, there's certainly hiking, but it could be quite a shock to go from working in a busy San Francisco law firm to living in a small settlement on the coast."

"Well," said Blossom, "there are various possibilities. For one thing, I've always regretted not having more time to pursue painting and photography. I'm hoping to do some of that kind of thing while I'm here and see how it goes. But I might also do some pro bono legal work. You know, work with environmental organizations or something. Or do some other kind of volunteer work. Not right away, but maybe at some point. Maybe take some shifts at a crisis hotline."

Lily was impressed. Other than doing some decorative painting around the house, and taking ordinary personal photos, she had never pursued her own interest in art In any serious way (that was Amber's area, she told herself). And it had never occurred to her to take up volunteer work. Would there be time to do anything like that now that she was running a B&B? Once more guests began to arrive, that is ... which she certainly needed to have happen soon.

MEAGHAN
LAKEISHA AND SAPPHIC ROMANTASY

Meaghan had begun to get together with Lakeisha fairly regularly, although this was usually at Lakeisha's convenience as she was the one with a car; Meaghan could borrow her mother's car now and then for errands, but Lily didn't like to be left without transportation, especially given that she didn't really think Meaghan was a good enough driver to trust with a fairly new and now somewhat underinsured Mercedes. Nor did Amber care to have Meaghan borrowing her own car too frequently, as she pointed out that she needed the relatively ramshackle vehicle to haul scrap metal and other materials for her sculptures, as well as to shlep the finished pieces to the gallery that displayed and sold them.

As both Meaghan and Lakeisha were temporarily lodging with parents after several years more or less on their own, both were eager to spend the daytime hours out in the world, even if "out in the world" largely meant meeting up to spend hours in Mill Valley's several coffee shops. There, they developed a routine of coffee purchase followed by ten or fifteen minutes of conversation, after which they typically worked diligently for two or three hours straight—for Lakeisha was firm that she needed to work on a schedule in order to complete her drawings and books, and Meaghan, impressed with such industry, followed her example. As Meaghan had already developed reasonably consistent work habits during her time with *The New True Bernal Journal* (although more of the time at the newspaper had been taken up with research and interviews than with actual writing), she found it not too difficult to turn her mind to polishing up her old stories to post online, and then to get going on new ones that were specifically intended to please an audience seeking short morsels of sapphic romantasy.

"Work on your craft with the short and free pieces," Lakeisha had counseled, "and once you've got some loyal fans, you can add a paid-subscribers-only area. Not everyone will convert to paid, 'cause not everyone has the money, but if you can serve up some juicy tales with super world-building, they'll soon be begging for more."

Meaghan took this advice to heart, figuring that Lakeisha was already making respectable money in her own niche and knew what she was talking about. To supplement Lakeisha's advice, Meaghan also diligently read online columns on how to succeed at genre fiction, and devoured as much romantasy—sapphic or otherwise—as she could find. But while she had some ideas, and had written a fair number of stories in the past, it looked like before long she would need to zero in on just exactly what kind of sapphic romantasy to specialize in, because while this was a niche area, it was nonetheless a niche with sub-niches. Yes, she could write in more than one of these sub-niches, but maybe not for a while. Would it be elf-girls in a world of fae untroubled by humans? Would it be human girls unexpectedly encountering lovely elf-maidens? What about sexy witches running competing magical teahouses or bakeries or pharmacies? Would her characters live in the modern world and communicate via cell phone as well as magic, or would they live in King Arthur's time or ancient Ireland or in the days of the Vikings? Should she specialize in lovers discovering their sexuality, or in slightly more experienced vixens? Would the stories be relatively cozy or involve danger and deception? It appeared that the best option would be to experiment by writing very short pieces in many of these sub-niches and see what readers began to respond to—

as well as seeing what she liked best and felt she handled the most skillfully.

"This is crazy hard, making decisions about some of this stuff," she said to Lakeisha as they settled down with their lattes to work. "I mean, there are so many possibilities! What if I like writing all kinds of different sapphic romantasy?"

Lakeisha laughed. "Girlfriend, you make this too hard for yourself!" she exclaimed. "If you write enough of this stuff, you can be queen of multiple series of different subgenres. You just need to separate out your book series once you get going. Like, say you do one series with magical pirate ladies, but a different one with gardening witches. You make clear they're different series with your series titles and your cover designs. But right now, just work on your craft with the short stuff and post new ones online regularly."

"Yeah, I know," said Meaghan wistfully. There was Lakeisha calling her Girlfriend again, and looking so enchanting with her cascade of a hundred or so long little tawny braids falling forward as she drew … and the thoughts of Shaun were gradually fading along with the pain of the breakup, but … was Lakeisha *attracted* to her or were they just destined to be friends who both happened to love to read (and invent) sapphic romantic fantasy? It wasn't as if, given that they were both staying with family, it would be easy to have actual romantic trysts. Not in the winter, anyway! Lakeisha's father was usually at home rehearsing or writing music, and Lakeisha's mother was in and out with no obvious schedule, plus Lakeisha also had a sometimes annoying younger brother. Lakeisha was looking for a place of her own, but even with an income, that was tricky in Marin, and Lakeisha was particular.

Then there was the whole B&B thing going on at home, with that woman Blossom Hinckley staying on the same floor as Meaghan's own bedroom! Meaghan tried to be grateful that Ms. Hinckley had come to stay, since obviously they needed the money, and it wasn't that she disliked Ms. Hinckley or anything like that, but the whole thing was just not ideal. Ms. Hinckley always looked so elegant, so … *soignée* … even in jeans and hiking boots, like she never slipped and fell in the mud or ever did anything stupid or clumsy. Meaghan could see that her mother and Ms. Hinckley were becoming friends, and that was fine, but living on the same floor as Ms. Hinckley and sharing a bathroom with her (while having to keep her towels and toothbrush and so forth in her own bedroom, really!) was kind of weird.

But at least Amber had come up with the money owed Shaun for December's rent and utilities—Amber said she had borrowed it from Greg Stover, so it would absolutely have to be paid back as soon as Meaghan was earning some money—and Amber had also fronted some money for bus fares and coffees, because Amber could understand that she needed to get out of the house and work … although Amber had also suggested that with all this time spent in cafés, perhaps Meaghan could learn to be a barista in order to bring in some immediate cash …

Meaghan sighed and kept writing, with only brief glances up to take in the glorious sight of Lakeisha at work drawing big-eyed, pointy-eared, sassy-talking, unbelievably cute manga girls (and some boys) in wild adventures.

AMBER

THREES?

The New Year's Eve orgy so imperiously called for by Tippy had been a success, if not exactly the gigantic piggy pile that Tippy might have been hoping for. While Amber hadn't been the only person at the table who joined Greg and Tippy at home for an after-party, the others had drifted home after a very short while, some with demurs of not having brought condoms or other useful items, and others making jokes about needing to get home to pay the babysitter or let the dog out. Amber too might have drifted home in a similar style, had Tippy not made very clear that she was to stay.

Amber did have a twinge or two of unease as the other guests departed—what if Tippy was actually planning to kill her, either with Greg's help or with Greg as Victim #2? However, Tippy made clear (while Greg looked slightly embarrassed) that, first of all, the days of marital separation were over, and that, secondly, nobody need feel left out or abandoned, because from now on, Amber was to be part of the family.

"Polyamory is the way to go," announced Tippy. "It's the wave of the future and jealousy can go fuck itself!"

Greg had smiled a little nervously at Amber, without saying anything to dispute this pronouncement. Amber, meanwhile, wondered what Tippy had been reading lately to prompt this seemingly new turn in the Stovers' marital life, but she figured that so long as everyone stayed friendly, and so long as the sex was good rather than cringe-worthy, then well, why not give it a try?

·   ·   ·

And the sex had been good enough that Amber was open to (carefully) continuing along this polyamorous path. She knew, to be sure, that polyamory wasn't just about sex—successful polyamorists made sure to address feelings of jealousy and loneliness that if left ignored could easily destroy the intricate relationships among the group members. Also, time would tell whether this particular configuration was to consist mainly of Greg as nucleus circled by Amber and Tippy as electrons, or whether the sex and relationships would develop in a genuinely triangular manner, with each of them equally connected to the other two. Given that there was a long history now of Tippy versus Amber, each struggling to gain primacy and exclusivity in Greg's life, there was going to be a lot of actual work needed if they were to reformulate! Were they all, for instance, going to continue living in three separate homes, or would they (not immediately, but at some indeterminate future point) decide to gather together in the redwood house currently occupied only by Tippy and Brayden? While Amber was all for saving money on housing, she wasn't ready to give up her very sweet deal on the place she was currently renting, where she contributed a certain amount of maintenance and other labor in exchange for low rent (not to mention that she had actual studio space there). Besides, were there even enough bedrooms at Tippy's place for three adults plus Brayden? She rather doubted that a guest bedroom would be enough space for her needs.

And yes, Brayden—what did Tippy have in mind about him? He couldn't always be shunted off to his Grammaw's. Amber wasn't eager to start spending time with a prepubescent (or was he pubescent now?) boy, but she also felt that Brayden had some rights here. She supposed that as a Marin County kid, he probably knew plenty of kids with two moms or two dads or maybe even more than two of each, but as someone who had grown up with the traditional one parent per gender, she admitted to a slight bias toward the standard configuration. Besides, while she was sure that many of Brayden's peers had step-parents or gay or trans parents, she doubted that his friends were all living in the midst of communal poly households.

Still, Brayden was hardly Amber's main concern at this point. More important at this point from her perspective was whether she and Tippy and Greg could make this new arrangement work for the three adults. If it worked for the adults, then it would (probably, eventually) work for Brayden, but if it didn't work for the adults, then it wouldn't work for anyone.

LILY
OTHER GUESTS

Lily bade Blossom Hinckley goodbye with a real sense of loss.

"I'm going to miss you!" she said as lightly as possible when the day arrived for Blossom's departure. "It's been such fun getting to know you." In addition to their breakfast chats, Lily had introduced Blossom to Gail and Margo—and as a foursome, or even five if Meaghan joined them, Scrabble and other games had been a winter-evening delight.

"I'll probably be back," said Blossom, who was heading further north to the Sonoma coast to see what she thought of the Bodega Bay area. "I've really enjoyed my stay here. Being your first guest has been a very special experience, and I'm sure that once word begins to get out, you'll have guests lining up to get rooms."

"It's a little hard to imagine," admitted Lily, increasingly aware of the limited bathroom facilities and equally limited parking options. "Naturally it's important to start attracting more guests, but I can't help thinking that'll be so different." Would future guests prove to be as considerate or as good company as Blossom had turned out to be? While initially Blossom had been rather reserved, she had gradually opened up after revealing that she hoped to start a new life following Julie's death. Not surprisingly, their shared recent widowhood provided an important emotional link, although neither woman had proffered specifics about their spouses' deaths. That, Lily thought, was something that need not be discussed yet, although she was curious about Julie and could imagine that Blossom was at least somewhat curious about Don. Lily had made occasional references to Don—his role in fixing up the house years ago, for instance, and how Thousand Island had remained his favorite salad dressing no matter how often she tried to tempt him with bleu cheese and vinaigrettes—but she hadn't wanted to bring Don into the conversation any more than necessary. It was one thing to mention ordinary and trivial details about him often enough not to seem secretive, especially when Margo and Gail were around, but there was no reason to burden Blossom with too much talk about Don. She found that to some extent she wanted to close off that part of her past and consider it finished. Whether Blossom felt similarly about Julie, she couldn't quite tell, but it seemed possible. After all, their relationships were surprisingly parallel; they had both met their spouses in college, had spent many years with them, and now they were both recent widows. If Lily and Blossom did continue their friendship, then more details were likely to gradually emerge on both sides.

"You have a very hospitable nature," said Blossom. "I'm sure there'll be more guests as spring approaches."

Spring, thought Lily, was rather far away considering that it was now late January, but she appreciated the thought. She looked over at Blossom as they stood beside Blossom's Miata, the luggage already packed into the car's tiny trunk, and she marveled that Blossom had ever managed to fit both winter clothes and painting supplies into such a small space. Today Blossom was clad in the camel-hair coat again, although Lily thought a jacket would be more sensible to drive in, and the cream beret was back on Blossom's glossy dark hair after weeks of a nondescript black one (easier to replace if lost, Blossom had noted). Lily now knew that there were some gray strands hidden among all those nearly black ones, but they were few—certainly not as many as in her own lighter hair. Now that Lily could no longer afford to get her hair touched up, the amount of gray mixed in with the dark blonde was startling.

"I'll miss you," said Lily. She thought quickly. "May I give you a goodbye hug?" she asked shyly.

Blossom smiled. "Of course."

•   •   •

After Blossom's departure, Lily felt curiously empty. While to her relief some short-term bookings rapidly materialized—both rooms were booked for Valentine's Day, in fact—the house seemed empty, especially as Meaghan was constantly hightailing it out to meet up with Lakeisha.

"You know, honey, it's okay for you to have friends come here," she told Meaghan, "especially when there aren't any guests. This is still your home, and I won't bother you if you want to hang out in your room or in the living room or in the downstairs. You could play ping-pong for hours downstairs."

"We're working on stuff," Meaghan claimed. "It's easier when we're sitting at a café."

Lily privately thought that Meaghan ought to be getting a job sometime soon, perhaps as a barista—that seemed like a suitable in-between kind of job for people in their twenties—but she wasn't ready to push Meaghan on this yet. Meaghan still seemed mopey, although less focused on Shaun than she had been, and it wasn't really any more expensive (as far as she could tell, anyway) to have Meaghan in the house than not. Lily supposed they could wait a little longer before she got after Meaghan to start contributing to the household expenses. In the meantime, she had taken out a home equity loan, which would keep them afloat for a while if they were careful. Getting a succession of short-term rentals seemed like it could be key, because while those would be much more work than having a long-term guest like Blossom, people renting for a night or two would pay full price, whereas it was only reasonable to discount a bit for long stays.

Lily knew that Meaghan wasn't exactly thrilled to have B&B guests staying upstairs with her in Amber and Tiffany's former rooms, but Meaghan had behaved herself about it so far, and neither Meaghan nor Blossom had reported any problems regarding sharing the bathroom or anything else. They had simply taken to rather different schedules and mostly spent their evenings in different parts of the house; Meaghan tended to retreat to her room to read and do whatever on her laptop and phone, all of which was standard for Meaghan and had been so since childhood. Blossom had spent some evenings upstairs as well, but had soon more often joined Lily for Scrabble on the dining-room table or for a movie in the living room. Meaghan was a good enough Scrabble player, but her taste in movies seldom aligned with what piqued Lily and Blossom's interest. And so what exactly would things be like when Meaghan was confronted with a more changeable set of guests, some of whom might be men or couples?

•   •   •

Lily soon had an answer to the question of what things *could* be like, when two men, apparently in their early thirties, booked Amber and Tiffany's old rooms. Trent Hoskins and Hunter Cassidy arrived in a sporty BMW and quickly proved to be a loud-voiced pair who tracked a remarkable quantity of dirt and sand into the house. These characteristics, while not ideal, could have been overlooked had Trent and Hunter seemed like endearingly good-natured fellows, but the longer they were in the house, the more they grated on Lily's nerves. They weren't interested in hearing any of her instructions about the rules of the house, so they parked the car right in front of the garage, slammed doors, shouted to each other when inside the house, and generally gave the impression of being overgrown high-school boys.

"They're gross," said Meaghan promptly.

"They're only staying two nights," said Lily.

"That's two nights too many," retorted Meaghan. She repeated, "They're gross."

Lily sighed. She didn't like them much either, but they were paying guests. So long as their payment had gone through with Airbnb and they didn't damage or destroy anything, she supposed she could tolerate them. "Just avoid them and don't say anything to make them feel unwelcome. You can sleep in the downstairs with me if you'd rather."

"They're not going to push me out of my bedroom. I have a door lock now, remember?"

"Right, but you might need to get up in the night."

Meaghan made a face at this idea. "I do not get up in the night. Why would I get up in the night?"

"Honey, you might need to use the toilet," said Lily, who found that she herself usually got up at least once and sometimes twice for that reason.

"I'm not an old person. I only get up if I'm sick."

"Your mother," said Lily with steely calm, "is not an old person yet but she does get up at night."

"Well, I'm not old enough for that. I'll just barricade myself in my room and ignore the dudes, and in the morning I'll use your old bathroom instead of the upstairs bathroom."

"Okay," said Lily. She didn't think there was likely to be any real problem, but it was best to be careful. And she didn't believe for one minute that Meaghan never needed to get up in the night. It was just not every night.

• • •

The first night of Trent and Hunter's stay seemed off to a rather tense but not actively distressing start when the two returned from supper decidedly inebriated. They had driven into Sausalito for the meal—not dreadfully far if you lived on the coast and wanted a change of pace, but an odd choice for guests who had chosen lodgings on this side of the hills. Their voices had continued to be loud even late at night, although as neither Lily nor Meaghan were required elsewhere in the morning, this was not a major problem and Lily decided not to remind them about night-time quiet hours.

In the morning, however, Hunter somehow became confused by the bathroom sink's water faucets, and actually broke the handle on the hot water when it wouldn't turn in the direction he imagined it ought to go. Lily was in the kitchen working on breakfast when she heard him let out a loud bellow and then, after some curses followed by laughter (apparently Trent was amused by the mishap), Hunter stampeded down the stairs so noisily that she thought he was going to break the steps, yelling "Hey, I don't know what I did, but the faucet up there broke!"

"What?" exclaimed Lily in dismay, looking up from the pancakes she was flipping.

"Friggin' faucet handle came off in my hand! First it wouldn't turn, then it broke off!"

Lily dropped her spatula and hastened up the stairs. Sure enough, the faucet handle lay in the middle of the sink like a bizarre meteor fallen from the heavens. This wasn't a cheap faucet assembly, either; Lily remembered choosing it with Don at a high-end bath-and-plumbing showroom. Nor was this something she was going to be able to fix herself; she'd have to call a plumber and might even have to buy a whole new faucet. That would almost certainly cost more than she was making on the two rooms for two nights—although she supposed it might be possible to bill Hunter for the damage. She'd have to check with Airbnb on how to do that, maybe even before calling the plumber. This was awful! She checked to see whether the other handle still functioned—luckily it did.

"Well," she began, "I'm afraid that you're just going to have to stick with cold water at that sink until I can get the plumber out."

"That's crazy," said Hunter, "crazy cheap faucet that breaks off in a dude's hand!"

"I'm sorry," said Lily, "but that is not a cheap faucet and I'm afraid you broke it."

"The fuck I did," said Hunter, "it was stuck and then it came right off in my hand."

"Dude!" hooted Trent, arriving to stand in the bathroom doorway. "Incredible Hulk the Faucet-Breaker!"

"Shut up, dude, piece of crap broke on me!" retorted Hunter. "Not my fault!"

"I'm sorry," said Lily again, "but you're responsible for any damage incurred. We've never had a single problem with that faucet."

"Mom!" came Meaghan's voice now. "What's going on? Why is everybody hollering?"

"The faucet's been broken and we're going to have to call the plumber," said Lily as she caught sight of her daughter standing behind Trent wearing Hello Kitty pajamas and exhibiting an alarming new bald spot. "Meaghan, I need you to run downstairs and take the pancakes off the griddle. Stack them on a serving plate and take them into the dining room while I come down and see which plumber I can get to come out at this hour."

"It just came off in my hand," reiterated Hunter grumpily.

"I don't want to hear any more excuses," said Lily. "You guys are responsible for any and all damage incurred. Now get yourselves dressed if you expect to get any breakfast. I need to finish getting it ready, so no more trouble out of you."

She turned and descended the steps wondering whether it was a terrible mistake to treat her paying guests like naughty children. But what other option did she really have than to insist that they behave? She wasn't running a four-star hotel that could afford to have rock stars (or overgrown frat boys, or venture capitalists, or anyone else) trash the place.

TIFFANY
NAUSEA

By late January, Tiffany was in full retreat—from Jason, from her family, from work, from decisions about the pregnancy. She was sick daily, fighting the near-constant nausea with ginger tea and grated ginger, but losing the battle regularly, vomiting what little she managed to eat. She was no longer spending hours in cafés—that was too risky, and she'd already made herself unpopular with the baristas at two of her hangouts by publicly puking more than once in each.

"You're not well," one barista had told her. "Stay home. You shouldn't be out exposing people to your illness."

"I'm not ..." began Tiffany, weakly.

"You are *sick*," reiterated the barista. "Stop denying it. Go to the doctor and then stay home till you get better. What are you, one of those anti-vaxxers or something?"

At that point, another barista had intervened and told the first barista to have some compassion and shut up, but even that barista had recommended that Tiffany stay home. Well, all right, she'd stay home! She'd stay home and drink ginger tea all day and eat bananas for potassium and see if she could keep enough whole-grain crackers down.

She was still reading romances, book after book, most of them short ones, leaning at times toward the hyper sweet-and-clean in which no sex intruded, and at other times toward dark, even violent, tales of women in love with mafia men or werewolves, where at times the sex was not entirely consensual. She buried herself under the bed covers to read, with a bucket beside the bed in case a bout of vomiting came on too quickly to reach the bathroom; some days she bathed obsessively and on other days she refused to wash at all.

Her mother called every few days to ask how things were going, but she pretended things were relatively normal, saying she'd seen Jason after Christmas, that she was still deciding about the baby, that she was eating nutritious meals and was still working at the boutique.

But most of the time she was lying in bed or on the couch, staring at the ceiling or keeping her eyes closed pretending to sleep, keeping the shades closed on the living-room window and keeping the TV on at a low level to game shows and infomercials. She couldn't imagine what was going to happen next, past the next bout of nausea and vomiting and feeling drained. Her life was, she felt, on hold.

AMBER
A VALENTINE INVITATION

"You've got to come to Calistoga with us for Valentine's Day," announced Tippy.

"Um, that could be fun, but exactly what did you have in mind?" asked Amber warily. Things were going well enough so far with this new arrangement—she was spending three or four nights a week with Greg and Tippy at the big redwood house—but nonetheless she felt she had to tread carefully.

"Spa time! Wines!" said Tippy.

"Yeah, I know that's usually what people do in Calistoga," said Amber, who had gone once or twice herself to soak in the hot springs, "but maybe you could be a little more specific. Like, are we talking about a day trip or an overnight? How much spa and how much wine-tasting?" She was trying to get a sense of how much this was going to cost and whether she'd be expected to pay a third of the bill, but she didn't want to come out and say that if she didn't have to.

Tippy giggled. "Well, I think we should stay at least *one* night. After all, Valentine's Day!"

"Yeah, but have you already made reservations? Valentine's Day is almost here. We can't just show up and expect to get a room." Surely Tippy knew this and had booked months ago. Spontaneity was all very well, and Amber considered herself to be a pretty spontaneous person, but you couldn't be spontaneous about everything. Certain things definitely required planning ahead, and holiday bookings at hotels normally fell into that category.

Tippy giggled again, and Amber wondered if she was stoned on something. "Reservations, schmeservations. That's Greg's department. It'll be fine. We'll have mud baths and bubbly. Stay in a super-duper elegant hotel. Do the whole lovers' deal. And chocolates! Plus trays of Sweetheart conversation heart candies in pastel colors! Be mine! Only you! Cutie pie! Kiss me!"

Amber sighed. Now she was pretty sure Tippy was either drunk or high. Who on earth went around quoting candy hearts at people from memory, especially when discussing going to a hot-springs spa for mud baths? "Sounds fun," she said. "I just want to get a clearer picture of what we're planning. Which hotel, what kind of spa package, how long we're staying, all that kind of thing."

"Oh, my little bird," cooed Tippy, "you're so detail-oriented. So cute. It'll all flow. Go with the flow, Geronimo."

Amber was tempted to tell Tippy that Tippy was being naughty and was asking for a spanking if she didn't straighten up and provide the necessary information, but she didn't think she could probably get away with that. For all she knew, saying something like that would result in Tippy bending over and offering her butt for paddling, which was not really of much interest to Amber. She needed to know how much money she was going to have to come up with, and it sounded like she was going to have to ask Greg about that.

•   •   •

"Yes, Greg," said Amber later, "I actually do need to know these details."

"This is really Tippy's department, though," said Greg. Whined Greg? Almost whined, thought Amber.

"Tippy did not really give me enough information," persisted Amber. "You know I live on a limited budget."

"Well—" huffed Greg, as if he were trying to blow himself up into some sort of large and imposing figure—"you're not expected to pay for everything. We're paying for the hotel, all that stuff. You'd only have to pay for incidentals, your own stuff."

That was clearer, but … "You know I don't want to be leaning on you financially for everything."

"You aren't. You don't. Tippy and I can afford it."

"But Greg …" So frustrating. After all, she'd borrowed money from him to cover Meaghan's rent and utilities, and hadn't had a chance to repay that yet. "Are you even sure I should go?"

"Listen," said Greg, patting her hand. "Tippy's decided she likes the idea of our being a throuple, so that irons out a lot of problems, right?"

"Yeah, I guess, but …"

"You're not getting cold feet about the arrangement, are you?"

"No, it's fine so far, but relationships take work to maintain, and the more people there are, the more effort everyone has to put in." Amber had been reading up on successful polyamory; classics like *Polyamory* and *The Ethical Slut* (books nearly as old as she was!) now sat on her bedside table. If she was going to be in this kind of relationship, she wanted to make a success of it, but she suspected that Tippy had simply decided that life should be one perpetual orgy, not a well-designed effort at ethical nonmonogamy. Tippy had been pretty wild in bed so far, which could be fun, but were the three of them really going to keep having wild and even exhausting sex several nights a week? Amber wasn't sure that was truly sustainable without a little more care on Tippy's part.

"Hey, I'm sure it'll all be fine," said Greg. "You both used to stress out about each other, and now that's over. Tippy's decided she likes you, and you seem to like her too, so that's all good."

"No, that's just a starting point," persisted Amber. "She seems to think the three of us are on some kind of extended honeymoon, and nothing wrong with honeymoons, but they don't last. If we're going to go on as three, we have to figure out the finances and the ground rules and—"

"Amber, just let it be a honeymoon for now," interjected Greg. "Yeah, I know they don't last, but why not enjoy it while it's happening?"

MEAGHAN
LATTES AND ONLINE STATS

Meaghan and Lakeisha carried their lattes to their chosen table and began to set up for the morning's work. The winter sun was streaming in the windows of the café, requiring some adjustments of position from what they chose on rainy or overcast days, but that was fine with them.

"It's so shiny out!" exclaimed Meaghan delightedly. "And those annoying dudes who broke our faucet yesterday are leaving."

"I don't get how any normal human could just, like, break off your water faucet," said Lakeisha.

"Me neither," said Meaghan. "It's like they had some kind of unnatural faucet-breaking superpower. Mom said she thinks the guy tried to turn it the wrong direction, but still. I don't see how that would actually break it off."

"Barbarians," said Lakeisha. "Some boys are just barbarians. Did your mom get it fixed yet?"

"Yeah, she got a plumber to come out, but I guess it wasn't for hours, and then it was expensive. She says that whenever you call a plumber or an electrician, they charge for the visit plus whatever they need to do, plus parts, so it's more cost-effective to fix more than one thing at a time. But we didn't have any other plumbing problems to fix."

"I'd hate to be a plumber," observed Lakeisha. "One of my uncles is a plumber. He likes installing stuff, but there's all that time he spends fixing toilets and dealing with actual backed-up shit in pipes. No thank you!"

"I know, it's nasty," said Meaghan, giving her latte a cautious sip. "And my mom says we'd've been better off just never having those particular guests in the first place. Which is so true! They were a pain. I wanted to have my door locked the whole time they were there—they could've been a pair of rapists, who knows?"

"Maybe your mom needs to stick to renting only to women," said Lakeisha.

"Her friends think she's going to find Husband #2 this way. I don't think so."

"Husband #2! Your dad hasn't even been dead all that long! I mean, you said it was just last year that he passed!"

"Exactly. They were married over thirty years. He could be kind of a dork, but it was True Love. When her friends start in on finding a new Mr. Right, she looks at them like they're deranged."

"I think my ma would tell 'em to shut they mouths, if it was her."

"She kind of does, they just don't listen, 'cause they've known her forever. When that lady Ms. Hinckley was staying with us and we'd all play Scrabble together, they'd tell her Mom needs a new love in her life. It was so *cringe*." Meaghan sighed deeply.

"Well hey," said Lakeisha, "why don't we start the day by taking a look at your online stats? When did you last check?"

"Oh god," said Meaghan, "not for days. It was so scary checking at first when I knew no one was reading yet."

"Well, dang, Girlfriend, you've been posting stuff for a while now, time to check and see what people're saying."

Meaghan sighed again. "There's prob'ly still nobody. I mean, I had a few followers last time I checked, but …" She opened her laptop and set to signing in to the site they had chosen for her short fiction. Surely there would be little or no change from last week, and it would begin to look sad, and maybe her stories weren't really very good yet. She knew that romance was a very crowded field, and while romantasy was less so, there was still a lot of it. Even sapphic romantasy had quite a few practitioners, or at least a lot more than she'd expected to find when she began exploring what was out there. While she hadn't seen any on the shelves at the Mill Valley Book Depot or at Book Passage in Corte Madera, it hadn't been hard to find such books on Amazon, mainly as e-books. So that was both good and bad—good because she wanted to read and study the genre, but bad because there was obviously competition, and would she be able to gain a share of that market?

Lakeisha was moving over to her side, peering over her shoulder, braids even cascading onto that shoulder. "Girlfriend!"

Meaghan saw it too.

"Look at that!" crowed Lakeisha.

And there it was: comments, quite a few comments, studded with words like "swoony" and phrases like "honey-dripping" and "girl power" and "super-hot fae girls."

"I think you're rolling now," observed Lakeisha. "Readers telling you to bring on more!"

Meaghan wanted to swoon, herself. Swoony super-hot fae girls! With swoony super-hot Lakeisha as their publishing doula!

AMBER

CALISTOGA

The hotel was sybaritic, Amber decided. First they'd had contact-less check-in. Social distancing according to federal and international guidelines. Complete sanitation and disinfection. Wellness checks. Tranquility.

Their suite—not a mere room—boasted a king-sized feather bed with a down duvet. There were thick white terrycloth robes for each of them. A mini-fridge and room service. A flat-screen TV. And all of the products in the suite were described as being from reputable and eco-friendly local brands.

You could soak in the hot spring water, or alternatively plunge into cold water filled with ice cubes—in fact, you were encouraged to alternate hot and cold several times. There were eucalyptus steam baths and a mineral-rich pool fed by the aquifer underlying the town.

There were so many massage options—Swedish with light to medium pressure, "deep release" with firm pressure, Loma-Loma; massages with topical cannabidiol; massages with warm honey, ginger, jojoba, and coconut oil. You could add warm lava stones or salt stones, get a scalp massage, or foot reflexology. You could be wrapped in Bentonite mud (Amber gathered that Bentonite was an unusually absorbent type of clay), add a coffee scrub to the Bentonite mud, add seaweed, lemon verbena, peat, or (of course) CBD; or you could choose a volcanic ash mud bath instead. Calming and professional touch was key, and two, three, or even four people could share the same private treatment room.

There were facials of numerous kinds. There was Reiki and Aromatherapy. There was sound-based healing, incorporating chimes and musical bowls. Amber had seen the website and the brochure, which cooed: "Stimulates immune function!" "Aids restful sleep!" "Assists bodily healing!" "Encourages natural detoxing!" "Eases tense muscles!" "Improves healthy digestion!" "Helps regenerate collagen!"

All that was good, but most of those choices of treatment weren't included in the price of the room, which was the main thing Greg and Tippy were covering on Amber's behalf. And while Amber was willing to splurge on having one treatment—would it be a mud bath or a massage?—she was not about to pay extra for add-ons. Likewise, she expected she'd need to pay for her own meals; clearly she'd be eating a lot of salad and pasta.

Tippy was bouncing around, flinging herself onto the bed, then leaping up. They'd all had an evening soak after arriving in the Tesla (*not* the family SUV and certainly not Amber's elderly car), but they'd only snacked at supper-time before Tippy had called for an anointing with a bottle of CBD-laced massage oil that she'd brought along.

"We'll get the bedclothes all yucky," Amber had protested.

"The hotel'll wash them!" said Tippy.

"Not before we sleep in them," objected Amber. "I don't want to sleep in oily sheets."

"Oh Amber, they won't be *that* oily," said Tippy. "Our skin will absorb the oil. We'll have silky smooth skin filled with nutrients."

Greg, meanwhile, was sitting in the armchair eating handfuls of Spanish peanuts and raisins from a Ziploc bag—one of his favorite snacks, and one he usually carried with him—showing no interest whatsoever in being anointed with massage oil.

"Well," said Amber, "who's going to massage whom? Are you asking for a massage or are you dying to get one? I mean, tomorrow we'll be able to have massages from actual masseurs."

"Oh, sometimes you're so literal," said Tippy with a little laugh. "Yes, I do want a real massage tomorrow from a pro, but tonight we can pour on the oil and lie on each other and rub the oil in with our bodies. It'll be fun. It's not like we haven't done it before at home. Are you up for it or not?"

Amber considered the idea. It was true that they'd engaged in this kind of play a few times already, beginning with New Year's Eve. It could be fun, when everyone was in the mood. Being a little tipsy or just a little stoned didn't hurt, although being too drunk wasn't a good thing. Mainly, the question was whether she felt like doing this tonight.

"Come on, Amber, let's do it," said Tippy.

Greg and Tippy were paying for the suite, and Greg had lent the money for Meaghan's expenses. Amber supposed that it was probably a good idea to go along with Tippy's whims so long as they didn't actually offend her, at least while they were on this junket; she had no real objection to participating, just wasn't currently panting to do it the way Tippy evidently was. "Okay, why not," she said.

"Oh, good sport!" exclaimed Tippy. "Yay Amber! Greg, you gonna roll with us?"

Greg yawned. "Nah, I think I'll just watch for now. My two favorite babes."

Greg was just going to watch while they rubbed massage oil into each other? Amber was mildly annoyed, not really in the mood to put on a show, but she put the feeling aside, figuring it didn't matter all that much one way or the other.

Tippy was already pulling off her long-sleeved cotton top and flinging it aside, revealing a lacy hot-pink bra. Amber approached, divesting herself of her own black turtleneck and simple black bra. Tippy reached for her, and although both were still half-dressed, pulled her laughingly onto the bed.

"Hey, let's at least take the bedspread off first," protested Amber, thinking but not commenting that they didn't know whether *everything* had been laundered before their arrival. Sheets, certainly, but bedspreads and duvets? Maybe not!

"Okay, okay," said Tippy, making a pouty face for a moment before springing up to help Amber open up the bedding and then removing the rest of her clothes. "All right, Amber, you lie flat and I'll do the honors."

Amber, now also nude, obeyed, choosing to stretch out on her stomach with her head resting on the pillow and her arms. The white cotton sheets were cool and soft beneath her—the mattress beneath them was giving—and she closed her eyes to focus her attention on the sensations, letting her breathing slow for the moment, the air reach her skin all along her back, willing her irritation away, feeling the slight liquid surprise of the oil being poured in a line down her spine, then Tippy's hands rapidly spreading the oil more broadly, and then Tippy's entire body settling atop her, belly and breasts to her back, writhing gently, rubbing the oil in, gripping her hips between strong thighs and knees ...

•   •   •

The next day, Amber awakened cradled between Tippy and Greg, still slightly oily in places but mostly, as Tippy had predicted, with her skin feeling vaguely enriched and supple. The sun was filtering in the window, a weak wintery sun, but sun nonetheless; she could see from the hotel clock that it was just after eight o'clock. She knew that they would have a sumptuous breakfast, perhaps by room service; and so she spent a while pondering whether she would like to have eggs in egg cups to eat with a small spoon with which she could delicately dig perfect scoops of white and runny-centered yolk from the expertly broken shell. Or would she prefer a poached egg or an over-easy egg? What about muffins—bran or English? Or would simple pieces of whole-grain toast be better? And fruit—yes, there should be fruit, slices of several kinds, fresh whether or not in season (even in California, February could not really be considered fresh-fruit season, it must mostly be coming from somewhere else, perhaps Mexico or Chile?). She would want tea, not coffee—preferably herbal, but potentially black, with milk. Potatoes? Probably not. Oatmeal with nuts and dried fruit? Possibly, but she was leaning toward egg, toast, and fruit. It had been some time since she'd had a restaurant or hotel breakfast, so she spent a good while dreamily thinking over the possible options before turning her thoughts to whether to have a mud bath or a massage. By the time Tippy and Greg awakened, Amber had concluded that this time she would try a mud bath, as she'd had massages before but never submerged herself in mud, therapeutic or otherwise. The rest of the time, she thought, she could enjoy simple soaks in the hot spring water, for which there was no extra charge.

LILY
BLOSSOM'S RETURN

No guests so far had been quite as troublesome as Hunter and Trent, but Lily was not finding any of them to be nearly as congenial as Blossom Hinckley, never mind that "congenial" in the sense of a Miss Congeniality was not exactly a word Lily would have chosen to describe Blossom; she was a little too reserved for that. But Blossom's slight reserve was one of the things Lily felt to be part of the woman's appeal; Blossom did not intrude or insist on telling you all about herself, yet at the same time she could be drawn out and laugh, and even reveal snippets about herself. On the other hand, Mr. and Mrs. Peterson had been a little grumpy, Ms. Aroian had done a lot of some kind of fairly noisy calisthenics that had annoyed Meaghan, Ms. Gooch was an extreme vegan who refused even honey, the Santillans both had food allergies, and Mr. Moritz left far too many beard trimmings in the sink. These were not Lily's idea of ideal guests, and they were certainly not guests that Meaghan expressed any enthusiasm about either. Not, of course, that Meaghan had to like any of the guests, but Lily had hoped that it would not be difficult for Meaghan to coexist with any of them. After all, this was still Meaghan's home, and Meaghan was at least not being too sulky about the situation, nor completely refusing to help out, despite her habit of ducking out for most of the day to hang out with this Lakeisha instead of lending a hand for the morning cleaning and laundry. This disappearing to the cafés of Mill Valley irked Lily (surely she made good enough coffee? Couldn't Lakeisha come to the house now and then?), but she could understand Meaghan's need to escape, so for the most part she let the whole thing slide.

But Blossom Hinckley! Lily missed Blossom. She even occasionally admitted that she pined for Blossom, although she always told herself that it was silly to pine for someone she hadn't known all that long. After all, she didn't pine for Gail or Margo when they left town, and she'd been friends with them for decades. But then, she was used to Gail and Margo; they were her closest friends. At this point there was not all that much new to discover about them. She knew exactly what kind of movies and TV shows they would like, was well acquainted with their tastes in art and music, had heard all about their extended families and met numerous of their relatives, had commiserated with them about their ex-husbands and various boyfriends, knew their favorite foods and their go-to choices of soft drinks, wines, and cocktails. There were so many things she knew about Gail and Margo, and they knew almost as many things about her, except that since she had remained married to Don, and had had children with him, there were some things that she had always kept to herself on the grounds that her family members deserved at least some degree of privacy. There was, however, so much about Blossom that remained tantalizingly unknown, yet potentially discoverable. And while Blossom had gone north, she had not disappeared; Blossom texted with some regularity, although often in the form of photos rather than words, photos of places she was visiting or considering living in, photos of various coastal areas like Jenner and Sea Ranch.

And then came the text inquiring whether Lily might have another longish vacancy for Blossom to schedule a second stay. Blossom had enjoyed the more northerly coastal areas, but the ability to alternate a relatively remote location with access to the towns and cities of the greater Bay Area was proving to have a very strong appeal.

Upon seeing this note pop up on her phone, Lily found herself smiling; the corners of her mouth leaped to an upward curve and her gaze, too, leaped up, her eyes sparkling. She even felt a little pleasantly wriggly in the shoulders and torso, as if some invisible person had turned on her favorite dance music. Blossom wanted to come back, and not just for a night or two! Lily definitely wanted to dance about if that was in the offing. She hastened to look over her bookings, not that Blossom couldn't verify the schedule herself on the Airbnb website. Yes, of course there was space—it was still wintry out, after all, even if winter in coastal Northern California was on the mild side.

While Californians ventured to a wide range of outdoor spaces at all times of year, beachgoing was not exactly most people's top choice in cold weather. San Franciscans who wanted to stroll on the beach in wintertime had their choice of Baker Beach, Ocean Beach, Seal Rocks, Crissy Field, and several others right there within the city limits, plus the southern tip of Marin County, with its Golden Gate National Recreation Area—just across the Bridge—offered additional beaches suited to an afternoon's drive and stroll. Granted that there weren't many beaches lining the Bay inside the Golden Gate—the ocean provided the majority of beaches—still there were a few, supplemented by the various waterfront paths that constituted the Bay Trail's planned 500 miles of walking and cycling pathway. And so, demand for beach-adjacent lodging at this time of year was only sufficient to bring in driblets of income. Lily reckoned that she could easily block out a month or perhaps even more for Blossom to stay, so long as they set up the booking right now before someone else took that second bedroom and before people realized that spring was just around the corner. In the next week or two, Lily could stock up on some of Blossom's favorite foods, get the garden in tip-top winter condition (Meaghan could help with that!), locate some more board games from where they'd been tucked away, and pick up some tempting used books to add to the shelf.

• • •

"Blossom, what a delight to see you again!" exclaimed Lily when Blossom appeared at the front door not too many days later. She had gone into an absolute frenzy of cleaning and decorating in anticipation of Blossom's arrival—fresh flowers and artfully arranged branches were everywhere (most from the garden, but some had had to be purchased), the oak and teak furniture was freshly oiled, a new welcome mat graced the front door—and she had sifted though her closet trying to decide whether to greet Blossom wearing one of her prized now-vintage Laura Ashley dresses or something more recent but similar from April Cornell. In the end, she had gone with a looser-fitting April Cornell option, as while years of exercise classes and a pandemic-purchased Peloton machine had helped keep "menopause belly" at bay, months without the classes made her hesitant about the more fitted Laura Ashley waists. The long flowing lines and floral prints typical of both designers always made her feel both feminine and elegant, and she recalled that Blossom had complimented her when she had happened to wear one of the April Cornells during the earlier stay.

"It's so nice to be back!" responded Blossom. "And you look like a harbinger of spring today."

"Thanks!" said Lily, almost blushing. Blossom herself was neatly dressed in cream corduroy trousers and a thick cable-knit pullover in oatmeal wool, an ensemble that Lily felt to be a perfect expression of Blossom's personal style. "Come on in and I'll make some tea for us. And there are fresh scones!"

"Ooh, what kind?" said Blossom, setting down her suitcase beside the door next to the shoe rack.

"I made both blueberry and cheddar-chive."

"I can hardly wait," said Blossom with a smile.

"Earl Grey?" inquired Lily as they entered the kitchen.

"Of course." Lily had learned that it was one of Blossom's favorites, along with Gunpowder green tea and several other varieties.

Blossom seated herself at the counter while Lily put the kettle on the stove for their tea. "Your kitchen is such an enchanting space," she observed. "I've missed sitting here with you, looking out those big glass doors to the garden." The doors in question were a wood-framed pair— lighter, newer wood than the hundred-plus-year-old board-and-batten wall—each holding one large pane of clear glass. Through them could be seen a small area of patio with pots of flowers and shrubs, beyond which stood a tall hedge of glossy-leaved camellias. "And then there are those wonderful tiles behind the sink and stove. Portuguese?"

"I believe they were."

"It's all like being in a fairy tale. The whole house. But you, I think, are the good witch in the fairy tale who brings it all into existence."

Lily beamed, again verging on a blush. "I've spent so many years making it my own. Don helped, of course, and even the girls, but I do feel it's largely my creation. It was a little scary to take on when Don and I first bought it, because it's old and not everything had been well maintained, and we were young and didn't really know what we were doing, but gradually things got fixed up. I found things at flea markets and craft fairs and interesting little shops, it all began to come together."

"It must have been quite strange opening up to paying guests," noted Blossom, "or wasn't it? You seemed well prepared when I came along, anyway. Or were you just good at hiding nervousness?"

The kettle began to whistle and Lily poured, then placed the scones on a colorful majolica plate. "Nervous? I'm sure I was a little. But it was an adventure. I was excited that I might have come up with a good way to make a living. Now I'm not so sure."

"You're brave. I could never have turned my home into a B&B. Not that it was big enough for that, of course. But isn't it going well?"

Lily sighed. "I suppose it's hard to tell yet whether it's going well. Opening in January when the main attraction here is the coastline probably doesn't give me a very good idea of how many people will want to stay here in the summer."

"True enough."

"I was also planning to have all three upstairs bedrooms available, although I knew there was a chance Meaghan might need to come home. But I certainly wasn't expecting her to move back in before I even opened for business!"

"How's she doing?" Blossom was aware of the major facts regarding Meaghan's breakup and return home, but they had never discussed the matter in detail.

"Well, Shaun basically threw her out, so they weren't getting back together even if Meaghan had made peace with Shaun transitioning. That's probably for the best. I mean, I hate to say it, but when both of them are figuring out who they are—to the extent that both of them seem to be—the chances of the relationship holding together can't be very good. Don't you think?"

"I suppose not," said Blossom. "Some people can manage it, most probably can't."

"And so," Lily continued, "I'm relieved that Meaghan mostly seems to be getting over this breakup, although I wish she would get a job. She's gotten into this odd routine of leaving the house nearly every morning and catching the bus to Mill Valley—so obviously she could get up and catch the bus to go to work—but instead of getting a job, she apparently meets up with some pal from high school named Lakeisha, who is not anyone I remember her hanging out with in those days, and allegedly they sit in cafés and write and draw all day."

Blossom made sympathetic noises and wrinkled her brow, then said, "Do you think that's actually what they're doing?"

Lily sipped her tea. "Well, I just don't know. It's not impossible, of course—Meaghan wants to be a writer of some kind, and she did have that job at that strange little newspaper in Bernal Heights until the owner went and got indicted for money laundering. And she says Lakeisha makes a living drawing manga. I don't know—is that plausible? Do people really make a living drawing manga?"

Blossom smiled. "Well, I'm sure some people do. It's very popular with people their age. So, maybe Lakeisha's a luminary of the manga world. She probably isn't, but I wouldn't discount the possibility."

"I have been kind of worried about the whole thing, because Meaghan's not that helpful around the house and she's not making any money that I know of, so I hope they're not involved in anything illegal."

"Let's hope not," said Blossom. "How are the other girls?" Blossom had met Amber once or twice, but she and Tiffany had not crossed paths during the previous stay.

Lily shifted uneasily. "Amber seems to be doing fine, still making and selling those bird sculptures that tourists go for. I thought she was going to break up with Greg, but I guess she didn't, because they went off to Calistoga together for Valentine's Day. Tiffany … I'm kind of concerned about her, because she hasn't been over here in a while and she's not answering my calls very often. She usually seems to let everything go to voicemail and then not call back, likewise doesn't text me. Still, she's like that sometimes. I wouldn't worry about it much except that she and Jason are separated right now."

"That's too bad," observed Blossom.

"Yes, it's not ideal," said Lily. She hadn't previously mentioned either the reason for the separation or that Tiffany was deciding whether to keep a pregnancy; she supposed that by now Tiffany must have decided about the pregnancy, but what else was going on? She turned the subject back to the bed-and-breakfast. "Anyway, they've had their little dramas, or not so little dramas, and I've been dealing with a string of guests who mostly have just not been all that nice! Not at all like having you here. So I was very, very glad when you said you wanted to come and stay again."

TIFFANY
AMBER BRINGS FOOD

Tiffany's phone was ringing. It seemed to ring a lot these days, usually blaring the ringtone associated with her mother. Most of the time she let it go to voicemail; she was always tired now, even when she wasn't nauseated, and she didn't think she had all that much to say. Her mother always wanted to know how she was doing, whether she had seen Jason again, and similar hard to answer questions.

This time, however, the ringtone informed her that Amber was calling. Amber didn't often call; at most, Amber normally sent a text. What could Amber be calling about? Tiffany stumbled to her feet and over to the table where she had left the phone, next to a bottle of Gatorade, which was what her mother had always kept on hand for quick rehydration when they were sick. Although she'd never liked the stuff, lately she'd been downing it for electrolyte balance. She figured it had to help, given how often she was vomiting.

"Hey, Amber," she mumbled.

"Tiffany, you there?" demanded Amber. "I can barely hear you."

"Yeah, I'm here," said Tiffany more loudly.

"Good! That's better. Look, how're you doing? Mom says she can never get hold of you. You don't answer her calls and texts."

"I do too," said Tiffany. "Answer them."

"She says you mostly don't."

"Well, not—not *all* of them. She calls like every day these days. It's too much."

"She's calling because she doesn't know what's going on with you. Yeah, I know it can be annoying, but why don't you just answer now and then? She doesn't even know what you decided about the baby. Hell, I don't know either. It's kind of a big thing, that first you say you're pregnant and then you never tell her if you still are. Not to mention the situation with Jason. I mean, I know it's your life, but you can't just tell her the first part of the story. Either keep the whole thing a secret or keep her updated."

"There's not that much to tell," said Tiffany. She settled herself on the couch and closed her eyes.

"Oh, criminy, you're such an idiot sometimes. Look, what're you doing tonight?"

"Nothing."

"What're you having for supper?"

Tiffany resisted the urge to hang up. "I dunno. Soup?" She thought she still had a couple of packages of butternut squash bisque in the cupboard. She'd turned to having groceries delivered so she didn't have to go out, but her orders had mainly involved a lot of crackers and Gatorade.

"Look, I'm going to get us some basic Chinese takeout and come over. Any requests?"

"No …" moaned Tiffany, both to requests and to the idea of Amber bringing food at all.

"I'll be there in half an hour."

Tiffany dropped the phone and slumped back against the couch, letting herself go limp. She felt, she thought hazily, like a dead jellyfish. Amber was coming over—she knew she ought to get up and fix things up a little around the apartment, maybe even get dressed, but that all seemed like far too much effort.

•   •   •

"Let me in, Tiff," said Amber, a little crossly. "It's cold out here. Look, I've got the takeout." She waved the sack containing the takeout containers.

Tiffany stepped out of the doorway and Amber plunged into the living room.

"Man, it's dark in here! Why've you got all the curtains drawn—it's not dark out yet. Turn on a light, at least!"

Tiffany flipped the switch by the front door, flooding the room with the relatively dim light from the overhead fixture's twin sixty-watt-equivalent bulbs, and revealing the rumpled throw piled on the couch, the tablet e-reader that had slipped to the floor, and, on the table, the box of saltines and bottle of Gatorade.

"This looks kind of grim, Tiff," announced Amber as she gazed about and slightly wrinkled her nose, suggesting that she smelled some odor imperceptible to Tiffany. She moved rapidly to place the sack on the table, continuing to look searchingly about. "Are you depressed or something? Or sick?" She paused a moment to unload the sack and turn on an additional light. "I brought chow mein and Buddha's Delight. Let's get the plates on the table so we can dish things up, and then you're going to tell me what's going on."

Tiffany didn't move. "I'm barfing a lot."

"What, today?"

"A couple of times."

"Look, are we talking morning sickness or sick-sickness? If it's just morning sickness, you should eat. Maybe not if it's the flu."

"It's different times of day."

"Yeah, but morning sickness isn't always in the morning. What do you think is causing this barfing?"

Tiffany sat back down on the couch. "Well, I'm still pregnant."

"Okay, and so how long have you been barfing? Two days? Two weeks?"

Tiffany avoided looking at her sister. "It feels like forever."

Amber threw her hands in the air. "So, then I guess morning sickness. If you're pregnant, you gotta eat. Your body needs food. Nina Taylor Swift Simone or whatever you're calling it needs food. This is basic." She headed for the kitchen and returned in a moment with plates, forks, and chopsticks. A set of white paper napkins in a Polish ceramic holder with a blue tulip pattern already sat on the table; it had been a wedding gift.

Tiffany continued to lean lifelessly against the back of the couch. She said "I'm not hungry."

"Bull," retorted Amber.

"I'll have some later."

"Right—after you have some *right now*. Get your butt to the table or I'm bringing some of this to the couch and feeding you like a baby, you infant-carrier."

It was as if they'd returned to childhood, Tiffany thought, when Amber used to boss her around and tell her what to do. That she had to play some particular role in a let's-pretend game, or surrender a toy of Amber's that she had appropriated, or stop wearing something that looked too babyish. She forced herself off the couch and lurched toward the table where Amber was dishing up helpings of the chow mein and Buddha's Delight onto their two plates.

MEAGHAN
GROWING THE FANBASE

After choosing one of the popular online writers' platforms to host her stories, Meaghan quickly began to make use of tips posted on the site, plus advice from Lakeisha and any other resources she could find. She followed other writers working in the same subgenre and commented on their work; she welcomed anyone who followed her; and she requested comments and suggestions on her own stories. These strategies rapidly began to pay off in terms of a growing readership, although Meaghan was not yet in a position to charge fees to readers—both Lakeisha and the platform advised that in this particular corner of the writing world, building a fandom came first. Once she began to write longer stories that could be serialized chapter by chapter, the short fiction and initial chapters would be available free to entice readers into paying for more. In the meantime, she had her work cut out for her: not just writing new stories and interacting with others online, but beginning to craft social media posts to attract readers who were not yet members of her specific platform. She created a new Instagram account separate from her personal account, she developed a TikTok account where—from her bedroom if no guests were down the hall, or otherwise from out on the beach or the trail—she recounted her struggles and triumphs as a newbie writer and directed viewers to her profile and stories; she looked into other social media arenas where, even if she didn't plan to be active there, she could create a profile and place links to her work.

"This is a business," Lakeisha had said. "Yeah, we're doing what we love, but it's a business and we have to treat it that way to monetize. You wanna earn, not have to work as a barista or something, you gotta treat this very serious. We spend hours creating, but then we spend more hours working the business side. Getting the word out. Building the fanbase."

Meaghan always listened raptly to Lakeisha's opinions on the business side of writing—after all, Lakeisha was making a living already. Maybe not a huge living yet, which was why she was taking her time looking for the right affordable apartment and putting up with living with family for the time being, but Lakeisha had shown Meaghan some of her monthly earnings statements from the major online book retailers, and they were certainly respectable. Lakeisha was bringing in more each month than Meaghan had been paying in rent living with Shaun, and the Amazon reviews of the books were enthusiastic, so clearly Lakeisha had established a fanbase that could only grow.

Lakeisha refused, however, to read Meaghan's stories yet. "I will, Girlfriend, I will," she stated, "but first you grow yourself some fans who don't know you, because this is a good platform for you to do that. Perfect your craft. Then, when you're still not real well known but aren't totally obscure, then I can swoop in as a more recognized name and say wowza, check this girl out, she's fantabulous."

"How long do you think that might take?"

Lakeisha looked at Meaghan, head cocked to one side. "You tell me, Girlfriend. You in the driver's seat here. The more and better you write, the more and better you market, the sooner I enter the picture. Now look, it's nine o'clock, so let's us settle down to work now that we've had our morning chat!"

Oh, Lakeisha was so inspiring! So smart, so talented, so gorgeous, so all-around perfect! Meaghan was always tempted just to sit and gaze at her with puppy-like adoration, memorizing every curve of her face, the colors of her eyes (streaks of brown and gold, but which exact shades of brown?), the subtle fullness of her lips, the delightful way her countless tawny braids framed her face … but Meaghan knew that that wouldn't get any words on the page, plus Lakeisha was bound to notice and be distracted from her own work, and it would be very cringe for Meaghan if Lakeisha noticed this adoration when they were supposed to be working. It'd be different, of course, if at some other moment Lakeisha noticed and … well … leaned over and kissed her or something. But Meaghan couldn't tell yet whether Lakeisha was interested in her in that particular way. Yes, obviously Lakeisha was eager to pursue their friendship; this was way beyond the extent to which they'd hung out together in high school. And yes, Lakeisha had expressed her excitement at the idea of Meaghan writing sapphic romantasy, which Meaghan didn't suppose Lakeisha would have been nearly so enthusiastic about if Lakeisha didn't find girl-on-girl sex swoony. But Lakeisha's own books were very inclusive in their characters' gender identities and sexual orientations, as well as inclusive in being multi-ethnic and diversely abled, so while Meaghan found this hugely admirable, it wasn't as clear a signal as she would have liked that Lakeisha definitely personally longed for a girlfriend, or more specifically had a yen to kiss and cuddle with *her*. And so Meaghan always obediently settled down to write once Lakeisha gave the signal that their morning chat was at an end. Because Lakeisha was certainly right that in order to start making money, she needed to perfect her craft by writing every day, seeing what resonated with readers, and growing that fanbase!

LILY
HIKING THE DIPSEA

"You know," said Lily to Blossom, "last time you were here it was really too wet out to hike the Dipsea Trail, but I don't think it's nearly as muddy now. We could check online and see what people are reporting about the trail conditions."

"I would definitely like to do the Dipsea," replied Blossom. "And yes, it was disappointing to have so much rain before—granted that we needed rain after so many years of drought, but still. I felt like I was mainly hiking along the water and not exploring the inland trails."

The Dipsea was a rather famous trail that took the hiker over the hills between Stinson Beach and Mill Valley—a distance of about seven and a half miles. Although quite popular, it was definitely considered a challenging hike, with nearly seven-hundred steep stairs at the Mill Valley end, which was where the annual Dipsea Race began. The race, which intrepid souls had been running nearly every year since 1905, with cancellations only during the Depression, World War II, and the first year of the COVID pandemic, included some alternative segments of trail where diverging and converging paths added an element of strategy for the runners.

However, neither Lily nor Blossom were serious runners, and Blossom had been hoping to hike from Stinson to Muir Woods and back, not all the way to Mill Valley. The Stinson-to-Muir-and-back version constituted more like ten miles, and was estimated at close to six hours, not counting any hiking done while visiting the Woods.

"Let me just take a quick look at the conditions," said Lily, reaching for her phone and executing a search on it. Peering down at the screen, she reported "A hiker from a few days ago says there was mist and some sprinkles, but not much mud—more soft ground than muddy. He says he did a double-Dipsea, saw great views. It looks like some people are just wearing sneakers, not hiking boots, but personally I'd say boots."

"That sounds great," said Blossom. "Maybe tomorrow if the weather holds."

Lily continued to examine her phone. "Looks like tomorrow ought to be fine. That could change, of course, but the forecast is good."

"Lily," began Blossom, "do you have anyone else scheduled to arrive?"

"Not for a few days. Why?"

"I was thinking that if you don't have anything pressing on the horizon—like new people arriving—would you like to join me on the hike?"

Lily flushed, to her surprise. Hike with Blossom? What a wonderful, unexpected, invitation! "Hike the Dipsea to Muir Woods? I'd love to! I don't know when I last did that. I might be a little out of shape, but I still hike partway up now and then. We could leave early in the morning and take a picnic lunch."

"Definitely a picnic lunch," agreed Blossom.

"We could have an egg breakfast—nothing too heavy, but eggs for protein—and take sandwiches with carrot sticks or some kind of salad plus some other treats. Cookies or maybe brownies, for instance."

Soon they had planned out the entire hike, including shorter possible add-on trails to take once they reached Muir Woods. Lily tried not to show it, but she was thrilled. While never a hardcore hiker, she had always enjoyed the occasional day hike, and southern Marin was blessed with numerous options for those, given the hilly terrain of this part of the Coastal Range. The area was largely under the protection of entities such as the Golden Gate National Recreation Area (administering the Marin Headlands at the southern tip of the county, west of Sausalito); Mount Tamalpais State Park with its redwoods, oaks, chaparral, and grasslands; the Marin Municipal Water District's lands northeast of the State Park; and of course the Muir Woods National Monument and the Point Reyes National Seashore. All of this was within just a few miles of the house, never mind the many trails elsewhere in the Bay Area or indeed in Northern California more generally.

When she and Don had first married, and Don had still been relatively athletic, they had spent many weekends exploring the different trails. They had scaled back once the girls were born, but before too long they had begun taking the family on some of the shorter and easier trails. Muir Woods would have been perfect—its flat Main Trail was suitable for small children and the disabled—but the need to reserve parking in advance, plus the length of time spent in bumper-to-bumper traffic on the way to the parking lot, had significantly limited their visits until everyone was old enough to hike their way in. And, as the girls got older, often they had wanted to do other things on their weekends than go for day hikes, so Lily and Don had gradually gotten out of the habit. These days Lily's hikes were mainly a matter of heading down to the beach and walking along the coast, or of spending an hour or so on the Dipsea or the Matt Davis Trail, both of which began fairly near the house.

•   •   •

The morning of the hike dawned promisingly. While fog was visible along the water, sunlight and a clear sky were to be seen atop the hills behind the house. Lily and Blossom arose early, a little before the sun itself peeked over the hill, and Lily put the kettle on for some English Breakfast tea. She had decided on a hearty scramble with onions, mushrooms, dried tomatoes, jalapeños, and bell peppers, sprinkled with grated cheddar and some salsa, with whole-grain toast and some orange slices on the side. Blossom soon joined her in the kitchen, dressed in a well-cut pair of perfectly aged jeans (nicely faded but devoid of holes) topped by a long-sleeved T-shirt of golden hue; over one arm she carried her oatmeal cable-knit pullover and a windbreaker, which she took out to the entryway to hang up. Lily herself was also in jeans, with a pastel plaid flannel shirt; good, they'd be wearing similar weights and types of clothing on their hike, making it a little easier to time when they might pause to zip or unzip jackets and such.

"That looks very tempting!" said Blossom, leaning to examine the pan of eggs.

"I certainly hope so!" replied Lily. "Sit down, everything's just about ready to eat."

Blossom sat, and Lily turned her attention to plating the oranges and toast, and to pouring their tea.

•   •   •

The trail ascent began with relatively gentle steps and a wide reddish-dirt path rising parallel to the coast in a more or less southeasterly curve. Not yet surrounded by trees, instead they walked between low masses of shrubby vegetation, at times catching panoramic views of the ocean to their right or if they stopped and turned. After about a mile from the trailhead, they entered the State Park and soon began hiking under a lush canopy where the air grew cooler and moistened noticeably.

"This is lovely!" said Blossom, gazing up at the trees.

"It won't last long unless we veer off on a different trail, the Steep Ravine," replied Lily. "Which is also an option for hiking to Muir Woods, but I thought we might stick to the Dipsea all the way there and then possibly take an alternate route back. Dipsea will give us some stunning views of the ocean and possibly even San Francisco, depending on whether there's fog, and I'm betting we won't have fog this time."

"All right, I'll let you be guide," said Blossom.

Sure enough, in very little time they reached the intersection with Steep Ravine.

"See, off to the left that trail ascends through a narrow band of redwood forest, while to the right it goes down to the water at Rocky Point, a little south of Stinson. Steep Ravine basically follows Webb Creek. Now, right here we're at something like 600 feet. Both Steep Ravine and Dipsea start to really climb after this point—they've both got sets of stairs. With Dipsea, we'll have a whole lot of steps right away, well over a hundred, while Steep Ravine spreads out the steps more, but in both cases we're in for a serious incline."

Fortunately, most of the Dipsea steps were under cover of the trees, keeping them cool as they climbed—not that it was exactly warm out yet even in the sun. After the second, quite long, set of steps, they left behind the redwoods for a more diverse type of woodland, and almost immediately came to a third long rise of steps.

"There won't be any more steps after this for quite a while," said Lily.

"That's good … I think," responded Blossom.

They moved now through varied and changing micro-environments that included many ferns and other low-growing plants, plus some very large spruce trees and a couple of dense groves of younger redwoods. Once high enough and emerging from the trees onto a relatively level area of chaparral, they could see clumps of conifers here and there as well as a considerable amount of both land and water—soon, in fact, they came to areas with splendid views that included far-off fairytale-like shorelines blue with distance.

"The sky's so blue this morning!" exclaimed Blossom as they paused a moment to gulp a few mouthfuls from their water bottles. "I'm so used to fog."

"It's just luck," said Lily. "This can be pretty foggy too. Some of what we're seeing is actually San Francisco," she explained. "If you look carefully, you might even notice some skyscrapers punctuating the skyline here and there."

"I'm not sure my eyes are good enough for that," said Blossom.

"Well, it really depends on the day," said Lily, pressing her sunglasses just a fraction of an inch higher on her nose. She wasn't quite sure whether she was seeing any skyscraper tips today or not. Still, she felt you really couldn't beat this weather for hiking the Dipsea, especially when showing it off to someone who'd never been on the trail before. Blossom was proving an excellent hiking companion, and while both needed to stop and rest from time to time, they were easily able to hike at about the same pace.

From here they remained in the open chaparral, ascended a few more steps, stopped at a bench to rest and enjoy another view, and finally reached a drinking fountain at what Lily noted was Cardiac Hill, the highest point. The hill itself was dotted with stands of dark conifers and areas of the kind of shortish brushy vegetation that they had already frequently observed. Now they were starting to meet up with other trails again, as well as an increase in the number of westbound hikers and runners; at the bench they'd stopped at, the Old Mine Trail had forked off to the north, followed by the beginnings of a southbound creek and now a fire road that crossed the trail and led to the Coast View Trail, after which soon came the TCC Trail.

"It's as if we've reached some sort of massive intersection, except that there's very little traffic," commented Blossom.

"On race days—and the Dipsea isn't the only race that follows this trail—I'm sure it's swarming with runners," said Lily. "Always check to make sure you're not accidentally hiking this during a race!"

"I used to jog," said Blossom, "but I wouldn't care to try jogging what I've seen of the Dipsea. I'll stick to hiking, at my age."

Lily thought Blossom looked in fine shape; she was pretty sure that if Blossom wanted to get back into jogging, she'd be just fine, but she didn't say so. You never knew when someone might have a slight disability that wasn't obvious to others. Besides, she didn't know exactly how old Blossom was. They certainly looked around the same age, but looks could be deceiving. (Still, surely Blossom couldn't be more than a few years older than Lily, if she were even older at all! Blossom looked youthful in every respect without actually looking young—good skin, few gray hairs, vigorous step …)

After Cardiac Hill, they had mostly left the open chaparral and rejoined the trees. Most were relatively slender-trunked, but here and there was a thicker, more majestic specimen. They'd technically been in the National Monument since meeting the Coast View Trail, but this was not yet the part of Muir Woods famous for its old-growth redwood groves.

After another fire-road crossing and an intersection with the Ben Johnson Trail, Lily said, "Okay, from here we're going to be on a pretty steep descent through the trees down to the Muir Woods parking lot and visitor center. If I remember right, it's about two more miles. Now, that Ben Johnson Trail that we just saw would be an option for the return trip. It'd take us along the northern edge of the Muir Woods boundary instead of skirting the southern edge. We can see what we think about that when the time comes." Lily had made a point of reviewing the various trails and routes the night before, and just hoped she hadn't missed noticing any mentions of closures and detours. Sometimes, especially when it had been a rainy winter, there could be significant rerouting.

As they descended, the fire road descended with them, so that one moment they might be surrounded by misty, verdant forest and the next moment see or even cross the open fire road in sections of wild grass and chaparral once again. Then as the trail began its final descent through the damp forest, with its large and small mossy trees and profusions of ferns and other flora, they found that they'd have to detour on the fire road to get to the Visitor Center.

"Rats," exclaimed Lily, "I don't know how I missed this when I was checking for routing problems last night! I think it's because they close the footbridge to the parking lot every winter for salmon spawning—which I'd totally forgotten about—so it's not something unusual. I must have been just blind! Anyway, this detour adds on almost a mile. Sorry!"

Blossom assured her that it didn't matter, but added that she was looking forward to sitting down for a while once they got to the parking lot or thereabouts.

"I know, so am I!" said Lily. "It just feels cruel to have expected that we were nearly there, only to have to add on a big detour. I guess we should have taken Ben Johnson when we had the chance."

"Well, we'll love being there once we get there," said Blossom. "I've always loved visiting Muir Woods—I've just never hiked in before. It's such a special place."

Luckily, there were no more disagreeable surprises on their way to the parking lot, which was unsurprisingly entirely full. They walked on to the entrance, where after a stop at the restrooms they found an unoccupied bench and decided that they were ready for lunch.

"We're not allowed to picnic on the viewing paths, so we'll need to eat somewhere near the Visitor Center," said Lily.

"Well, maybe we're best off eating right here," observed Blossom. "We might not find a better location—there don't seem to be a lot of other benches."

Having decided, they unloaded the lunch from Lily's daypack and devoured sandwiches of roasted vegetables with hummus on whole-grain, complemented by Honeycrisp apples and brownies.

"I needed that!" said Blossom afterward, as they stowed the reusable waxed-cloth wrappings in Lily's insulated fabric lunch tote.

"Me too!" agreed Lily.

Somewhat restored after their morning's hike, they agreed to spend a while strolling the broad boardwalks and paved pathways along the valley floor that constituted the primary visitor areas of Muir Woods.

"I will never tire of walking in the redwood forest," said Blossom as they stopped to examine an outcropping of shelf fungus on a fallen log. "Hiking, maybe, but not of simply spending time."

"I know what you mean," said Lily. "And especially here, where the trees are like some kind of natural cathedral."

"Well, there *are* a lot of people here, so it's like a cathedral in that respect too," said Blossom, "but at least we're all here to appreciate the forest. They talk these days of 'forest bathing,' and that's exactly what we're doing, immersing ourselves in nature and particularly in the woods."

"I'm so glad you invited me to join you today," said Lily. "I've been spending way too much time indoors, especially since deciding to run the house as a B&B. Well, even before that. Don and I weren't going on many walks the way we used to; he'd started spending so much time online in addition to all the time he spent at work in San Francisco. This is really a treat. And look, there's a banana slug over by that clump of sorrel!"

"I'm not a big fan of most slugs, but I do adore banana slugs," said Blossom. "What's not to like—they're bright yellow, they eat forest floor detritus, and they're hermaphroditic."

"They're what?" Lily wasn't sure she'd heard what she thought she'd heard.

"They're hermaphrodites and so when two of them mate, each one fertilizes the other. That seems like such a convenient, egalitarian way to be."

"I guess it could be," said Lily dubiously. She supposed it probably worked a lot better for slugs than it could ever work for humans.

There was a pause. "Does it bother you to have a gay daughter?" asked Blossom.

Lily was not expecting this, even after the hermaphroditic banana slugs. "Bother me? No, I don't think so. That is, the fact of it doesn't bother me. But it bothers me that I didn't know earlier. I was used to thinking of her in one way and then suddenly I found out she was different than what I thought she was. And that was pretty soon after I found out that my husband was different than what I'd thought—or at least at the end of his life he was different—and everyone in the family seemed to be having some kind of crisis all at once. Well, maybe not Amber. But all the rest of us. So it hasn't been just finding out that Meaghan's gay and I have to get used to the idea, it's a whole mess of stuff. I haven't told you most of it, obviously."

"Oh," said Blossom. "I suppose I really only know that your husband died last year and that Meaghan's at home after a breakup and some kind of strange end to her job."

"Well, Don's brain tumor made him very unpredictable, which seems to be why he suddenly put all our money into crypto and consequently lost it. There's more, but that's probably enough for right now."

"I'm so sorry," said Blossom quietly. "I don't like to say a lot about losing Julie, either." She put her hand very gently, tentatively, on Lily's hand, which was holding the wooden fence rail too tightly as the two women leaned against the fence looking at the forest floor.

Lily allowed her grip on the fence rail to relax just slightly. She turned to Blossom and said "Thanks for understanding."

•   •   •

After strolling some more of the valley floor and pointing out small flowers, elaborate spider webs, new shoots from old burls, and also helping a woman whose wheelchair had run into trouble on an uneven part of the asphalt trail, Lily and Blossom decided that it was time to start on the return hike. This time they took the Ben Johnson Trail until it met up with the Dipsea in the western end of the National Monument, pushing themselves up the incline until Cardiac Hill and the more level open section prior to the descent to Stinson Beach. By the time they reached the house, it was late in the day and turning very chilly; they were ready for slippers, a hot beverage, a supper of supermarket-deli chowder, and an evening of Scrabble in the living room. Meaghan was nowhere to be seen, but Blossom reported that she could be heard reciting something not entirely comprehensible up in her bedroom, so they let her be.

What an absolutely glorious—tiring, but glorious—day it had been, mused Lily as she ladled the chowder and glanced appreciatively at Blossom, who held a hot mug of tea between both palms, her head tilted slightly back, eyes closed, and a faint smile on her face. Just a wisp, just a few strands, of straight gray-and-black hair fell across Blossom's cheek, unnoticed and so for once escaping her normally perfectly smooth coiffeur.

AMBER
CHOOSING THROUPLEDOM

"I really had no idea Tippy was going to suddenly decide she wanted to have orgies or a throuple or whatever the hell else she's been into lately," said Greg, gesturing as if to wipe his brow, although there was no other evidence that he might be sweating.

Amber and Greg were seated on Amber's couch, with its view of the ocean, but neither of them were looking out the big front window. It was a rather foggy day anyway, so there wasn't all that much visible beyond about twenty feet.

"You seem to be okay with it, though," said Amber.

"Well, it's not like I have a problem with it," said Greg. "I just had no idea she was suddenly going to go in that direction, so it's taking me some time to get used to the idea. Anyway, you've seemed like you were okay with it too."

Amber's chin was in her hand in a position that she vaguely recalled, from her college art history intro course, was associated with both melancholy and contemplation. Hundreds of years earlier, the German artist Dürer's print *Melancholia* had shown a winged seated woman in this pose, and a seeming gazillion other artists had followed suit, with even the Early American painter Copley using it to make the silversmith Paul Revere look like a man of intellect. Amber did not recall much from her college art history classes, but occasionally tidbits like this popped into her head. She said, "I'm not against it, if it works out, but it was pretty unexpected. And remember, it's not like Tippy and I exactly knew each other very well before New Year's Eve. We've mostly avoided each other the whole time you and I've been together, up until that night. The two of you were separated but dealing with Brayden, I was waiting for the divorce you kept saying was going to happen, blah-blah-blah. You and Tippy were together for years before you separated, then you and I've been together a few years. So you're the one who knows both of us. Whereas me, I have no history with Tippy beyond whatever you said about her and whatever I gleaned running into her at the store now and then."

"I get what you're saying," said Greg uneasily, picking at something stuck to his sock.

Unable to stop herself, Amber interjected "I think that's just where your sock has pilled in the wash."

"Huh?" Greg stared at her.

"Your sock. Never mind. Anyway, I just don't know Tippy well enough to understand where she's coming from, that she suddenly wants to be so lovey-dovey with me after years of us avoiding each other. What does she want from me?"

"If you can't beat 'em, join 'em?" said Greg. He had now withdrawn his hand, carefully, from any contact with his nubby pilled woolen sock.

"But why now?"

"Midlife crisis?"

"Oh come on, Greg, she's too young for a midlife crisis. She's in her prime. How old is she now, like thirty-five?"

"No, she's older than that, I think thirty-eight now. That's old enough to have a midlife crisis, isn't it?"

"Greg, with women we usually talk about menopause. It's men who have midlife crises. I seriously doubt that Tippy is menopausal already. Like I said, she's in her prime."

"Well, maybe she's just realized that she was missing out on too much sex while we were separated. She has a pretty high sex drive, after all."

"Yeah, I've noticed that."

"We didn't separate over sex," asserted Greg. "The sex was always good. It's even better as a threesome."

"Agreed that she's a good fuck," said Amber. "And I don't suppose for one minute that she was pining for sex the whole time you were separated. I think she was getting plenty … somewhere."

"Wait," said Greg hastily, "if you're saying I was banging Tippy the whole time we were separated, I was not! Now and then, okay yes, I admit we sometimes did have a go. But not … come on, I was normally with you, not with her."

"I didn't say you were her primary source of sex, did I? Although thank you for confirming that you were sometimes the one providing the sex-high."

Greg flushed.

"Tippy has quite the collection of sex toys, so there's partly the solo sex option, but I think she probably got into some of the local sex party action. You do know that kind of thing happens, right?"

"Well, yeah, but …"

"That is my guess, Gregory, because you've never mentioned her acquiring any new boyfriend. Or girlfriend. I have friends who are into that scene, and they say that sounds very likely. They don't know if they've seen her at any of those parties, but that's not too surprising since there's nothing all that unusual about her looks."

"She has that butterfly tattoo …" said Greg.

"There is not a great current shortage of women with butterfly tatts on their butts," said Amber. "Believe me, my tattooist friend says that there was a time when that was very, very popular. He still gets requests for it, along with requests to remove 'em, which he doesn't do because that's a medical procedure."

"Tippy's never said anything to me about getting into the sex party scene," said Greg. "The only time we had anything like that was on New Year's Eve before the other people went home, and they went home pretty soon."

Amber gave him a skeptical look. "Remind me," she said, "of some of the big reasons you've said the two of you separated."

"Well," said Greg, "there was a lot of tension. It started to seem like there was always tension between us, and I mostly couldn't figure out why. Okay, some of it was about Brayden, normal parenting kinds of tension about who was doing what and when, and why we were doing this or that for him, like what to feed him or how to toilet train him or what kind of toys he should have. Where he should go to preschool. That sounds like a lot of Brayden-related tension, and maybe it was, but it was still the kind of normal stuff parents have to negotiate, it wasn't severe. But it also seemed like Tippy was not a good communicator. She could say what she thought Brayden should have, but apart from that it usually seemed like I was just supposed to magically intuit her feelings and what she needed or wanted."

"Yeah," said Amber. "I'm remembering that."

"And I would try to get her to articulate stuff, and she just wouldn't and instead she'd get huffy and pouty and we'd have a fight. That's one of the reasons I was attracted to you when we met—you're more communicative. You usually make clear what you think and what you want. It can be annoying, but at least I'm not left wondering all the time. I know I'm a guy and I have my own communication issues, but at least I try."

"So," said Amber, "here's what I think. I may be wrong, but this is my theory. I think Tippy always wanted the wild and crazy sex life but didn't know where to find it or have the nerve to admit it to you. So even though by your account the two of you were having pretty good sex, this wasn't addressing her personal fantasies."

"She didn't have all that many partners before me," said Greg. "Or at least that's what she said. Very few and she said they were no good in bed compared to me."

"Well, that may or may not be true, but we'll assume it's true, since plenty of guys are not impressive lovers. So we assume she got some of what she wanted with you, but it wasn't enough or not what she was really looking for, and she couldn't admit it. Therefore, big tension."

"Maybe," said Greg. "Could be."

"And once you split up, she was older, she knew her way around better, she could hunt for what she really wanted."

"Maybe …" said Greg again.

"But she still liked you, was still attracted to you, you're the father of her kid. And I didn't seem to be going away. She'd gotten more confident about asking for what she wanted. She'd learned how to maneuver with two or more partners doing things at the same time, how to handle pleasuring at least two and directing some of the action."

"Yeah, could be. She's pretty good at orchestrating moves for all three of us. I was surprised how well she seems to handle directing the action without making it all about her. I mean, of course it's all about her pleasure, but it's also about *our* pleasure."

"Exactly. I think she's been doing sex parties and now wants to bring what she's learned home. I'll bet she'll still want to go to sex parties and play with other partners, but if she can pull together a functioning throuple, the sex parties would be more of a now-and-then thing. Life might be a little easier if most of the action is at home. After all, she's got a kid to bring up."

"He's also my kid," interjected Greg.

"Well, and it's easier for two people to bring up a kid."

"I've been bringing him up too!"

"I think she wants you on the scene more."

"If it's actually going to be a throuple, she probably wants you to co-mother, though."

"I'm not a very maternal type."

"Maybe not, but I think you're more maternal than you realize. You look out for your sisters, after all."

"That's not maternal, that's something else," objected Amber.

"It's similar, though. You're never mean to Brayden, you're just not that involved with him, which isn't surprising given that he lives with Tippy. Do you think we could make a throuple work?"

Amber threw her head back against the sofa cushion. "Hell, Greg, how should I know?"

"But are you up for trying it out? Tippy's not a bitch, and she seems to like you so far. Even if the two of us divorced, I'd still need to be in touch about Brayden. I love you a lot, I really do, but I also still have a lot of love for her. And if the two of you could also love each other—not just enjoy the sex—that'd be just stellar."

"It sounds like a lot of work," said Amber. "I also like living where I am, with my art studio right here."

Greg took her hand in both of his. "All relationships are a lot of work. You wouldn't have to move into the house full-time to do it. I wouldn't want you to give up this place unless it was clear we all really wanted to live together, and it's too early to know that. So whadda you think, are you okay with continuing our test run?"

Amber snuggled up against him. "I guess I'm game to give it a go."

MEAGHAN
TRULY MONETIZING

Meaghan had now been writing and posting short sapphic fantasy romances since the beginning of the year, averaging one or two new stories per week, and the engagement and response from readers was growing in a most gratifying way. Readers were commenting on and recommending the stories to friends elsewhere on the platform, and the analytics provided by the platform were beginning to give her some solid demographic data about these readers. Most were in their teens and twenties, based in North America, but some were older and some were in other English-speaking parts of the world.

"I think I want to move to longer stuff now," Meaghan told Lakeisha. "It's been fun writing these shorts, but there's not a lot of room to develop the story in two thousand words. Especially since the readers are starting to ask when I'm going to write longer ones."

"That's a good sign," said Lakeisha. "Do you have an idea for something longer yet?"

"Oh yeah!" exclaimed Meaghan. "I have three or four ideas for books in my notes, and I've already written a few chapters on one of them."

"Excellent, Girlfriend! You want to be ahead of the game. Having more chapters written than published is golden!" Lakeisha's eyes sparkled as she offered this praise. "The reader comments you've quoted to me are dynamite—you're finding your target audience! These gals are full of, like, *quivering delight* as they devour your tales. Golden, Girlfriend, pure gold!"

The phrase "quivering delight" was straight from a recent reader comment that had had both Meaghan and Lakeisha chortling with glee. Quivering delight! Wasn't that the epitome of reader engagement in just about any form of romance?

"I *hope* I'm ready to go long!" said Meaghan. "That seems like it'll be really fun, and—"

"That's where the money is!" finished Lakeisha. "Money-money-money!"

Meaghan's eyes grew dreamy. "I know! I mean, I want to be the very best writer I can be, but I also really need the money."

"You can do both," pronounced Lakeisha. "You can definitely do both so long as you're working in a popular genre—which romantasy is—and get your branding right. And you're on the right track with all that. You are getting these readers *panting* for more!"

"Well—" Meaghan blushed just a little—"I figure that if I can write scenes that make *me* pant for more, maybe that'll be just as exciting for my readers."

Lakeisha cocked her head and regarded Meaghan. "Girlfriend, I told you not too long ago that I wasn't going to read you yet, that at a certain point I would read and give you a big public boost. Well, I have a confession to make! I've gone and read these stories now, and ooh, do they sizzle. Maybe it's that you're so *hungry for love* yourself, but dang, that last one about the kinda curvy earth girl finding the luscious brown elf-maiden made me so hot-and-bothered, I had to run to the bedroom and—" she leaned over to whisper loudly in Meaghan's ear—"pleasure myself right then!"

Meaghan's blush went crimson at this.

Lakeisha leaned back in her seat and said, "You don't think, Girlfriend, that I haven't noticed you surreptitiously *feasting your eyes* on my little self? And then writing your glorious not-so-secret longings into your ever-so-steamy stories? My oh my!" Lakeisha made a show of fanning herself.

Meaghan couldn't bring words to her mouth; she just kept blushing, her gaze mostly downcast but flickering repeatedly upward to take in Lakeisha's mischievous but smiling face.

"You play so shy," said Lakeisha, "but you a volcano underneath!" She added, hastily, "In a good way! I mean to say, I hope one of these days to see, once I have my own apartment again, that volcano in action!"

Meaghan caught her breath. Was Lakeisha inviting her to make love once there was a place away from parents and Lakeisha's annoying brother? "Your apartment?" she ventured.

"Girlfriend, sometimes you're so slow—but it's cute. Yes, when I have my own apartment, I want you to come butter my muffin. In person. You have an eye for me, well I think you're pretty tasty too. Once you have some money, maybe we could even share that apartment."

Meaghan was relieved to note that no one was sitting all that near their table, which was in a dark corner of the café. Could Lakeisha really be saying these things? She could feel herself warming and moistening down there at it all. "I would love to share with you," she breathed. "You are just the best—the best ever—I can't even believe it. Are you really saying everything I think you're saying?"

Lakeisha laughed merrily. "Girlfriend, you are just the bee's knees. I don't get this flirty unless I mean it. I'm gonna do a big social media promo on you when you launch chapter one, and I'ma tell the sapphic world plus anyone else interested that you are a pearl of an emerging romantasy writer. With any luck at all, a whole new slew of readers are going to come your way and, um, probably cum in their little panties too, and you can start to monetize and we can afford to get our own apartment."

Meaghan managed a dazed grin. "You are so wonderful. You're like a dream. Can I kiss you even before the apartment?"

"Well dang, Girlfriend, obviously. You can even give me a big smackeroo right here in the café."

Meaghan leaned over with joy and threw her arms around Lakeisha. It was a little hard to kiss over the table-top, but not actually impossible.

TIFFANY
A MEDICAL SITUATION

Tiffany looked in horror at the bloody globules that had just fallen into the toilet. Traces of the things were also visible on the crotch of her underpants. What on earth was she seeing? Surely it wasn't a miscarriage—a miscarriage would be bloodier, wouldn't it, and not look so much like … well … tiny grapes? She felt faint just to see this horror-movie stuff. She already felt faint much of the time these days, but the sight of these alien things—

.   .   .

"Amber!" she breathed into the phone back in the living room, her underwear now stuffed with toilet paper. "You have to come over. Something really weird's happening."

"Really weird? Like what?" Amber sounded testy. "Your body, or someone's breaking in, or what?"

"Uh, I don't think anyone's breaking in," said Tiffany, looking around in a panic at the idea of this too potentially happening.

"Be *specific!*" exclaimed Amber. "What is going on?"

"I don't know! Just come over! I can't deal with this."

Amber gave a loud sigh. "Okay, but if it's a medical emergency you need to call 911, not tell me to come over."

"I don't know what it is!"

"Coming," said Amber gruffly, and hung up.

Tiffany threw the phone at the far end of the couch, emitted a muffled groan, and flung herself down in a heap upon the couch. *Why me,* she kept thinking. *Why has my life imploded?*

. . .

"Okay, what's happening?" demanded Amber when she arrived twenty or so minutes later, rousing Tiffany from the couch to realize that Tiff was wearing only a T-shirt and the toilet-paper-stuffed panties. "Let me in, you're not even dressed. What's going on? And let's at least get a damn bathrobe on you, it's still cold out."

"I don't know what it is," murmured Tiffany, accepting the pale pink bathrobe that Amber located and pressed upon her. "It's in the bathroom. I shut the lid."

"You aren't saying something swam up the toilet pipe, are you?" demanded Amber. "Are you hallucinating or what?"

"No, no ..." said Tiffany. "Go look, it's horrible ..."

Amber strode rapidly to the bathroom, saying "You aren't having a miscarriage, are you?" and then, after the sound of the toilet lid meeting the tank, "Ewww, what is this stuff?"

"It came out of me!"

Amber shut the lid again and emerged. "Is there more of it or was that all of it?"

"I think there's more—I don't know—I stopped peeing when I saw it—"

"Clothes on, we're heading for Kaiser," directed Amber. "Terra Linda Kaiser has emergency, and who the fuck knows what this might be. Get something warm on and wear socks."

Tiffany felt dazed. Kaiser Permanente? Emergency? She hadn't seen a doctor in months.

"You do still have Kaiser, don't you? Where's your purse? You'll need your insurance card."

Tiffany stumbled into the bedroom to locate socks and a pair of pants while Amber sighted the purse on one of the chairs and began checking Tiffany's wallet.

"Found the card," Amber announced. "Now let's go. Shoes! Coat! You don't need to go to Kaiser in your bathrobe, Tiff—my god!"

Within moments they were in Amber's car and turning onto northbound 101; the apartment in Strawberry was practically next to the freeway, a fact that until now had made Strawberry a desirable location only in that it made Jason's bus commute an easy one. Up they now went, over the big grassy hill to Corte Madera, Larkspur, and Greenbrae; past the turnoff to the San Quentin prison and the Richmond Bridge; up through San Rafael, the county's largest city; then veering westward into the Terra Linda district to pass Frank Lloyd Wright's futuristic Marin Civic Center and the Northgate Mall in order to reach the Freitas Parkway and make just a couple of turns more.

"I guess it's a good thing you live so close to the freeway," remarked Amber as they entered the Kaiser Permanente parking lot. "That didn't take long at all. How're you feeling?"

"I dunno," whispered Tiffany.

"Well, you're going to have to say more than that when we talk to the ER people." The car now parked, Amber hopped out and came around to open the passenger-side door. "Up you get, Tiff. You can still walk, right? I don't need to get them to come out with a wheelchair?"

Tiffany hadn't really thought about wheelchairs or what might happen once they got to Kaiser. But then, she hadn't been thinking about much of anything lately. She allowed Amber to pull her forward out of the car and stood, a little unsteadily, as Amber picked up her purse and slammed shut the car door.

They walked, more slowly than was typical for either of them, over to the building and located the Emergency entrance. Fortunately, it didn't look like too wildly busy a day in the ER, but then you could never really tell just by looking at the waiting area. There was no easy way of knowing how many heart attacks, strokes, broken limbs, power-tool injuries, falls from ladders, drug overdoses, and suicide attempts were occupying the medical personnel in the rooms beyond—but at least Marin County wasn't a major locus of gang activity or shootings.

At the intake desk, Tiffany and Amber began the laborious process of explaining that Tiffany was pregnant but had not gone in for any prenatal care because she'd been uncertain whether to keep the pregnancy ("You haven't been in at all?" exclaimed Amber in disbelief); that she'd had terrible, relentless, nausea; and now had produced strange little globules along with some blood …

•   •   •

Later on, in Tiffany's hospital room, a doctor explained to Amber, Lily, and Meaghan what she had already gone over with Tiffany, namely that this hadn't been a normal pregnancy, but something called a molar pregnancy.

"It's nonviable. A fertilized egg does implant in this kind of situation, but it's an empty egg—it lacks a nucleus, so it can't develop. Even if it does become an embryo, it's not properly formed and can't survive. The placental tissue grows abnormally, and a tumor develops in the uterus, with fluid-filled cysts that look a little like a bunch of grapes."

Lily gasped.

"The tumor isn't cancerous," the doctor continued, "but it has to come out in order to avoid serious complications—which could include developing cancer later. Some people have a miscarriage. Otherwise, surgery is needed to remove the pregnancy."

"I've never heard of this," said Lily. "How common is it?"

"It's fairly rare—about one in a thousand pregnancies. So, not *extremely* rare, but definitely not common. Normally," the doctor said, "we discover molar pregnancies when the patient comes in for routine prenatal care."

"And what's the prognosis?"

"Most women who experience a molar pregnancy will recover completely and be able to have a perfectly normal pregnancy later on.

However, it's important to wait six to twelve months before attempting another pregnancy, in order to ensure that the treatment has been successful and there is no remaining abnormal tissue."

Tiffany listened silently to this recapitulation of her situation. She had learned that her severe nausea and vomiting had been a symptom, but molar pregnancy was by no means the only cause of excessive vomiting. Most of the possible symptoms, in fact, were also symptoms of other conditions, but the tiny grape-like sacs of fluid were specific to molar pregnancy. Had she gone in for prenatal care, routine first-trimester tests would have alerted her doctor to the situation—her abnormally high level of pregnancy hormone and her ultrasound would have revealed it.

LILY
FINDING A FUTURE

Lily had been stunned when Amber called from the Emergency Room and told her to come to the hospital—and said that Meaghan might be smart to come too. Lily'd been worrying about Tiffany, but there'd been so many different things to worry about lately. She'd been telling herself that while it was upsetting that Tiffany rarely responded to her calls and texts, Tiffany was a grownup now and had a right to her privacy while dealing with her current messy situation. And while Lily naturally wanted to know just what was happening between Tiffany and Jason, and certainly wanted to know whether she was soon to have a grandchild or not, she had repeatedly told herself that it was Tiffany's life and it was up to Tiffany to choose what to reveal and when.

But this was quite another matter! Lily and Blossom had been sitting cozily in the living room playing backgammon when Amber's call interrupted their afternoon, while Meaghan had been up in her room doing who-knew-what after returning from the cafés of Mill Valley—recording herself for TikTok, apparently. Blossom had quickly assured Lily that it'd be fine to finish their game later, the important thing was for Lily and Meaghan to get themselves to the hospital. She would manage on her own and, not being really acquainted with Tiffany, would not intrude.

"It wouldn't be intruding," said Lily breathlessly, "but you're right, you and Tiffany don't really know each other yet, so it wouldn't make sense."

Once arrived at Kaiser and listening to the doctor explain the situation, Lily was stunned anew. Tiffany had neither scheduled an abortion nor embarked on prenatal care? How could this be? It might be difficult to decide whether now was the right time to be pregnant, but surely Lily had brought her daughters up to be more responsible than this about their health, and certainly about any possible pregnancies! Tiffany was not indigent and uninsured, nor living in a state with laws that restricted pregnant women's options—she was a married woman with insurance through Jason's company, living in California's Bay Area where doctors and hospitals were numerous. For heaven's sake, even Amber had health insurance, thanks to the Affordable Care Act; Lily really could not see why Tiffany had failed to go to the doctor, if only to have her drugstore pregnancy test verified.

Lily knew, however, that this was not the time to lecture her daughter on the importance of scheduling routine medical visits. Everything had clearly gone wrong for Tiffany. First there'd been Jason's revelation and the separation, then the unexpected pregnancy, and now this bizarre abnormal growth that, in Lily's view, didn't even deserve to be called a pregnancy. After all, how could you have a pregnancy if there was no embryo? Or, if somehow there was some sort of early embryo, it had no ... well ... nucleus ... and couldn't develop? If it was really a tumor, why call it a pregnancy? The term "molar" pregnancy made it sound like a tooth had somehow lodged itself in the womb, although the doctor explained that in this case "molar" referred to there being a mole. That sounded even more confusing because, apart from the small mammals that lived underground, the only moles Lily could think of grew on people's skin and were usually just ugly brown spots. (Well, unless they turned cancerous—but still, they were on the skin, not inside people. Weren't they? So confusing!)

And—while Lily couldn't see much of the evidence when Tiffany was under the covers in the hospital bed—apparently Tiffany's nausea and vomiting had passed into the territory of hyperemesis and resultant weight loss. Ordinarily, Tiffany was both slender and healthy, a young woman who ate a pescatarian diet and got plenty of exercise from walking, jogging, Pilates class, and so forth. Now, however, her face looked gaunt and Lily suspected that so did the rest of her.

Lily had wanted to weep, but throughout the visit she kept a firm hold of herself, feeling sure that it wouldn't benefit Tiffany in the slightest to see her dissolving into tears.

•　　•　　•

Instead, Lily waited until she and Meaghan had returned home and Meaghan had gone upstairs. Blossom was sitting quietly in the living room reading by lamplight. When Lily, who had entered the house via the back door with Meaghan, came into the living room, Blossom put down her book and said "Is she all right? Are you all right? I can go upstairs if you'd rather be alone."

"She'll recover," said Lily wearily. "She has some horrible weird thing called a molar pregnancy that isn't a real pregnancy, but the doctor said she'll be fine. And I'll be fine too, I guess, but don't go—" she began to sob now—"so many things have been so hard for a long time now, but it's been such—such a help having you here. You're such—such a treasure. It's—silly of me to say this—but—I wish you could stay forever."

Blossom took her hand in both her own, gently petting it. "Dear Lily," she said slowly, "I'm here if you want me to be here. I'm slow to heal from my own heartache, but if I can help you with yours, I'll gladly try."

"Oh Blossom—just your presence—you calm me when I think I'm going to—going to explode with pain—no one else brings me the strength that you do—"

Blossom too began to weep, but more silently. "Lily, you give strength too. I didn't want to say this, but you are my anchor. You've helped me want to live after Julie's death. You are the ray of joy I try to follow as I rebuild my life."

"Oh Blossom," cried Lily again, "you are so dear to me." She gulped. "Sometime when we're not so—so overcome—we'll have to tell each other more, explain more about Don and Julie and so on, but for right now it's enough just to have you with me."

•   •   •

Easter came late that year, and although Lily was not exactly religious, she considered herself to value the spiritual aspect of life. Marin County being part of the greater Bay Area, she naturally had friends who celebrated Jewish, Muslim, Hindu, and Buddhist holidays, and probably others as well, but of the major religions' spring holidays, it was Easter that she felt most at home with. Easter, she thought, would be a good time to celebrate renewal and new beginnings.

Therefore, although money was still tight, Lily planned a holiday luncheon for the family and friends. Nothing so elaborate as Thanksgiving or Christmas, of course, but nonetheless it would be festive.

When the day arrived, the table was soon set with a lavender jacquard cloth and cream napkins; the centerpiece consisted of a simple glass vase of pussy willows flanked by chocolate rabbits and some candy eggs in the wooden egg cups Lily had inherited from her mother. None of the family ate red meat anymore, so there was no ham, but rather a large crab and shrimp quiche accompanied by dishes of fresh asparagus, snow peas, and buttered carrots with tarragon; a basket of hot baking-powder biscuits; a plate of deviled eggs; and a strawberry-rich fruit salad. With Meaghan's help making some of this and Blossom contributing Chinese red-bean buns, the three soon had the main elements in place, which would be augmented by whatever the others brought.

Gail and Margo arrived first, with Gail carrying a bottle of Prosecco and Margo bearing her standard spring-and-summer Jello salad, which was justly famous despite the decline in popularity of anything involving Jello—to the box of lemon Jello, she added chopped celery, julienned raw carrots, apple slices, both cottage cheese and sour cream, and finally sliced almonds.

Tiffany arrived just in time for lunch, accompanied by Jason and carrying a tall "daffodil" cake from a recipe that Lily's mother had often made, combining angel food and sponge cake batter in glorious swirls of yellow and white. Amber, meanwhile, had indicated that she would stop by later, as she would be decorating eggs with Greg, Tippy, and Brayden.

"You always do such a lovely holiday table," exclaimed Gail delightedly, "and this one is an Easter delight."

"That's for sure," said Margo. "To be honest, I wasn't sure you'd have the energy to keep up doing this kind of thing after becoming an innkeeper."

"Well, there's no question that my energy took a real hit after Don died," said Lily. "You know how I've struggled with quite a few things in recent months. The whole family has had a lot to deal with, some of which I've told you about and some of which I haven't mentioned."

Gail and Margo nodded; they'd heard about troublesome B&B guests, Meaghan's job and the breakup with Shaun, and more recently Lily had told them that Tiffany was recovering from a molar pregnancy and would have to go to the doctor regularly for months, possibly even a year, in order to make sure that no molar tissue was continuing to grow. Surely that was more than enough to deal with after losing both spouse and financial security!

"I'm feeling better about things now," Lily went on, "but this will be a long road and we can save talking about some of it until everyone's here. Amber doesn't expect to get here until mid-afternoon at the earliest, since she's over at Greg's teaching egg-decorating techniques. I think they're doing *pysanky* in solidarity with Ukraine. You know, those amazing intricate designs they do using wax, sort of like batik."

"She's so talented!" exclaimed Margo.

"All of my girls are talented," said Lily automatically, although so far Amber was the only one whose talents were known, as far as she knew, outside the immediate family. She supposed that Meaghan's writing had gotten her at least the one job, short-lived though it had been, and Tiffany had briefly been on the Tam High swim team.

"Of course!" said Margo. "And by the way, Tiffany, that's a lovely ensemble you've put together, a real vision in pink and white. Are you back at the boutique?"

"Yes," replied Tiffany. "I'm lucky that Maeve took me back after I missed a lot of time with my medical situation."

Jason put his arms protectively around Tiffany from where he stood behind her. "And *I'm* lucky that Tiffany took me back after we had some serious misunderstandings."

Lily hadn't fully explained the nature of Tiffany and Jason's separation to Gail, Margo, or Blossom, as she felt it was up to the couple to decide how much of it to make public, but she knew that in the hospital Tiffany had consented for the family to contact Jason, who had rushed to her side. There had been considerable discussion between Tiffany and Jason after Tiffany's D&C removed what was hoped to be all of the molar tissue, and Jason had asserted that while yes, he did find men attractive, it didn't negate his love or attraction for Tiffany; he had experimented with a few hookups during the separation but hadn't enjoyed them nearly as much as he'd hoped. And so, he'd said, couldn't he be one of the many bisexuals who was content to lead a monogamous life with a beloved partner? Tiffany had agreed that they could at least give the marriage another try.

"We're glad to have you back in the family with us," said Lily. "We missed seeing you at Thanksgiving and Christmas."

"I love both my families," said Jason. "Tiffany and I are going over to my parents' later on."

"I'm an aunt now!" said Tiffany. "I can't believe I missed all the excitement."

"Meaghan, are you looking for another job in journalism?" inquired Gail.

"Not right away," said Meaghan.

Lily told herself not to say anything; it wasn't the time to press Meaghan to get a job.

Margo asked, "Are you planning something new and different? I remember you really enjoyed the job at the paper."

"Oh, I did!" said Meaghan. "But there aren't a lot of jobs in print journalism these days, or even online journalism. Newspapers are disappearing, and a ton of companies are using Artificial Intelligence to write copy instead of hiring real people." Her chin tilted upward. "So I'm doing something else, I'm writing stories online, where if you get enough subscribers, you start to earn money. My friend Lakeisha told me about it—she's a manga artist and she makes a living from that."

"How's it going?" asked Margo.

Lily's ears perked up; she was definitely interested in whatever Meaghan was about to reveal, as Meaghan had not exactly been very forthcoming about whatever she and Lakeisha had been up to every morning in the cafés of Mill Valley.

"Well," said Meaghan with shining eyes and a little smile, "it's actually going *brilliantly*. Romance is super popular and I'm starting to monetize and Lakeisha and I are going to get an apartment together. She found one in Greenbrae that we think would work."

Lily was astounded. She had certainly not expected this. "Honey, that's wonderful! I had no idea."

"Well, I didn't know whether writing romance stories would really work," said Meaghan. "It's not like most writers make money, but it looks like I will."

"That's exciting!" said Margo, and everyone else offered their congratulations as well.

"You'll have to bring Lakeisha over so we can get to know her," said Lily. "I'd really feel more comfortable knowing the person you're living with, especially after that embarrassing confusion about Shaun."

"Oh, Mom, I've known Lakeisha since high school," said Meaghan.

"Yes, but I don't think I've ever met her. Just bring her over sometime before the two of you get the apartment. I'm sure she's wonderful, but I'd like to meet her." Lily was seriously annoyed with herself about never having met Shaun; she suspected, of course, that Lakeisha was Meaghan's new love, and that was fine, but it was especially important to meet Lakeisha if Lakeisha was going to be more than just a roommate. She looked over at Blossom, and the two exchanged meaningful glances; they had wondered whether Lakeisha would prove to be Meaghan's new partner, but it had seemed too early to tell.

•   •   •

After lunch, as midafternoon approached, Amber arrived bearing chocolate eggs and several brightly colored *pysanky*.

"Those are just gorgeous!" Lily exclaimed, and everyone else added their oohs and ahs as they examined the eggs. "You'll have to teach the rest of us sometime."

"It's complicated to do the traditional types of designs," said Amber. "You need a steady hand applying the wax. But a person doesn't need any art training, you just learn by doing and experimenting once you know how to apply the wax effectively."

"Was there a big group?"

"No, not especially. Just Greg and Tippy and Brayden and a few other friends."

"I'm surprised you're hanging out with Tippy," said Tiffany.

"Well, she's not so bad. We're getting along all right," said Amber, in tones that suggested the subject need not be further pursued.

"Well, we've had some important news from more than one person today," said Lily. "A little while ago Meaghan told us that she's starting to earn some money as a romance writer and expects to move in with her friend Lakeisha soon."

"Very cool," observed Amber.

"And now that you're here too, there's more news to announce," Lily went on. "Running a B&B in the house has been an interesting experiment, but I'm not sure it's one that I'll be continuing long term.

Renting out just the two rooms, or even three once Meaghan and Lakeisha get a place together, is more time and trouble than you might expect, and it doesn't bring in as much money as I'd hoped, either. But what it did do was bring Blossom to join us! I think you all know that Blossom has been looking for a place to move after losing her wife Julie last year." She paused, glancing around the room.

Blossom, standing next to her, gave a tiny nod.

"And so," Lily went on, taking Blossom's hand, "after many conversations, we've decided that Blossom will move into the lower floor of the house, where I've been staying lately. I'll continue to rent out the upstairs rooms for now, but we'll see how that goes and reassess the B&B later in the year."

"Wow!" exclaimed Gail.

Margo added, "Welcome, Blossom! I hope this will work out like a real dream for both of you."

Blossom smiled. "I'm very much looking forward to this new phase of my life. Meeting Lily and spending time with you all has been a lifesaver. After Julie's death, I didn't feel like going on with the life we had in San Francisco."

"Wow, Mom, this is so unexpected," said Tiffany. "I had no idea. I was just getting used to the idea of you running a B&B." Jason massaged her shoulders as she spoke, leaning protectively toward her.

"Well, Tiffany," said Lily, carefully keeping her tone gentle, "you've had a lot of other things on your mind lately. Blossom has spent quite a bit of time here since she first arrived in early January, so the two of us have gotten pretty well acquainted. I think you'll like each other very much once you get to know each other."

"Mom's seemed a lot happier with Blossom here," Amber put in. "If she and Blossom like living together, that seems like a win to me, especially if it means not having to rely so much on random B&B guests for income."

Lily's grip involuntarily tightened and Blossom squeezed her hand in return. "It's been hard for both of us, losing our spouses last year," said Lily, "but we're helping each other to process our grief." She thought, but didn't add, that while there was definitely grief, both she and Blossom had experienced a certain ambivalence about their spouses' deaths. There had been love and sadness, but also anger and weariness and disappointment. Like Don, Julie had committed suicide—but after many years of struggle with depression. Julie had taken an overdose of pills, and Blossom had been the one to find her. Lily could certainly understand Blossom's reluctance to discuss Julie's death, and also Blossom's desire to leave behind reminders of a past that had often been painful.

"Well, I think it's wonderful that you've found each other," said Gail staunchly. "Not to mention that Blossom is a fantastic Scrabble player and is teaching us Mahjongg! Now Lily and Margo and I don't have to rely on one of you girls to help make up an impromptu foursome at games."

Amber laughed. "That's good, because you know Meaghan and I aren't the ideal regulars for game nights. I do spend a lot of evenings with Greg, and Meaghan probably has some new plans for her evenings too."

Meaghan said "Lakeisha and I are working creatives. Making a living from our art and writing takes a lot of time. It's not just making the work, but we have to spend a lot of time marketing it and engaging with our fans. It's a full-time job."

Lily smiled. "Yes, I'm sure you'll need to put in a lot of work, honey. I know that writing is closer to your heart than helping me run a B&B." She paused. "Say, did you ever hear anything more about your old boss at the newspaper?"

Meaghan's eyes grew large. "Yes!" she said dramatically. "I heard something just the other day from one of the other reporters. Britt says the money-laundering case is scheduled to go to trial soon."

"That's just wild," said Margo, and everyone nodded in agreement. "So crazy that you would have ended up working for someone who was money-laundering for the Russians!"

"Yeah, the Russians, of all people right now!" said Gail, hastily adding "Slava Ukraini!" Support for embattled Ukraine remained strong among just about everyone they knew.

"I'm glad you're out of that job, sweetie, even though it seemed like a dream job at first," said Lily. "Money-laundering for the Russians, I mean really, what can that woman have been thinking?"

"I don't know," said Meaghan. "I really liked Carole and her vision for the newspaper, so it was a big shock to hear she was using the paper to support the Russians. I mean, I don't know if it was the Russian government, but if not them, probably the Russian mob, so it was just awful either way."

"Well, I think maybe we're all—not the Ukrainians, but us in this room—better off than we were a few months ago," asserted Lily. "This past winter was kind of a tough time for the Simone family, anyway. And now things are looking brighter."

Her daughters nodded, and Blossom, Gail, and Margo smiled.

Lily was tempted to lean over and give Blossom an impetuous kiss, but there would be plenty of time for that. She was still getting used to thinking of Meaghan as an adult with same-sex preferences, and of Jason as a bisexual man who was choosing through love to stay with Tiffany rather than pursue the other side of his attractions. She didn't know exactly what was currently going on with Amber and Greg, but something seemed different than before. Becoming accustomed to her own new feelings for Blossom could be taken slowly. They had exchanged some long and deep kisses by now, and some caresses, but both were cautious, not wanting to move too rapidly and run the risk of damaging this delicate new relationship. They would see if it worked to share the downstairs space while Lily continued to rent the upstairs bedrooms to B&B guests, but Lily would be able to sleep in her old main-floor bedroom—now the B&B office—if either of them felt a need to be alone.

Lily wasn't sure at this point just how she felt about Don. They'd been in love when they married, and they'd had a mostly satisfactory marriage, but over the years her feelings had changed, and she thought his probably had too. Would they have remained married had he not developed the brain tumor? Maybe yes, but maybe not. She really wasn't sure. They might have discovered a renewed closeness as they aged, or they might have grown further apart and divorced. At this point, she had no way of guessing which way things would have gone. And now, she found that she liked the idea that, a little like Jason, she could love a person without that person's sex or gender being a deciding factor. Perhaps she and Blossom could build something that would sustain them throughout the years ahead. She knew, at least, that Blossom was financially secure and not about to squander her savings on questionable investments—Blossom was a partner she felt she could rely on, and she hoped that Blossom would always find her a reliable partner as well.

Lily looked out the front window to the sea, for once fully visible under a cloudless blue sky. She turned back to Blossom, who smiled warmly at her. And then, despite herself, she stood on tiptoe and gave Blossom an impetuous kiss after all.

"Let's all have some of those chocolate eggs now, shall we?" she said.

END

ABOUT THE AUTHOR

Dolores Street grew up in California and spent many years living in the San Francisco Bay Area. Although life eventually took her to the East Coast, she frequently returns to the Golden State. She enjoys exploring both California's cities and the state's natural environment and is particularly fond of the majestic redwoods. When not at home writing in a cozy chair, she can often be found at a nearby café with a nice cup of chai. She loves to read many kinds of fiction, and her favorite nonfiction author is Mary Roach. Unlike her characters, she has never run a B&B, worked for a newspaper, gone to Burning Man, or attended Tam High.

NOTE FROM DOLORES STREET

Word-of-mouth is crucial for any author to succeed. If you enjoyed *A Marin Bed and Breakfast*, please leave a review online—anywhere you are able. Even if it's just a sentence or two. It would make all the difference and would be very much appreciated.

Thanks!
Dolores Street

We hope you enjoyed reading this title from:

BLACK ✿ ROSE
writing™

www.blackrosewriting.com

Subscribe to our mailing list – *The Rosevine* – and receive **FREE** books, daily deals, and stay current with news about upcoming releases and our hottest authors.
Scan the QR code below to sign up.

Already a subscriber? Please accept a sincere thank you for being a fan of Black Rose Writing authors.

View other Black Rose Writing titles at
www.blackrosewriting.com/books and use promo code
PRINT to receive a **20% discount** when purchasing.

Made in United States
Orlando, FL
07 June 2025

61901267R00132